DEATH'S APPRENTICE

DEATH'S APPRENTICE

A GRIMM CITY NOVEL

K. W. Jeter & Gareth Jefferson Jones

THOMAS DUNNE BOOKS
ST. MARTIN'S PRESS
NEW YORK

THOMAS DUNNE BOOKS.
An imprint of St. Martin's Press.

DEATH'S APPRENTICE. Copyright © 2012 by Gareth Jefferson Jones and St. Martin's Press. The Grimm City trademark is jointly owned by St. Martin's Press and Gareth Jefferson Jones. All rights reserved. Printed in the United States of America. For information, address St. Martin's Press, 175 Fifth Avenue, New York, N.Y. 10010. Grimm City is created by Gareth Jefferson Jones

www.thomasdunnebooks.com
www.stmartins.com

Library of Congress Cataloging-in-Publication Data

Jeter, K. W.
    Death's apprentice : a Grimm City novel / K. W. Jeter & Gareth Jefferson Jones.
        p. cm.
    ISBN 978-0-312-54771-4 (hardcover)
    ISBN 978-1-250-01345-3 (e-book)
    1. Paranormal fiction.   I. Jones, Gareth Jefferson.   II. Grimm, Jacob, 1785–1863.   III. Grimm, Wilhelm, 1786–1859.   IV. Title.

PS3560.E85D35 2012
813'.54—dc23

                                                                                  2012030864

First Edition: November 2012

10   9   8   7   6   5   4   3   2   1

For Jacob and Wilhelm

DEATH'S APPRENTICE

1.

The music was jacked up so hard and loud, every note felt like a punch to the head.

Nathaniel shouldered his way through the club's fevered crowd. The black T-shirt under his jacket turned darker, soaking up the mingled sweat of too many bodies packed too close together.

From up on the club's stage, the bass line set the air vibrating like a chrome hammer, cutting through the old-school *schranz* pumped out by a pair of sequenced TR-909s. The DJ, a near-comatose gearhead slumped behind the equipment rack, paid minimal attention to the Serato cues scrolling by on his beat-up laptop. At 180 BMP, the raw-throated vocal samples sounded like a Thai slasher flick with all the silences and dialogue spliced out. The crowd loved it, writhing wide-eyed into each other with wild abandon.

As Nathaniel watched, he felt the distance between himself and the dancers expand. He knew that they belonged here; he didn't. They were enjoying themselves, in their own frenetic, addled way; he was on the job. He felt hollow and cold inside, envying those who knew so little about death and darkness.

One of the dancers, in a spangly silver outfit that barely covered her hips, threw him a flirty look. *She likes you,* Nathaniel told himself—the spark that sizzled between her eyes and his seemed to tell him as much. But maybe it meant nothing at all. He didn't know.

"Beat it, punk." To Nathaniel's relief, the girl's obvious boyfriend showed up next to her. Tank top showing off 'roid-enhanced muscles, a forehead that could be spanned by the width of two fingers.

Nathaniel didn't feel like messing around with the guy. Or the girl, or anybody else. He had work to do. He closed his eyes and drew the club's smoke-laden air deep inside himself. He didn't let it out. Instead, a little room opened at the center of his skull, a space he had been in before, and that he had come to dread. But that was part of the job as well. Dark things were in there, and he let them slip out, silent and fatal.

Outside himself, he could hear the music slowing, the beats per minute dropping into the double digits, the treble dopplering down into the bottom octaves, the rumbling bass fading into unheard infrasonic. The crowd's screams and laughter morphed into the dying groan of some immense, wounded beast.

Then there was silence. For which he was grateful. He let the breath out of his aching lungs, and opened his eyes.

Nothing moved. Nothing would, until he let go.

The light had shifted down into the slow red end of the visible spectrum. Across the club, the dancers were frozen in the murky haze, like an ink-wash illustration in some ancient travel guide through the more disturbing circles of Hell. He glanced back over his shoulder and saw the girl, now with wild outflung hands, teeth clenched in the raging sway of the silenced beat and whatever crystalline substance still glittered at the rim of her nostrils. Her hair swung across her face and to one side like a raven's wing. Nathaniel could have walked back over and kissed her, and it wouldn't have been anything more to her than a hallucinated spark inside her brain's overamped circuits. He had done that kind of thing before, when he had first started out on this job and halting Time had been a new thing for him. But he'd stopped when the realization had sunk in that whatever he did, the ones he held in the grip of his power would always have something he could never have. There wasn't a stolen kiss hot enough to thaw the ice that had formed around his heart.

He walked farther across the locked-down tomb that had been the club's dance floor, before he'd willed it otherwise. He looked up at the ceiling's high-domed skylight. Frozen rivulets of rain streaked the glass panes; the storm clouds hung low enough to be edged by the glow of neon from the streets outside. A bright, jagged tangle of lightning cracked the night sky, caught before it could flash back into the dark.

He looked back down and stared at the crowd for another moment. He knew he should be getting on with the job, the reason he had come to the club. But the work he had done already tonight— this was the last one, the last name on the list he carried inside his head—had left him more than tired. Envy and disgust soured his guts.

One thing to stop Time. Another to waste it. Nathaniel headed for the back of the club, brushing past the frenzied, motionless bodies. He knew without glancing over his shoulder—he'd seen it before—that he'd left something behind. His shadow was still there, caught where the reddened light had still been in wave motion, before he'd stopped that as well.

He kept walking, shadowless now.

Should've waited, Nathaniel told himself, *until I got where I needed to be.* That was one of the main problems with stopping Time: if people were in the way before, when they were still moving, they were ten times as much of an obstruction after they'd been frozen in place.

Especially someplace like the back of a nightclub, where people went to do the things they didn't want to be seen doing in public. He squeezed past the inert, inconvenient bodies in the tightly packed corridor behind the stage. Some of them were caught against the walls in full-on, stand-up sexual passion, hands and faces all over each other's sweating bodies; they probably wouldn't have noticed him pushing his way past, even if all the world's clocks had still been ticking.

There were others, more furtive and hyperaware of their surroundings, their paranoid, over-the-shoulder scans of the darkened space stapled to their visages by Nathaniel's power. Beneath the dangling lightbulbs and the asbestos-wrapped ductwork, they stood trapped in tight knots, their hands caught passing folded wads of money and receiving little foil-wrapped bundles in exchange.

He managed to get past the various deals going down, both sex- and chemical-driven, all the way to the toilets at the rear of the building. He shoved open the men's room door and stepped inside.

More bodies were frozen in place. Some of them were caught hunched over the white porcelain sinks, vomiting up the hard kick of whatever they had purchased in the corridor outside. Others splashed cold water straight from the taps into their smoke-reddened eyes.

Nathaniel stood in the center of the tiled space, searching for someone. Someone in particular.

"You've done well." A soft, emotionless voice spoke behind him. "Your powers are developing . . . immensely."

He looked behind himself. And saw Death.

"Thanks," said Nathaniel. "I've been getting a lot of practice lately."

"Indeed." Death's pallid face remained expressionless.

"Maybe . . . a little too much, actually."

Death slowly nodded. "Ten years you've worked for me. Without complaint." Death lowered his head to peer into his apprentice's eyes. "You've become nearly as proficient in these arts as me. I confess I find it surprising that you speak of weariness now. Now, when you're so close to being that for which I purchased you."

This kind of talk drew a layer of discomfort on top of the fatigue Nathaniel already suffered. Death had treated him kindly enough for the last ten years. Better than Nathaniel's own father would have. He had no complaints. But even so, whenever he came along on what he called Death's reaping rounds, a tension grew inside him. He had come to dread each encounter with those whose names Death gave him.

"Come on." Nathaniel looked away from his master. "Let's get this over with."

"Very well." Death's reply was as flat and uninflected as always. "This way."

Death led him down the row of stalls at the back of the men's room, then pointed to one of the thin metal doors. With the flat of his own hand, Nathaniel shoved it open.

A young guy knelt beside the toilet, but wasn't hurling up his guts. Instead, he had a pocket mirror set out on the seat's lid, with three lines of glistening white powder reflected on the shiny glass. From the pocket of his suit jacket protruded a ripped-open envelope, which had held the six-figure quarterly bonus from the hedge fund company where he was a junior stockbroker. Sweat pasted the guy's hair to his forehead as he looked up with an angry scowl on his narrow face, a twenty-dollar bill rolled into a tube in one hand. "What the hell do you want?"

"You already know." Death spoke in a whisper. "It's time."

Red-rimmed eyes snapping wide, the stockbroker scrambled to his feet. He looked up higher, as if finally noticing the silence, the pounding techno shut down with the other processes of Time. Panicking, he tried to shove his way out of the stall, but Nathaniel caught him with one hand against his thin shoulder. But the stockbroker got far enough to see out into the men's room; the sight of the figures frozen statuelike at the sinks and urinals visibly horrified him. He backed away, trembling hands upraised.

Nathaniel stepped forward. "There's no way to fight this. So, for your own good, try to relax. It won't hurt, I promise."

"But . . . It can't be happening. I'm still so young."

"Age has nothing to do with it."

He heard the soft, agonized moan that escaped the stockbroker's lips. He felt sorry for the man. Just as he'd felt sorry for all of them. But there was a job to be done. He went on, despite the man's mounting fear.

"It's all right." Nathaniel laid a hand back on the stockbroker's shoulder. "There's nothing to be afraid of. . . ." He slowly nodded, trying to reassure the man. "Just take it easy. Death isn't the end. Not completely."

The man turned away, unwilling to listen to the hard, simple truth. But Nathaniel knew that he understood, at least a little bit, what was about to take place.

Death slipped past Nathaniel and reached out to the man in the stall. His hand, with no nails at the ends of the fingers, might have been something fashioned from translucent candle wax. As Nathaniel watched, he could feel the metal panels trembling around them, echoing the man's pulse. The vibration hammered at his own spine, too, as the man's heartbeat raced faster and louder. The figure underneath Death's pale hands writhed in fear, his hands pressing at his own chest in an attempt to stop the glow that had started to rise within it. The light of the man's soul burst through Death's outspread fingers, hard and searing enough to blind. Nathaniel twisted away, shielding his eyes. Burned on his retinas was the blurred image of the stockbroker's rib cage, and the fiery ball pressed against it.

He turned farther, so that Death would not witness the agony that was mirrored in his own face, too, as the soul rose up. That dark suffering never ended; it returned with every soul that he saw gathered. All Nathaniel could do was hide his agony within himself, so that his master did not see.

Behind him, he could hear the body jolting against the side of the stall. And a smaller, sharper noise, as one by one the pins, which had held the divine and unsullied essence prisoner inside the corrupted flesh, snapped. The last one broke apart, and Nathaniel could sense the light slowly gathering itself into the air.

The soul floated free for a moment, caught between Death's waxen hands. Then, with a whispered incantation, Death lifted it further into the air and released it from the mortal world forever— sending it away to the distant realm of Purgatory, where its sins would be judged and its eternal fate pronounced.

The brilliance faded; soon enough, the pain Nathaniel had endured would diminish as well. He turned around again and saw the lifeless, blank-eyed corpse slumped between the toilet and the side of the stall. He tried to slow his own racing pulse, taking one deep breath after another. This part of the job was over.

Something had gone wrong. The pain filling his chest—it didn't pass, as it always had before. It sharpened, as though his heart were seized in a steel-taloned fist, tighter and tighter. A new fear, dark and unrecognizable, coiled around his spine.

Dizzied by his own unfamiliar panic, he gripped the stall's door to keep from falling. He could hear Death's musing words.

"Why are they always surprised?" Death sounded almost puzzled, even though it was the same question he had asked so many times before. "By something they know will come. From the moment they are born—they know."

Nathaniel tried to answer. But couldn't. The knifelike pain— blazing as it was sharp—had stabbed him when he had felt the fiery ball rising from the man's chest. Now it grew as large as the world, annihilating every thought. He screamed in agony, and the floor swung toward his face.

"Nathaniel . . ."

As consciousness faded, he was dimly aware of Death standing above him.

"What has happened to you?"

Through the bathroom's one small window, he could see the frozen lightning, caught as it streaked across the night sky. Somewhere, out beyond the rain and the stars, the gears of Time started up again. But not inside Nathaniel. In there, it was just blackness and silence . . .

Then nothing.

2.

Blake's worn-out boots hit the ground exactly as the lightning flash divided the night into jagged halves. Rain-soaked cracks and gouges in the ancient leather mirrored the white electricity above. The rumbling sky was the only sound; the broken soles seemed to make no impact at all on the cargo depot's sodden concrete.

Anyone watching might have thought he was just another ragged beggar—the city was full of them. But beggars—real ones—moved slow, one leaden shuffle after another. And this one moved fast. Glimpsed, then gone before the darkness filled up the crack that the lightning had rent through the night sky.

The wooden train carriage was empty and silent now, as though nothing more than a ghost had departed from it. A few damp splinters, brushed free by Blake's hands, drifted onto the oily gravel at the platform's edge; the freight door might have opened on its own accord as the train had slowed, so quick had been the man's touch upon it. His matted dreadlocks had trailed behind his head as he darted to the ground. Up ahead, the diesel locomotive gasped out its final sulphurous exhaust, winding to a stop.

The rain barely touched his face, deep mahogany beneath the dirt and grease smudged on it. Crouching on one knee where he had landed, he quickly scanned the freight platform, then sprang to his feet.

Yard Bulls, the private cops hired to keep drifters off the railway's rolling stock, glared at Blake as he slipped past the stenciled crates crowding the platform. The Bulls' eyes tightened as water trickled from the drooping brims of their hats onto the upturned collars of their rain-heavy coats—but they didn't pull their shotguns out from beneath and yell at him to stop. Any other time, the man's appearance—his long, matted hair, his grime-blackened hands, and the crudely stitched-up tears in his fraying overcoat—would have given the Bulls perfect license to splay him out, their boot heels pinning his wrists to the concrete. But the way the Rottweilers cringed and tugged at the leash chains grasped in the Bull's black-gloved hands, paws scrabbling at the wet concrete to put as much distance as possible between themselves and this spectral intruder—that gave their masters enough sullen wisdom to let the man disappear from view. These days, there were plenty of other, slower vagrants to bully. There would at least be a chance of catching ones like that.

Farther in from the tracks, the iron overhang cast the platform into nocturnal shadows, their edges rendered hard by the halogens crudely mounted above, power cables looped from one arching girder to the next. The raw, wooden flanks of unclaimed freight containers had been pried open by those desperate enough to risk sneaking past the station's guards. The cheap splendor of

Asian toys, spilling from the broken crates, had been imbedded into the concrete like a slurried mosaic of bright-colored plastic, the tiny fragments still sharp enough to draw blood from incautious fingertips. As the beggar moved catlike past the decaying freight, his momentary step raised no dust from the shards.

Another crackle of lightning broke across the night; Blake's narrow shadow leapt across the crates. He halted and looked behind himself, the grimy dreadlocks tracing across his shoulders.

A shift in wind blew the rain beneath the overhang and closer to his face. He could feel soot-blackened rivulets crawling beneath the rag knotted at his throat. The muscles of his chest and spine, tightened from days of hard jostling as he had slumped in the corner of an empty freight car, now began to ease. This place looked like hell—which he had known it would—but he was still oddly relieved to have reached it at last.

Wanted to come here . . . A frown tugged at Blake's mouth, the rain collecting in one downturned corner. *Why?* That was what puzzled him. Why would anybody want to drag their sorry ass to this dump? Even somebody who had been born here, the way he had—nobody ever got homesick for this. A guy would need to be a glutton for punishment to have managed to claw his way out, and then make his way back here again.

A fragment of the answer came into his consciousness, the dark ebbing from a corner of his memory, as though the freight platform's searing halogen beams had managed to penetrate his skull. He had come back here to kill somebody—that much he could remember. Which was enough for now. The knowledge comforted him. Now all he had to do was find someplace to sleep off the weariness of his long traveling, and the rest would come to him in the morning. It always did.

Shouts and yelling broke into his thoughts. From somewhere farther down the platform, where there weren't any lights, just the shadows of crates and boxes that had been plundered and abandoned so long ago that they slouched together like damp straw huts in a moonless forest. The shouts weren't the fun kind but instead shrieked with panic.

He swiveled around to look. For a moment, it seemed to him as though the storm itself had come onto the platform, its wind rolling across the concrete. A torrent of fluttering rags surged between the freight containers, heading toward him. It took another second for him to see the fear-contorted faces, and realize that the cries came from their mouths.

"They're cleaning us out!" The rags were men, or what had been men, but were now just the homeless creatures who found what shelter they could in the station's unlit tunnels and corners. "Tons of 'em!" The nearest, his running gimped by an improvised crutch under his skinny bare arm, locked a panicked stare into Blake's eyes. "Run! Go!"

A tide of other homeless men crashed over the emaciated figure; their rag-swaddled feet trampled over his back. Blake let them sweep by, then looked down to see what they had left behind. The cripple, facedown, was still breathing, red leaking from his mouth and bubbling with each panting gasp. Blake reached down and pulled the broken figure to his feet. The wet sounds from the homeless man's mouth were no longer words; he clawed himself away from Blake's chest, and flopped birdlike after the rest of the ragged pack.

Blake peered into the darkness from which the homeless had burst into view. The platform was quiet again, but he knew they were still around, probably cowering under the freight carriages and peeking out at him, to see what he would do. Which was to turn and step into that dark, just to see what had spooked them all so bad.

It was still a mystery, even when he stood in the middle of the homeless men's abandoned encampment. Water leaked through the soot and grime of the tunnel's low roof, pattering like soft finger touches on the cobbled-together shelters, the cardboard boxes with nests of rags inside, the sleeping bags so begrimed with filth and the sweat of bad dreams that they shone in the trace of light like cocoons of black silk. Food rubbish, plastic bags, and little Styrofoam boxes scavenged out of the city's alley Dumpsters drifted to his ankles as he stepped through the crowded space. A cooking fire smoldered in the center of the boxes, a mold-spotted potato skewed on a length of rebar propped above it.

Blake heard more shouts coming from farther down the tunnel. These running steps were hard-soled, though, and the shouts rang with the fierce pleasure that came with clenched fists and truncheons snapping bones.

"There's one! Get the filthy bastard!"

He saw another pack of men, younger, not yet broken by time and the world, running toward him. Their shaved heads shone as bright as the knobbed toes of their cherry-red bovver boots, khaki fatigues tucked inside the tight, shin-high laces. Spittle flecked their yelling mouths, and their wide-open, excited eyes glistened with the joy of anticipated carnage.

Blake didn't move, just watched impassively as the skinheads charged toward him.

"Mess him up, Charlie!"

The first one's suspenders tightened over his sleeveless T-shirt as he skidded to a stop less than a yard away, braced himself, then swung a dented baseball bat in a flat arc toward Blake's ribs.

"God-*damn*—" The skinhead's eyes widened farther as he gawped in amazement. The blow hadn't hit its mark, but had been stopped instead by the palm of Blake's outstretched hand. The force of the impact traveled back up the bat, hard enough to nearly throw the skinhead off his feet.

"Whuddaya screwing around for?" One of the skinhead's companions shrieked in fury. "Get him!"

Blake plucked the bat from the skinhead's white-knuckled fists as easily as pulling a twig from a shoulder-high tree. He swung the big end up and set it between the skinhead's goggling eyes. A short, fast jab sent the thug toppling backward, blood streaming down from the crushed bridge of his pug nose.

It seemed sad to Blake that these kids didn't have as much sense as the Yard Bulls, who had at least known when to leave well enough alone. If they had turned tail and run, either dragging their buddy with them or leaving him where he lay, they might have had a better evening of it.

Instead, their howls rang louder and more outraged against the bricks of the tunnel's roof. Eyes reddened, the tight pack clawed and scrabbled at each other's tangling arms in their haste to throw themselves on him.

More shouts sounded, coming from another direction. He turned his head and saw another tunnel branching off from this one, filled with another churning pack, their weapons waved above their bald heads as they ran to join the party.

He brought his gaze back around in time to lay his forearm across the mouth of the first one to reach him, breaking the yellow teeth to stumps and sending the skinhead staggering back against the others, gagging on his own blood and ripped tongue. Blake's hand shot up, grabbing the nail-studded slat swinging down toward his skull. He wrenched it from another skinhead's grasp and brought it around hard across two of their faces, tearing open one's jaw before imbedding the bloodied nail into the other's neck.

That didn't slow down the rest; he hadn't thought it would. It never did. The second pack was racing toward him now. Their shouts were mingled with giddy laughter.

"We got ya now, asshole!"

True enough—they had spread out across the width of the platform as they ran, pushing and kicking aside the smaller crates, swarming houndlike over the bigger ones. Their black-nailed hands clawed toward him—

But caught nothing. Stupefied, the skinheads gaped as the beggar ran up the tunnel wall, the ragged hem of his overcoat fluttering behind him. Before they could react, he had already grabbed two by their necks, cracking their skulls against each other. As they dropped, a spinning kick, launched higher than Blake's own head, smashed bloody the faces of another pair.

The others finally reacted—but not before Blake was able to dive past their outstretched arms. He landed yards away, poised for only a split second on his fingertips and the balls of his feet, then leapt from the concrete's edge and onto the iron tracks. A solid wall of freight train loomed ahead, trapping him as the combined packs rushed close behind him—

Blake didn't slow. Instead, he dove shoulder-first toward the sharp-edged wheels, swinging his cracked leather boots above his own head with enough velocity to set him in a horizontal run across the locked carriage door. Rain fell in the skinheads' faces as they stared up at him. He bent his knees and kicked himself away from the carriage, hurtling above the shaved heads and landing in a crouch behind them.

They didn't have time enough to turn around. He grabbed the necks of the two at the rear of the pack, hard enough to hear bone crack like thick-shelled eggs. That gave him enough room to launch a roundhouse kick, dropping another pair. A steel rod swept toward his knees, missing him by inches as he sprang upward. The rod clanged on the platform as he dove forward, catching the attacker with a forearm under the chin and crushing his trachea. He dropped the gagging body in time to whip his elbow into the next one's face, a blossom of red bursting from where the nose and mouth had been.

One of the remaining skins snatched up the steel rod and drove its end toward Blake's gut. He fell backward to avoid the rod, then spun onto his side as it arced down, grazing the back of his skull before its tip sent shards flying from the concrete. He rolled back onto his spine and grabbed the rod, yanking the skinhead off his feet and catching him with a heel to the gut. Red vomit spattered Blake's ragged trouser leg, the skinhead's eyes rolling blank as he dropped like a punctured balloon.

There were only a couple still in front of him, the others having turned and fled back through the homeless camp. A simple uppercut took out one of them, who had been too stunned even before that to scurry away. That left Blake, knuckles scraped raw by broken teeth and bone fragments, gazing at a skinny runt in a stained undershirt, barely old enough to shave.

"Kid . . ." It had been so long since he had spoken out loud that his voice rasped deep in his throat. "You just standing there isn't making me any happier."

The young skinhead just trembled and covered his ashen face with his hands.

Have it your way. He obliged the kid by picking him up, hoisting him over his head, and tossing him onto the railway tracks. The kid bounced once, then scampered away. Blake watched him, then turned back toward the empty platform.

He figured it would be morning before the homeless recovered enough courage to come creeping out from beneath the wooden freight carriages and back to their cardboard hovels. That would give him at least a few hours use of the warmest nest he could find, to sleep off the fatigue from his long traveling and the fight with the skinheads. And maybe something to eat—the recalled vision of the potato charring on a stick roused a grumble in his empty stomach.

Just how tired he was didn't register until he got jumped again. If his senses hadn't been dulled, he might have heard them coming up from behind. But before he knew it, as he was leaning down to lift the flap of one of the empty cardboard boxes and check the rags inside for lice, the back of his skull seemed to explode in a red-tinged, shimmering wave. Teeth clenched against the dizzying pain, he turned his head enough to see his attacker, face crusted with blood from the struggle before, whipping the steel rod down for another blow. It caught him on his ear and one side of his jaw; he could feel the rebound against his skull as he toppled onto his back.

Another skinhead planted knees on his chest and a choking hand at his throat. A nasty little short-bladed knife drove toward his ribs.

He avoided the knife by rolling onto his shoulder, shoving aside the rags and cardboard box. The blade missed his chest, driving through the front and back of his overcoat instead, the sharp metal point pinning the grime-darkened cloth to a crack in the platform.

With the last of his strength, Blake lurched forward onto his knees. The pain and blood from before was nothing to what happened next. The skin over his rib cage ripped away, the raw muscles beneath clenching in torment.

The two skinheads backed up, gazing wide-eyed at the sight before them. The rod dropped clanging onto the platform.

With the sound of ripping gristle, Blake staggered to his feet. Still pinned to the concrete, the red-drenched overcoat tore from his shoulder and dangling arm, revealing how it and the raw flesh beneath were fastened together, as though some demented surgeon had imagined himself a tailor, combining skin and cloth into a garment that could never be shed.

The pain wiped out all of Blake's thoughts. He might have stopped before, when the gangs had run away—but not now. Now it was too late.

His blood-spattered hand shot forward, grabbing one skinhead by the throat. He squeezed until he could feel the cartilage grinding and snapping, then slung the dead body like a club, knocking the other figure to the ground. He ground his boot into the second one's face, until the hands stopped clawing at his leg and dropped away, lifeless.

Blake slumped down onto his knees, in the widening pool of his own blood. He had just enough strength left to tug the overcoat free from the knife, then wrap the joined cloth and flesh tighter about himself, his fist clenched just above the pounding of his heart.

He let his head drop, eyes fluttering closed. The groan of pain and despair from his whitening lips was all that was needed to damn the curse that had made him this way.

3.

Only a madman would tend a garden in weather such as this.

The dark storm clouds hung low in the sky, filling every direction visible to the naked eye, from one horizon beyond the city's tall office towers to the masses of craggy hills that ranged even farther in the distance. Rain pelted down, hammering the streets as well as the people and cars on them. The gutters ran like rivers, swift and engulfing, the muddied waters sloshing across the sidewalks and into the doorsteps of the grey buildings. Yet somehow there were never enough streaming torrents to wash away all of the city's filth and grime. The rain sluiced down along the buildings, leaving them just as filthy and blackened with soot as before.

The madman was so lost in the swirling tatters of his thoughts that he might not even have felt the lash of the rain upon his bent back. Through close-shaven stubble, his scalp shone pale and wet as he scrabbled through the contents of the frayed gunnysack at his feet.

With elaborate, methodical care, the madman set out the elements of his rituals. From the sack, he took out a child's toy, a plastic action figure, worn and scuffed. Something that he had rescued from a rubbish can set out at the curb. The broken ends of a wooden toothpick had been stuck to the doll's forehead, giving it what might have been horns. The plastic skin of the toy's face had been painstakingly colored red with a marker. One of its feet had been snapped off and replaced with the cloven hoof of a farm-toy goat. The madman knelt down and set the ugly figure in place, digging its plastic feet into the wet ground so it would stand menacingly upright.

There was still more to be set out for the madman's devotions to be complete. He dug more small figures from the sack, then knelt down with them at one side of a massive peach tree at the center of the garden square. Its withered, leafless branches raked like skeletal fingers through the rain-filled air above his head. When he stood back up, three more plastic action figures stood on the rain-soaked ground. Rescued from the trash, each now held a twig in its small, upraised hands, as though brandishing a weapon. The madman stepped back, nodding his head in approval of the miniature tableau.

"You know that tree's dead, don't you?"

The voice wasn't one of those that nattered and yelped inside the madman's head. Even he could tell that these words were real. Anyone in the deserted square might have heard them.

Startled, the madman looked back over his hunched shoulder. Across the sodden rubbish and brown weeds straggling up between the paving stones, a figure sat on one of the broken benches at the side. Vandals' boots had broken apart the bench's wooden planks, leaving just space enough for one person to sit. The dim moonlight that managed to slide through the shafts of rain revealed only the glint of blue eyes watching the madman.

"You'd better get away from there——" The madman didn't like having his private rituals observed. "Before you get yourself in trouble."

"Trouble?" The figure sitting on the bench sounded amused. "What kind of trouble?"

The madman dragged his gunnysack closer to the blackened trunk of the dead tree.

"This place is dangerous," the madman muttered darkly. "*He* doesn't like people coming in without his permission."

"He?" A fragment of a smile emerged in the darkness. "Who exactly are you talking about, old man?"

"Him!" The madman could tell that he was being mocked. Face set in quivering anger, he pointed to the red-faced, cloven-hoofed toy figure imbedded in the ground. "If he sees you here, you're done for. I can promise you that!"

"But how would he see me?"

"From up there, you idiot!" The madman pointed beyond the figure sitting on the bench, to the black office tower at one side of the garden square.

The figure on the bench didn't bother to look up. "What's that thing sticking out of his chest?" He nodded toward the horned doll in front of the peach tree. "Is that a nail?"

"That's because they killed him!" The madman's voice rose in demented triumph. "Look——it's gone right through him." He snatched up the doll and held it out before himself. With the thumb and forefinger of his other hand, he grasped the iron nail that had been thrust into it. The plastic squeaked as he pulled the nail out a bit, then shoved it back in. "With a great big spear— just like this! Killed the evil bastard dead!"

In the shadows at the side of the garden square, a scowl replaced the smile on the watching figure's face.

"Killed him?" A sneer sounded in his voice. "But I thought he lives in that building? How can he do that if he's dead?"

"I . . . I don't know," muttered the madman. He pawed at the side of his head, as though he could somehow dig through the bone of his skull and release some of the chaotic images trapped inside. "It's all . . . mixed up. Maybe it hasn't happened yet. But it will!" His eyes shone with absolute certainty. "I know it will! I can see it! As clear as I can see you sitting there! It's all true—I know it is!"

"And who is it . . ." The watching figure's voice softened as he studied the madman crouched near the dead pear tree. "Who's going to kill him?"

"The three of them, of course—who else? Look—can't you see them?" With demented certainty, the madman squatted down and laid the red-faced doll at the other toys' feet, the fatal nail sticking up from its chest.

"Just like that! That's how they did it! That's how it'll be!" The madman gazed down at the toys, fixated by the depiction of their victory. "This one here—" He tapped a dirty fingertip on the nearest one's plastic head. "This one's name is *Courage*!" His hand moved to the next. "And this is *Self-Sacrifice*!"

"And the last one?" The sneer in the watching figure's voice had hardened to contempt. "What is he called?"

"That's the one the Devil fears the most!" The madman nodded slowly. "His name is *Resolve*."

Goaded into a flurry of action, the madman dragged more objects out of his tattered gunnysack. With the rain sluicing down his upraised face, he hung three more action figures on the lowest of the dead tree's branches. They slowly turned about as they dangled there, with crude cut-out paper wings taped to their shoulders.

"It'll bloom——" The madman muttered low to himself as he draped the leafless branches with salvaged holiday tinsel. "I know . . . I know it will!" He stepped back from the tree, looking at everything with which he had adorned it. The effect was of a handmade shrine, a place of single-minded devotion. "There'll be leaves . . . and fruit! Like you've never seen! And on the day that it blooms, there'll be an army, too . . ."

He drew out handfuls of other, smaller plastic figurines from the sack. Toy soldiers molded from dark green plastic—he carefully arrayed them in the grass at the tree's base, surrounding the three action figures with their twig weapons raised above the one toppled over, with its red-painted face and toothpick horns.

"Just . . . just like that!" He looked over at the figure watching from the shadowed bench. "But the secret is, this army, it's invincible! It's so tough that no one can beat it. Not even him!"

"Is that so?"

"Yes!" The madman stood up from his crouch, shivering in excited certainty. "When they come out to fight him, then you'll see. Because then it'll be all over!" He pointed to the dark office tower. "Over for him!"

"You seem very sure of yourself." The watching figure tilted his head to one side, studying the madman. "How do you know all this?"

"Because the archangels told me!" The madman pointed to the winged action figures dangling from the branches. "They know everything! They planned it all." His voice turned hushed and reverent. "They planted the tree, you see. To bring hope. To the people . . . to everyone . . ."

He didn't wait for any more words from the figure sitting on the bench. More objects came out of the gunnysack as the madman knelt down. Candle stubs, with burnt-black wicks at the center of the pale wax. With a half-empty book of matches, he managed to light them, their small flames wavering in the storm's cold wind. He leaned back where he knelt in the wet grass, delighting in the effect of the trembling glow, then glancing over his shoulder to see if the watching figure had noted it as well.

Just as he did so, a car passed by on the street beyond, the beam of its headlights sweeping through the garden. That was enough to illuminate the figure sitting on the bench. The madman drew back, his eyes widening at what he saw.

A man—but something more than that. Tall and powerfully built, in the full strength of his early fifties. That was what the figure looked like. Garbed in an expensive cashmere coat that was somehow not dampened by the rain that drenched the garden square, and with a leonine, tawny hue to his skin and hair, as though descended from the ancient kings of Persia. The hard, chiseled planes of his face spoke of a barely bridled virility, the kind possessed by those sharp-clawed predators at the top of the world's food chain.

The headlights swung off into the darkness, the garden square falling back into the night's deep shadows.

Cowering back against the dead tree, the madman kept his wary gaze upon the watching figure. In the chaos of his thoughts, a dreadful realization was forming.

"What else," the figure said slowly, "do you know?"

"There . . . there'll be a battle." As though hypnotized, the madman couldn't stop himself from speaking. And revealing the rest of the prophecy lodged in his addled brain. "When the tree springs to life and blooms for all the world to see . . ." He pressed his knotted hands against his chest. "That's when the people will know that the day has come. The day of the final battle. That's when the three of them and their army will face down the Devil and his demons. They'll fight—and that battle will decide the future of us all. . . ."

Another set of headlights, coming from one of the cross streets beyond, sent their harsh beam straight into the other man's face. His eyes now shone with the piercing, inhuman blue of burning sulphur.

The madman shrank back against the blackened trunk, terrified. The beam from the passing headlights disappeared. But the other man's eyes remained lit up, bright as two intense flames.

"Who . . ." The madman found his voice. "Who are you?"

"Why don't you ask your archangels?" The watching figure sneered at the madman's terror.

The figure stood up from the broken bench and walked forward, into the center of the abandoned garden square. The madman's sight dropped to the man's feet. He could see now that the figure's left foot was misshapen and heavy, producing a dragging limp.

"I know . . ." He looked up at the man's sneering face. "I know who you are . . ."

"As you said—" The Devil towered above the cowering lunatic. "I don't like anyone coming here without my permission."

"I . . . I'll go. Right now . . ."

"And then to hear all this . . . this nonsense." The Devil glared down at him, face tightening with rage. "Just as if I'd never had to listen to it before. I know all about your archangels, and your heroes, and their invincible army. I've been listening to that fairy tale for centuries. And you know something?" Eyes burning even fiercer, he leaned down toward the madman. "It's never come true. And it never will."

The madman crouched down lower, but there was nowhere else to go.

"But all the same, no one has ever been fool enough to come to my front door and talk about it to my face before." The Devil squeezed his hand into a fist. "Not until now."

The Devil looked up from the quivering figure at his feet. He brought his gaze to the paper-winged toys dangling from the leafless tree. They burst into flames, spreading to the tinsel draped across the branches.

Crying out in dismay, the madman sprang to his feet, trying to beat out the fire racing across the tree. The flames spiraled like luminescent serpents down its trunk, engulfing the candle stubs and action figures set out in the grass.

The fire dwindled away in seconds, its purpose accomplished. The dead tree remained undamaged. But the ashes drifted from its branches, like black snow settling upon the shapeless blotches of melted plastic below.

"You . . ." The madman turned his face, tears mingling with rain, toward the Devil standing behind him. From somewhere inside himself, amidst his disordered thoughts, he had found a spark of defiance. "You can destroy whatever you want—but you can't destroy my hope. The things they told me, they'll come true one day. And maybe that day will come sooner than you think."

One corner of the Devil's mouth lifted in an ugly smile. "Somehow I doubt that. But even if it does, it still won't come soon enough to save you."

He turned and gestured with an outflung hand toward the weeds choking the limits of the square. Rats, their eyes glistening like points of fire, rushed from their burrows, streaming across the matted grass.

The rats swarmed over the madman, their claws scrabbling up along his legs, then across his chest. His screams were choked off by the yellow fangs sinking into his face. He fell, hands futilely tearing at the sleek, grey shapes blanketing him from sight.

Only a few minutes passed before he stopped moving. His raw flesh, gnawed to the bones beneath, could be seen in the middle of a widening pool of red, blood seeping into the ground.

The Devil turned away. He looked up at the black reach of the office tower at the side of the garden. In the rain, it stood as daunting as an immense cenotaph, fashioned from some black stone quarried from the earth's depths. Others like it mounted toward the storm-darkened sky, mute guardians of the city's wealth. Only a few people knew what distinguished this building from the rest.

The clouds obscured the top of the building. Just below them, at the twentieth floor, light came from an expanse of windows. That was where he brought his gaze, head tilted back.

Someone watched him from those windows, so far above . . .

The Devil looked down at the dark figure standing in the abandoned garden. He could see that they both wore the same expensive cashmere jacket and open-necked silk shirt beneath. The same sulphurous blue flame sparked in their eyes. The figure below wore a heavy, clubbed shoe, concealing his cloven left foot—as did the identical figure on the twentieth floor.

Their twin gazes met for a second. Then the garden was empty of everything except the dead peach tree and the madman's bloodied carcass at its base.

The Devil closed his eyes and inhaled deeply, as though drawing part of himself back toward the core of his being—

He had other business to take care of now.

When the Devil turned away from the window, a face bright with anxious sweat looked up toward him.

"Can . . . can I go on now?"

Disgust filled the Devil's thoughts. That was the reaction produced by each and every pathetic example of humanity. The cringing, sniveling ones that came here to his office were the worst.

"If you must." He stepped away from the floor-to-ceiling windows, looking over the abandoned garden square below. "So, what exactly did you want to discuss with me?"

"I thought . . . you knew . . ."

"Sadly, I do." He turned and looked at his desk. It had been cut, a long time before, from a two-ton boulder of black lavastone. "What's all this . . . stuff?"

"I brought some photos—" The magnate's hands, rounded and plump as his gut, frantically rearranged the colored images. "So you could see what I've built up for myself, since the last time we spoke to each other."

"This is your wife, I take it?" He picked up one of the photos and regarded it. "A little out of your league, I would have thought."

"Well . . ." A nervous smile showed on the man's face. "I guess I did well for myself."

"Money has an attractive quality to it. For certain women." He peered at another one of the photos. "And this is your son?"

"Oh, yeah." The man's face brightened. "I took that at one of his soccer games. He's the top scorer in the city youth league—"

"Indeed." He bent down and prodded a few more of them about with a manicured fingertip. "Your daughters?"

"Twins. That was at their ballet recital. We had to donate a bundle to the local ballet company to get 'em into the school. But it was worth it. I want my money to do some good now, you see. For everyone."

The Devil could barely keep his gorge from rising. "And what a lovely home you have, too." His polished fingernail tapped another photo. "Three stories—more of a mansion, really. You must keep a troop of gardeners employed, to have all that landscaping so well maintained."

"Yeah . . ." The other man shrugged. "But what can you do? You gotta have it."

"Just so." He nodded. "You *must* have it. That's what you decided. What you wanted *must* be what you have." He had picked up a half dozen of the photos, and now tossed them onto the desk with the rest. "That's why we made our little deal, all those years ago. And you got what you wanted, didn't you?"

"Oh, sure—" The other man nodded his head frantically. "I got no complaints—"

"Then why did you come here? Why did you want me to see all . . . this?" He gave a dismissive gesture toward the photographs. "These pretty pictures."

"Well—"

"And especially *now*." He frowned as he shook his head. "I have to say that your timing seems just a little suspicious. Given that tomorrow is the exact anniversary, to the day, of the sealing of our contract with each other."

"I thought that maybe . . ." The other's voice was nothing but a hoarse whisper; he couldn't look up, but kept his lowered gaze on the photos. Even if he couldn't see them now. "Maybe we could work something out together . . . something else, I mean . . . about my end of the deal."

"Ah." The Devil tapped a fingernail on the photograph of the man's wife. "I see."

"Do you?" A hopeful gaze lifted toward him. "I mean . . . if you could . . ." The fat man spread his hands above the photos again. "Because it'd be a crime to just waste everything I've accomplished. Everything I've pulled together . . ."

"A crime. Yes, of course." He nodded slowly. "But let me show you something even more criminal."

The magnate cowered as the Devil leaned across the desk. The leonine features were contorted with a sudden rage.

"You!" He jabbed a finger into the fat man's chest. "You disgust me. We have a deal, you and I, a contract—and now you want to crawl out of it. And for what?" He slammed the flat of his hand down upon the desk. "For this trash? That slutty whore you like to call your wife? Your ugly pug-nosed children?" He swept his hand across the photographs. "And you dare say that this is what *you've* accomplished? Twenty years ago, you were nothing but a broken-down traveling salesman who had pawned his samples case for a bottle of cheap bourbon. And when the bottle was lying empty on the floor of your five-dollar-a-night motel room, you looped your belt over the water pipe in the bathroom and tied the other end around your neck. There would have been nothing left of you but another purple-faced corpse if I hadn't arrived in that moment to offer you a way out."

"I . . ." The pudgy hands hurriedly pulled back the photos into a ragged pile. "I know. And I appreciate it. Really I do. But I've got a family now. And they love me . . ."

"Do you really think that means anything to me?" The scorn in his face was more frightening than the anger had been. "What does a worm like you know of love, and things lost?" He raised the man's tear-wet face with a fingertip under his chin. "Let me tell you a story, maggot. Once there was a creation, a being holier than any of your tribe could ever be, immaculate in a newborn universe. An archangel, the first to be molded by God's hands, the first ever to have life breathed into his unstained heart. That archangel was given the duty of bringing light to all the worlds. And he was God's favorite, until God created . . . Man." The single word sounded like a curse on his lips. "And a thing like you, a thing of stinking flesh and callow, ignorant appetite, became God's favorite." His gaze turned away from the fat man on the chair, and locked onto a vision of millennia past. "Was I to thank him for that usurpation? No. Better I should rise up and rebel against my creator for the love He'd taken away."

Imbedded in the lava-stone desk, a series of arcane metal symbols appeared, turning incandescent with heat as the Devil spoke. The photos on top of the desk burst into flame, their edges charring black as the fat man scooped them up and held them against his heaving chest.

"Do you see those?" He pointed to the swirling, interlaced symbols. "That's the spell that God used to create me. And it is more a part of me than this." One hand laid upon his chest. "This flesh is but earthly corruption, a prison. If you could decipher what is inscribed in that stone, you would know what happened at the beginning of the universe. You would see the beauty of it, and realize the crime God committed when He turned against me. But of course . . . I had my vengeance in the end. When I tricked your naked progenitor into eating the forbidden fruit in Eden." His smile was one of malignant satisfaction. "Man was banished for that crime, and made into a suffering, mortal thing—as he deserved. As *you* deserve. But that is not the end of the story. No, for God is not so craven an opponent as to fail to recognize my cunning. And so, following that victory in Eden, I was granted the authority to test and try every human soul that is born to this world, to sort the worthy from the foul, and damn all who fail into a Hell of my own making. A Hell that has been waiting for you ever since the moment you signed our deal." He reached down and tapped at the burning symbols. "The metal here is magnesium. The metal of Heaven. The metal of eternity. But as fiercely as these would sear your flesh were you to touch them, the pit of your damnation rages hotter. And it is so close to you in this moment that I could pick you up and throw you into the fire from where I stand."

Curled into a ball on his chair, the fat little man wept, his hands full of the ashes of his life.

The Devil spoke softer now, as though his anger had ebbed back into its hidden sources inside him. "Did you really think I came to you that night, with no thought but to do well by you, and make everything your hand touched turn to gold?" He shook his head as he gazed down at the whimpering form on the chair. "Did I lie to you? Did I deceive you? Tell you that I was anything other than what I am? Or that the price of all the success and wealth I would give you, twenty years of every desire satisfied—that the price would be anything other than your immortal soul?"

"No . . . you told me . . ."

"Exactly. As I tell everyone who enters into such a contract with me. Whatever else I might be accused of, by God or Man, none can say that I'm not up front. When we sealed our agreement twenty years ago, I told you what would happen when your time was over. But now that it's within sight, when you have only one day left in which to enjoy all that I have given you, now you throw that last little bit away by coming to me, sniveling and whining for me to change my terms." His disgust became even more apparent, the corner of his mouth withering to a sneer. "The species of man is so predictable. Do you think you're the first one to have come here like this, begging for a reprieve? Everyone does, when the time for their final settlement approaches. But it does you no good. None of you. Once you're mine, you're mine forever. And if you don't believe that, see it for yourself—"

The Devil pulled open one of the drawers of his desk. From the drawer, he pulled out a handgun, its polished silver gleaming. "If you want to be free of me, this is the simplest way to do it. All you have to do is shoot me with this gun, and you can have all the freedom you desire."

"What . . ." The fat man cringed backward. "What do you mean?"

"Take it." He held the gun by its barrel, handle extended toward the other. "All you have to do is show the same strength of will that I showed against God, when I fought Him face to face in Heaven. If you do that, then I promise you, you can spend as much time with your precious family as you want. Watching your children grow up and your pretty young wife grow fat."

He forced the gun into the magnate's trembling grasp.

For a full, ticking minute, the fat man grasped the gun in his doubled fists, its snout wavering toward the Devil's chest. Then, at last, it dropped away, dangling between the man's knees where he sat. "I . . . can't . . . I want to do it. But somehow, I just can't . . ."

"No. Of course you can't . . . And I'd have been astonished if you could." With a thumb and forefinger, he plucked the gun away, turning to toss it onto the desktop. "I was making a point, that's all. About how unworthy an opponent Man has always been. And how easy it is to destroy you all, by taking away your will to act. That's what happens to all of you who take my hand. I rip the willpower out of you bit by bit, until finally it is gone completely. Making it impossible for you to ever return to the way you were before."

The Devil sank down at the desk, leaning his head against one hand, as though suddenly wearied. "Go now, and leave me in peace." His other hand made a curt gesture of dismissal. "There's no hope left for you. The arrangements to end your life tomorrow night have already been made. So, go home, and enjoy what little time you have left."

The heavy stone door swung open, revealing one of the Devil's secretaries. Well-dressed, glossily made-up, in the full sexual vigor of her midthirties—the woman would have been attractive enough if it hadn't been for the thin, malicious smile that revealed her to be one of the Devil's witches.

"This way," she said coldly. "Hurry along, now."

Beyond her, the fat magnate saw the office's lobby, crowded to the suffocation point with all the other supplicants who had come begging for a moment of the Devil's precious time. Young, old, healthy or sick—all forced to stand and wait, without even knowing whether they would be allowed to see the one whose mercy they craved.

Their eyes all locked upon the magnate, desperate to see some sign of hope, some indication that the Devil might be in a good enough mood to grant even a few small favors. Even a day's extension on the fatal contracts to which they had all signed their names . . .

The lobby looked less like a place of business than it did a slaughterhouse, helpless creatures crammed shoulder-to-shoulder, with no way of escape before them other than their own deaths. Their faces were lit ghastly by the churning red glow barely visible through the thick sheet of tempered glass that formed the floor beneath their shuffling feet. Above the supplicants' heads, a frieze of grotesquely carved statues adorned all four walls of the lobby.

"You clubfooted bastard—"

Those words brought the Devil's gaze back down from the lobby's hideous decorations to the shivering specimen of humanity still in front of him.

"Someday . . ." Trapped in the office's doorway, the press of sweaty bodies tight against him, the fat magnate had managed to summon up his last scrap of courage. Chin trembling, he glared at the Devil.

"Someday you'll find out what it's like to be so frightened." He raised his arm, gesturing toward the others packed into the lobby. "To be just as frightened and hopeless as everyone here—"

"Frightened?" The Devil barked out a harsh laugh. "Of who?"

"Of someone . . ." The magnate clenched his hands into trembling, ineffectual fists. "There are stories—a legend—of people you should fear. I just hope . . ." His eyes welled with childish tears. "I just hope that one day those stories come true."

Before the Devil could unleash the anger rising inside himself, his secretary pushed the magnate out into the crowded lobby. She pulled the door closed, leaving the Devil at peace in the empty office. The vision in the lobby, that of disgusting, cringing humanity, was removed from his sight.

He walked back over to the window, the cloven hoof inside his clubbed shoe dragging with each step. The supplicants in the lobby could rot, for all he cared. He had no interest in hearing any more of their whining pleas tonight. They would all still be there tomorrow, and for all the days to come, without end.

"Legends . . ." The Devil muttered to himself, gazing out at the city's dark skyline. "Prophecies . . ." It infuriated him that he'd had to listen to such nonsense twice in one night.

He looked down at the dead peach tree in the garden, its bare branches straggling through the rain falling upon it. That sight made him feel better. Just knowing that it would never bloom . . . that all those legends and prophecies were just pathetic fairy tales. Things that stupid human beings told to each other, trying to create some hope for themselves in the darkened prison of their world.

As he brooded, savoring the bleakness of his meditations, the dark grey clouds just above the windows suddenly darkened to black, their heavy billows etched by a flash of lightning. The blue-white electricity filled the window as it shot by.

Down below, the lightning struck the tree, filling the garden square with smoke. But when it cleared, driven aside by the rain, the Devil saw that the dead tree hadn't been broken into splinters. Instead, the slender trunk seemed to glow, as though the leaping energy still coursed inside, waking it from centuries of dormant slumber. Green shoots pushed through the bark of the branches, lifting skyward. He could almost imagine being able to catch the sweet fragrance of the scattered peach blossoms opening, delicate and papery white.

He stared down at the tree in horror. Beyond rage, as though still in shock from what he had witnessed. That he had never seen before . . .

"Prophecy," he whispered to himself. The word sounded different now, filled with dread meaning. He laid a hand against the cold glass, wondering if that day had arrived at last.

The one in which the fairy tale would finally come true.

4.

When you're seven feet tall, and nearly as wide, it's hard to sneak up on people. So Hank didn't try anymore.

Instead, he smashed open the crack house's boarded-up door and lumbered inside, his shoulders barely squeezing through the frame. His heavy workman's boots splintered the scraps of wood that his massive fists had so easily broken apart. The bare light-bulb dangling from the water-stained ceiling shattered against his brow, the hallway plunging into darkness as he brushed away the shards of glass.

"Holy shit!" At the end of the narrow space, a voice shouted in surprise, just as if the person had never seen a human bull-dozer before—and worse, one that was heading straight for him and his buddies. The skinny figure darted away, shouting a frantic warning to the rooms beyond.

Hank knew there was supposed to be about a dozen or so people inside the crack house. Heavily armed—weren't they always?—and one of the worst gangs in the city, murderously disposed even before they got themselves hopped up on their own merchandise. Cleaning up scum like this was business as usual for him, doing the sort of job that the municipal police couldn't be bothered with. A professional hit man such as Hank didn't let it bother him that he was getting paid by people who weren't much cleaner than the ones he took out.

The clatter of guns being scrambled for and loaded came from the other side of the door. That didn't bother him, either. As always, the only weapons he had brought were his fists. And they were more than enough to do the job.

As he plodded forward without hurry, a door flung open and a shotgun blast roared. The lead pellets ripped the ancient flowered wallpaper beside him to confetti. He had come close enough that he could grab the hot barrel of the gun, yank it out of the gang member's hands, then slam its worn wooden butt against the punk's head. He stepped over the dying body, ready for the next.

They came at him with their full arsenal. A rusty machete swung toward his face. He knocked it aside with his forearm, then rammed his other fist into the punk's gut. The impact doubled him over, right where Hank could bring a knee up, turning what had been a human face into a bag of broken bones, leaking red. A handgun sprayed its clip wildly at his back. He turned and grabbed the gun, its last shot singeing between his fingers, and crushed another gang member's hand into a wad of blood and cartilage around it. A blow to that one's chest dropped another lifeless body at Hank's feet. From behind, a heavy chain slammed across his shoulders. Not even bothering to look around, he clamped the linked iron in his grip and pulled, dragging another one within range of his fists . . .

He appreciated it when creeps like this, the ones he'd been hired to eliminate, came at him all at once; it saved time. The last thug placed himself in the doorway of what had once been the house's kitchen, and was now filled with a haphazard assemblage of lab equipment and empty plastic bins of drug precursors. Unsteady hands gripped a .357 magnum, the black hole of its snout aimed straight at Hank's chest.

From beside one of the corpses, he picked up a broken length of broomstick that one of them had laughably tried to use as a club; he hadn't even felt the blow crack on top of his head. Now he cocked his arm back, then whipped it forward. The wood tumbled end over end, then brought its splintered point straight into the gunman's brow with enough force to bury itself halfway through his head. The man dropped backward, the gun discharging a round into the ceiling as it thudded onto the corpse's chest.

When the noise of gunshots and hammer blows and bones being crushed finally faded, he figured that maybe ten minutes had gone by since he had slammed through the crack house's door. If it had been as long as twelve, that would have been a minute for each of the broken bodies he counted, laid out around him. About par for the course.

His breathing was still as slow and easy as it had been when he had started this job. He pulled back his jacket sleeve and the cuff of the faded denim work shirt underneath, and laid a couple of fingertips on the underside of his wrist, checking his pulse. That hadn't sped up, either. "Damn," he muttered. It didn't come as a surprise to him, but as a disappointment, the same he always felt.

He reached into the back pocket of his jeans, dug out a handker-chief, and used it to wipe the spattered blood from his face.

A moan sounded from somewhere nearby. A spark of hope leapt upward in his chest. This was the sort of opportunity he hardly ever received, given how efficiently he went about his work. He rushed past the bodies, peering down to see which of the gang members might still be alive.

By the crack house's front door, Hank found one who had managed to crawl that far. Blood still bubbled from the wound in the man's throat. The eyes focused enough to see the hulking figure that loomed over him, and widened in terror.

"Don't worry . . ." Hank leaned in close over the gang member, desperate to speak to him before it was too late. "I'm not here to hurt you. Not anymore. I'm here for something else now . . ." He brought his face down. "This is just between you and me . . ."

Chest heaving, the man gasped. "Wuh . . . whut . . ."

"Listen. You're finished, pal. So don't fight it." He reached behind the dying man's shoulders and lifted him closer. "Just answer me . . ."

He searched deep into the other's eyes, his own breath stopping in his chest.

"Are you . . . afraid?"

Blood draining from beneath his face, the man feebly nodded.

Breath moved inside Hank's chest again, his pulse racing. "Then tell me. Because I need to know. What does it feel like . . . *Fear?*"

There was no answer except gurgling blood.

"Please . . ." He shook the gang member's shoulders.

The man's eyes dulled opaque, and a last small bubble burst in the ruin of his throat.

"Damn." Hank straightened back up. His ragged fingernails dug inside his clenched fists. That time, he had felt really close. To finding out at last.

The rain had started up again, more of the city's relentlessly punitive weather. Hank zipped up his jacket as he left the crack house, and the bodies inside. The organization that had hired him for the job could go in and make their own count, and total up how much they owed him. He didn't care.

Across the street's mounds of rubble, yellowing scraps of newspaper turning into sodden mulch, the neighborhood's residents regarded him from under the eaves of the lightless buildings. Mainly whores and their pimps, the kind scrabbling out the final bits of their working lives, mixed in with addicts prowling for their connections. They blankly watched him go; whatever had gone down inside the crack house had been close to normal for them as well.

As his heavy step crumbled fragments from the edges of the broken sidewalk, he heard the sound of a car cruising slowly behind him. That wasn't unusual in a district like this; all sorts of types from the more prosperous parts of town came down here, looking to purchase something for their evening's entertainment, the transaction conducted through side windows rolled down only an inch or two. But this car seemed to be pacing him, which was an annoyance. He figured he had already plodded through enough work for one morning, and didn't want to be bothered with somebody wanting to mess with so large a target. He stopped and turned around.

Not just a car, but a shining black limo, its length taking up nearly half the block. He could see the chauffeur silhouetted behind the wheel. And dimly, another figure in the back.

The limo pulled up even with him and stopped. Its rear door closest to him opened up, pushed by the passenger's hand.

"Hank?" The passenger displayed a slight smile. "It's Hank, isn't it?"

"Might be." It took him a moment, peering inside the limo, to realize that he was speaking to a dwarf, shoulders hunched forward by a malformed spine. "Do I know you?"

"Not yet." The hand holding the limo door open bore a large magnesium ring, engraved with some starlike symbol unfamiliar to him. The polished metal contrasted oddly with the scabs and suppurating boils visible on the dwarf's skin. "But that's something we can take care of. Get inside, so we can talk."

Hank rubbed his chafed knuckles. "Maybe tomorrow."

"Tomorrow will be too late. Please, you'll find it worth your while, I promise."

"Maybe I will." Hank shrugged. "But like I said, I don't even know who the hell you are."

The dwarf leaned back against the soft leather seat. "Names don't really matter in my line of work. Let's just say . . . I'm a lawyer. With a very important client." The dwarf's smile was like a swath cut from a rotting pumpkin. "I have a job for you. A lucrative one. And dangerous, too."

His own gaze narrowing, Hank studied the smaller man. "How dangerous?"

"Probably the most dangerous one you'll ever have." He slid farther to the side of the limo, making room for Hank to join him. "Honestly, it's the opportunity of a lifetime."

The promise of danger proved too tempting for Hank. "Okay," he said. "I'll give you five minutes." He gripped the top of the door and began working his bulk inside. "But I'm just warning you. I'll be mucho pissed' if you waste my time."

The hollow sound of the rain drumming against the roof filled the limo's interior. The upholstered ceiling pressed hard against the top of Hank's head. Even given the spaciousness of the limo's interior, the dwarfish lawyer was squeezed tight against the other door.

"Let me begin by saying this—" The dwarf signaled to the chauffeur, and the limo began slowly rolling through the city streets again. "You aren't the only hit man that my client is employing today. In fact, as far as I'm aware, every other killer in the city is already on his payroll."

"So what does he want with me?" Hank had a close-up view of the dwarf. The rashes and boils covered the beak-nosed face as well, as if the small man wouldn't have been ugly enough without them.

"Quite simply, you're the best," continued the dwarf. "Not only because of your size and skill. But also, more importantly, because of your . . . *condition*."

Hank stiffened. "My condition?"

"Your *pantophobia*. That's the medical term for it, I believe. In layman's terms, a complete and utter absence of fear."

Hank growled. "How do you know about that?"

"I've read your medical records. Apparently, you've had it

since birth. The most extreme case ever recorded, they say. A real advantage for someone in your line of work." The dwarf displayed his yellow-toothed smile once more. "Which is why my client is so anxious to have you on our team."

"You've read"—Hank's growl grew worse—"my medical records?"

The lawyer acknowledged the comment with a nod. "My client likes to know who he's dealing with before he makes them an offer. To be precise, we know everything about you, Hank. We know exactly how many people you've killed in your current profession. And we know all about the trouble you caused at the orphanage, when you were a boy. You were sent there just after you'd killed your parents, I think. The first two deaths in a very long line."

Anger swelled in Hank's body; the limo's seat creaked, as though it were about to break. His fists clenched as he struggled to restrain the impulse to reach over and crush the lawyer's wiry-haired skull. *You sonuvabitch*. Hank seethed inside himself. The rage didn't come from this man knowing so much about him. And not from the bit about that pantophobia crap, or whatever it was called. No, it was the way that the lawyer had made it sound that somehow his parents' deaths had been connected to all the scumbags he had taken care of in his job as a hit man. When actually there was no connection at all, except for there having been dead bodies at the end of the process. He gritted his teeth, shoving that certainty tighter into his thoughts. No goddamn connection at all.

But he knew he was lying to himself. There was a connection, and he hated the dwarf for knowing it as well. The lack of fear, that pantaphobia thing he had been born with—it made it easy for him to kill criminals. But it was also why his parents had died. That was the connection.

He had been nine years old, his parents still alive. He'd been huge then as well, not as big as he was now, but going on adult size. Strong as an ox. And worse, fearless. Which got a nine-year-old kid into all sorts of trouble, whether he meant to or not. And his poor mom and dad, worried about what might become of him if he went on that way, had tried to cure him of it one Halloween. If fearlessness was the problem, then the cure was to somehow put fear into him. They tried the best they could: jumping out of the dark in his bedroom, draped in bedsheets to make themselves look like ghosts. It didn't work—he wasn't scared—but he did think that the ghosts were real. He could still see every detail in his mind, as if it were happening again. He saw that huge nine-year-old boy leaping out of bed with the baseball bat he kept leaned against the wall, then attacking the ghosts with a flurry of blows. The fear might not have been there inside him, but he had still watched in horror as his parent's blood trickled toward him from behind the sheets and out across his bedroom floor. . . .

Hank still felt sickened by it. He knew that everything he felt about that night would never disappear. How could it? The guilt had made him what he was. All through growing up in the orphanage—and then his career as a professional hit man—it had always been that guilt that had driven him forward. Driven him to try and cure the fearlessness that was his curse. The more dangerous the places and fights that he walked into, the better. Maybe one of them, someday, would be enough to bring that hotly desired but never experienced substance, that fear, into his heart. And then maybe he would somehow be at peace.

He opened his eyes and looked over at the dwarf. "You ever mention my parents again," said Hank, "and I'll kill you. My past is my own affair. The same goes for my condition, too."

The lawyer held up a mollifying palm. "If I've upset you, I'm sorry. Everyone needs secrets, and yours are safe with me." Beneath his insincere words rose the sound of the limo's wide tires rolling through the sodden streets. "The only reason I brought it up is because I wanted to make it clear to you why my client needs you on his side. All the details aren't in yet, but there could be a bloodbath in this city before this day is through. And it's vital that we have someone on our team who'll stick with the job to the end, no matter how tough the going gets."

Hank leaned back, still regarding the lawyer suspiciously. "This guy you work for, who is he?"

The dwarf's scabby finger tapped the starlike symbol on his ring. "Let's just say he's a businessman, with a vested interest in maintaining the status quo."

Hank's laugh was a quick, rumbling bark. "I've heard *that* before. And the targets?"

"There are three of them in total. Three men, by all accounts."

"And you're sure they're bad, these guys?" he asked. "Because I don't hurt innocents. Just people who are in a position to hurt me, too."

The dwarf acknowledged the comment with another nod. "Rest assured, these men are the worst kinds of scum you'll ever find. In fact, considering what they're planning to start today, you could even call them mass murderers." He turned away and glanced at the rivulets of water sluicing over the side windows. "So . . . can I tell my client you'll take the job?"

Hank had to admit that his interest had been piqued. "Okay," he said. "I'm in. What I need from you now are their IDs, and the address where I can find them."

"Ah . . ." The dwarf smiled apologetically. "I'm afraid it isn't quite as simple as that. You see, their identities and whereabouts aren't clear to us at the moment. All we know is that they must be here in the city somewhere. Either as a group, or on their own."

"But . . . if you don't know where they are, how the hell am I supposed to kill them?"

"I suppose by just . . . doing what you do best . . ." The dwarf folded his scabby hands to explain. "You see, my client has instructed me to inform you that despite your strength and skill, killing these three men will be far from easy. So, if that difficulty in killing them is the only way to recognize them, he suggests that you simply attack everyone in this accursed city who's dangerous enough to hurt you, and let us know when you finally meet your match."

Hank glared at him in disbelief. "Are you serious?"

"Completely." The dwarf's beady eyes didn't even flinch. "As I said, my client has every faith in you. So rest assured, however many people you end up killing today, he is more than happy to pick up the tab."

Every bastard who can take a shot at me . . . The danger of it called to Hank. *Every scumbag who might be able to do me damage . . . Then, when I meet someone who can do the business, I just ring up this dwarf and tell him that I've found his guys.*

Hank gave a nod, sold on the brutal clarity of it. "Okay," he said. "Sounds like a plan to me."

5.

He had already lost so much blood, he was growing dizzy.

The city's streets seemed faint and without substance as Blake plodded forward. With one arm, he clutched his blood-soaked overcoat to the torn flesh over his ribs. The red strings of the broken stitches dangled from under the coat's bottom hem. A trail of bloodspots, some as big as his hand, mingled with his muddy footprints on the pavement behind him.

He kept to the city's backstreets, trying to avoid anyone seeing him. But it was impossible. Even in this dump, a man staggering along, leaking blood, drew attention. And not the helpful kind. He knew that the sight of his begrimed, wounded form disgusted everyone who spotted him. Some people crossed the street to get away from this filthy specter; others took more direct action.

Children were the worst. Their parents might throw curses in his direction, but the kids used stones. Blake felt a couple of fist-sized rocks strike him in the back; he turned and glared at the little bastards, but the sight of his grime-darkened face didn't scare them away. Instead, the next rock hit him just below the eye, drawing another leak of his body's rapidly dwindling resources. He watched as a couple of adults came up behind the kids, putting hands on their shoulders, as though defending them from him. Too weak for a confrontation, he turned and stumbled on.

He managed to leave the crowd behind him, at least far enough to slip into the hiding place of an unlit alley. Sinking against the wall's base, he tried to recover his strength, one ragged breath after another. The blood dripping from underneath his coat made a darkly shining pool beneath him. He pressed his hand against his side. There were things that he needed to do, things he had come to this stinking city for—but the chances of pulling all that off were nonexistent if he didn't get the wound sewn up.

For a moment, he thought that the loss of blood had sunk him into delusion: somehow, he could hear animals whining from somewhere nearby. But when he raised his head and looked around, he couldn't see dogs or any other creature. He was still alone in the alley.

The whining continued, sharp and persistent. It sounded as though the animals, wherever they might be, were in pain. He spotted a courtyard at the far end of the alley, with some kind of shabby warehouse building at the rear of the space. The noises seemed to come from there. Blake got to his feet and stumbled toward the building. Maybe there would be some corner that he could creep into unobserved, where he could curl up and rest.

A row of windows along the ground floor had been white-washed to keep anybody from peering in. But one with a broken latch was slightly ajar, letting the whimpering animal sounds escape from inside. Blake pulled the window open farther, enough for him to get a look at whatever was happening.

He saw a surgical table, but not one big enough for a human being. The sheet covering it was soaked with nearly as much blood as his own tattered overcoat. Under a glaring fluorescent light, a balding figure in a red-spattered lab coat was hunched over a mongrel dog, its neck and haunches held down with leather straps. The fur and skin over the dog's ribs had been peeled back, revealing the pulsing organs beneath. The red mess eerily resembled the wound under Blake's overcoat.

The man in the lab coat was some kind of veterinarian, Blake figured—but not the kind that made animals better, or eased their pain. He watched as a scalpel dug around this dog's pinkish lungs, then dropped on to the table when the veterinarian picked up a portable dictation recorder in one latex-gloved hand.

"Considerable indications of advanced pulmonary necrosis present in test subject." Unaware of the man watching from the window behind, the vet bent down to peer into the animal's exposed thoracic cavity. "Increase in dosage of the experimental formulation appears to have had negative effects, with likelihood of eventual fatality. . . ."

It was some kind of vivisection going on—Blake mulled over the scene he watched. *Must be running tests*, he figured, *for some kind of drug company*. Technically illegal but the law was never enforced, at least as long as the grisly procedures were kept out of sight in a place like this. The Dumpster at the side of the building was probably piled high with eviscerated animal corpses.

But where there was a doctor, any kind of doctor, there would be needles and suture threads. The kind with which torn, bleeding flesh could be stitched back up. He pushed himself away from the window and stumbled toward the door a few yards away.

Pounding his fist on the door took nearly the last of his strength. He had to lean his shoulder against the frame to keep from collapsing. Through the dull haze blurring his senses, he was vaguely aware of footsteps inside, heading toward him.

"What—" Opening the door, the veterinarian, still in his bloodied lab coat, raised a hand to keep Blake from toppling in on him. Revulsion showed in the upcurled corner of the vet's mouth as he surveyed the dirty figure, red pooling on the doorstep. "Get the hell out of here!"

"Please . . . help . . ."

"This isn't a hospital—" The vet pushed the door against Blake. "If you're in trouble, go find an emergency room."

"Can't . . ." Wedging himself between the frame and the edge of the door, Blake rummaged in the pocket of his overcoat. "Here . . ." He pulled out a wad of cash. "I can pay . . ."

Eyes widening, the vet took the greasy bundle from the beggar's hand. "What's somebody like you doing with this kind of money?"

"That's . . . not your business . . ." He could feel his head swimming, as though the last of his blood had been drained from it. "Just help me . . ." Digging inside the coat again, he pulled out another wad of money and pressed it into the vet's hands. "That enough? I got more . . ." Another wad of bloodstained bills joined the others. "All you want . . . doesn't matter . . ." He dug into the coat once more. "Don't need it . . ."

A small mountain of cash filled the vet's cupped palms. He stared at the wads in amazement, then slowly nodded. "All right," he said, holding the cash tight against the bloodied front of his coat. "I'll get you fixed up. Come on inside."

From seemingly miles away, the building's door closed somewhere behind him. Blake let the veterinarian steer him down a corridor lined with filthy cages. The stick-ribbed animals they held regarded the two men with mournful resignation.

"Let's get a look at you." In the surgery room, the vet dragged a larger table under the fluorescent light. "Get up here."

"I can't . . ." Blake gripped the edge of the chrome table. "Can't . . . make it . . ."

The vet got a hand under his filthy arm and strained to lift him. Blake got a knee up on the table, then rolled heavily onto his side.

"You get into a fight or something?" The vet lifted one side of the blood-soaked overcoat, then dropped it. He staggered back into the wall, startled by the raw, red flesh he had just glimpsed. "Good God—you shouldn't even be alive—not like that!"

"Tell me . . . about it . . ."

"It's . . . it's joined to you . . ." The vet leaned forward, staring in mingled revulsion and amazement at what he saw. With one cautious fingertip, he prodded what seemed like an open wound running down from Blake's chest. The vet's eyes widened in horror as he saw the bloodied flesh respond to his touch, quivering as it pulled the coat's wet fabric along with it. "Like . . . it's all one piece. Like it's part of you or something . . ."

"It is," Blake said through gritting teeth.

"How is that *possible*?" A horrified fascination was evident in the vet's eyes as he wiped his hand on his lab coat. "How'd you get this way?"

"Long . . . story . . ."

"It must be, I've seen corpses in better shape than you." The vet recovered himself enough to be able to lift the edge of the coat once more and peer at what lay beneath. "Whatever it is . . . I need to get it cleaned up first."

"No . . ." The matted dreadlocks dragged across Blake's shoulders as he slowly shook his head. "Just . . . sew it back together . . ."

"But you'll get septicemia if we don't disinfect it—" The vet bit his own lip, hands tightening into knots. "If you haven't got it already, that is . . ."

"That . . . won't happen . . ." The beggar shook his head again. "Just . . . patch me up . . ."

"Okay, okay . . . ," muttered the vet. "But don't blame me if you don't pull through . . ."

Blake hissed with pain as the veterinarian stroked a wet swab, held in a pair of forceps, across the wound. "I said don't clean it!"

"You said no disinfectant. This is just water. Or are you saying that's out, too?"

"Can't . . . Can't clean myself with anything . . . Not ever. Just . . . sew it . . . please . . ."

The forceps clattered as the vet dropped them into a chrome tray. He drew the coat farther apart, and saw the metal military dog tags hanging around Blake's neck. "Army, eh? Which war?"

"The army?" Blake said, confused. "Was I . . . I don't

know . . . Not anymore . . ." He felt the needle in the vet's hand piercing the torn edges of his flesh. Everything in the room started to roll away from him, the space between the surgery table and the walls expanding with each labored beat of his heart. "I can't . . . remember . . ."

But the memory found him in his fevered dreams.

There was a cage. That part was clear and vivid in his memory, as though he were sitting crouched in it once again, his forearms hugging his knees to his chest, the sweat trickling down his neck and into his uniform. There was a patch on his sleeve that indicated his rank—master sergeant—and another, the insignia of the twelve-man alpha team that he led. He touched the patches, as though they helped him to remember who he was.

A soldier . . .

There were other things—worse things—he could remember.

He was leading his alpha team on an antiterrorist sweep through an Afghan mountain range. Death was just as close then as it was in the vet's office, but he didn't mind that. Not as long as he was with his buddies. They were as close to family as he'd ever had. The whole team had taken a sacred oath, sealed with blood and a bottle of whiskey, to protect each other through thick and thin, and to avenge each other's death, whenever that might come. To mess with any of Blake's alpha team was to wind up with all of them on your sorry, soon-to-be-annihilated ass.

Blake was the point man on the Afghan sweep. But the comm link to the rest of his team fritzed out while he was separated from them in one of the winding cave systems. Then there was gunfire, and a hand-to-hand fight. A pack of insurgents attacked him from behind. Too many for him to kill alone . . .

An ambush . . . he realized as the butt of an insurgent's Kalashnikov struck him in the back of the neck. *Got to warn them . . . Tell them it's a trap . . .*

The beatings started at the isolated farmhouse they took him to. Almost nonstop, they left him a bleeding near-corpse, slumped in the squat cage they threw him back into after every round.

"Why . . . don't you just kill me?" he asked after a week of it, raising his bruised and bloodied face to them in the candlelight of the farmhouse cellar. "What're you people waiting for?"

But the answer became obvious when he saw them set up a computer and video rig right next to his cage. They were going to execute him. Live across the Internet. As a propaganda coup in the battle for hearts and minds.

His captors left the farmhouse then; they had business elsewhere. Their leader promised Blake that they would return, sharpened knife in hand, in three days' time. After Friday prayers.

He looked up at the skinny teenager, hardly more than a child, that they had left behind. "You got a name, kid?"

"Adeeb." The kid didn't appear to be more than fourteen years old or so, his arms and legs thin as matchsticks. "I'm here to keep you alive. Until the others come back to kill you."

Blake let out a stilted laugh at the irony of it. "Where'd you learn my language?"

"My village had a school . . ." Adeeb spooned out a mess of rice and goat scraps, and passed the bowl through the cage's bars. "Before we were bombed."

"By us?"

Adeeb nodded. "My mother and father were killed. My sisters, too. The people here are the only ones I have now. Without them, I'd starve."

Blake scooped the food into his mouth with his fingertips. "Yeah . . ." He nodded. "Sometimes . . . war just sucks."

The kid was a kind enough jailer, and Blake found himself liking the boy more and more as the hours ticked by. In some ways, he even felt sorrier for the kid than he did for himself. Someplace else, with maybe a living mom and dad, Adeeb might've been just an ordinary kid, doing ordinary things. But he supposed that might have been true for a lot of people, himself included.

Sitting in a cage left him with plenty of time over the next couple of nights to get himself ready for death. That didn't take much, since he had been expecting it for a long time even before the insurgents had captured him. As far as Blake was concerned, it pretty much came with the job, and the life—however short—that he had chosen for himself. The only thing that bothered him was Adeeb. He didn't want the kid to have to see him die. The insurgents had left Adeeb an old M16 rifle with which to guard their captive; he slept with it, over in the corner of the room.

Something happened, though. On the third night, while he was waiting for the insurgents' return. Crouched in his blood-stained cage, he nodded in fitful sleep, shifting between dream and waking. Sometimes he couldn't tell the difference. That was the case when he lifted his head and gazed out through the bars. The candles guttering on the shelves and ledges suddenly glowed brighter, their narrow flames reaching like golden threads toward the ceiling. Bright as daylight, as though in his dream he had turned his open eyes toward the sun. . . .

"Hello, Blake." A voice, soft and soothing, spoke aloud. "I'm here to rescue you. If you'll accept my help."

He brought his face close to the bars, peering at the figure of the man who had appeared before him. Elegantly dressed, a cashmere jacket visible beneath the unbuttoned overcoat. A real gentleman, with the wealthy's easy smile and charm. It was only the misshapen, heavy-soled shoe that spoiled the man's appearance.

"I . . . know you." The thought prickled the hair along Blake's forearms. His mind overflowed with dark memories from his life in the slums. "Or at least . . . I heard stories about you, back when I was a kid." He pointed to the clubbed shoe, and the cloven hoof that was reported to be inside it. "But I didn't believe you were real back then."

Or maybe . . . He thought about another possibility. *Maybe this is still a dream?*

"No. It's not a dream, Blake," the Devil said, reading his thoughts. "And luckily for you, it's not a nightmare, either." His clubbed shoe scraped on the ground as he approached the cage. "I'm really here. And I'm here to help."

Blake moved his face back from the bars as far as it would go. He looked over to Adeeb, but the boy was sound asleep against the wall. "What do you mean, help?"

The Devil crouched down to face him. "Friday prayers are over, and those murderers will soon be back here to cut off your head. But if you'll trust me, and do exactly as I say, I can get you out of this and back to your barracks."

"To my barracks?" That brought a sudden laugh from deep inside Blake's throat. "Do you think I'm stupid? If you're really who I think you are, then the only reason you're here is to steal my soul. But you won't get it. Even if I have to die to keep it, my soul is mine."

"You're right, of course—" The Devil's eyes glittered in the wavering light from the massed candles. "But you're also wrong. I do often trick people into parting with that most precious thing inside them. And under normal circumstances, I'd love nothing more than to carry off your gleaming soul. But that's not the reason why I'm here now. It isn't my greed for souls that's brought me to you, but my pride."

"Your pride?"

"Oh, yes . . ." A sneer twisted a corner of the other's mouth. "Poets have written whole books about how proud I am. So it should come as no surprise to you that I take my reputation very seriously. Ultimately, I'm here for myself tonight as much as for you."

Blake eyed him suspiciously. "What do you mean?"

"Simply put, I'm here because you were born and raised in my city. I know those slums where you grew up like the back of my hand. They are *my* slums. I made them. Most of the people you grew up with serve me daily. And in return for that service, they receive protection from me, no matter where they go."

"So, what does that have to do with me?"

"Well . . ." The Devil fixed him with his sulphurous eyes. "It happens to be a well-known fact in certain circles that no one is permitted to kill a child of my city without my express consent. That's what helps to keep my people satisfied, and under my control." He gestured contemptuously to the cage and the video equipment around it. "But this here . . . This flies in the face of my authority." The Devil moved his body closer, his voice lower and more intimate. "If they were going to murder you on the quiet, Blake, I wouldn't be bothering with you. But the fact is, these butchers aim to transmit your dying screams around the whole globe. If people back in my city learn of that, and realize that I've been powerless to stop one of their own brothers from being slaughtered like a pig, how do you think they'll react?" He shook his head, appalled at the thought. "My authority over them would be weakened for years to come."

Blake felt his gut go hollow at the mention of his slaughter. The candles' flames wavered as a bone-chilling draft touched the air. "So you're saying that this is somehow all to do . . . *with you*?"

"I'm saying that strange as it seems, our fates are linked together on this one. Which is why I need to free you." He glanced over his shoulder to make sure that Adeeb was still asleep in the corner, then turned back to Blake. "I need to get you out of here in one piece and back to your barracks. And in order for me to do that, I need you to trust me." The Devil's manicured fingers waved the objection away. "It's hard, I know. But if you insist upon it, I even promise not to shake your hand, or offer you any other kind of contract so long as we're together."

As a sign of good faith, the Devil made a gesture with his hand. The rusted padlock fell from the outside of the cage to the floor. Then the manacles parted from around Blake's wrists and ankles. He stared at them lying in the dust at his feet, then looked up as the cage's door swung open.

"But in return . . . " said the Devil, "I'll need your complete cooperation. Before it's too late."

Blake could almost feel the Devil's words setting a hook in his thoughts. He glared at the open door for a moment. Then, head lowered, he pushed himself out of the cage and stood up. His spine creaked, stiff from the long days of captivity.

"All right. You win." He rubbed the chafed skin of his wrists. "But I'm warning you. If you're not being honest with me, I'll—"

"Quiet—" The Devil held up a finger as he looked behind himself, up through the walls to the farmhouse's courtyard. "They're returning. Eleven of them. All outside."

Blake tried to hear them, too, but couldn't. "Should I run?"

"No—" He shook his head. "If you run, they'll come after you. It's safer if you fight." The Devil pointed to the M16 propped in the corner by Adeeb. "Take the boy's rifle. I'll make sure he doesn't wake up."

Blake took the rifle and the extra ammo clip from the corner. Adeeb stirred, as though troubled by bad dreams, but his eyes didn't open.

"There; the rear stairs." The Devil pointed to the opposite side of the cellar. "We'll head outside and circle around the back of them. They won't be expecting an attack from behind."

"But it's too dark out there." Blake kept his voice to a whisper. "I don't have a scope. And if I can't see them, I won't be able to take them out."

"Don't worry about that. I'll be with you, and that will be enough."

Outside, the moonless Afghan night was so dark that Blake couldn't see his hand in front of his face. He moved stealthily away from the farmhouse, then crouched down, wondering what to do next.

"Go left." A voice whispered at his ear, startling him. "About three yards. Then wait."

For a moment, he thought that the Devil had followed him out through the window, and was still beside him. He reached over with one hand, but felt nothing.

"Go," the disembodied voice commanded. "Now."

Following the voice's directions, he found himself tucked behind a slight rise, the M16 resting on a stone outcropping.

"They're right in front of you." The Devil's voice whispered once more in his ear. "There's a bluff on the other side of the farmhouse. Pull the rifle back so they won't see the muzzle flash, and fire into that."

Blake had already figured out the Devil's strategy. The sharp crack of the rifle shot, and the rocks dislodging from the bullet hitting the bluff, drew a flurry of surprised voices from the insurgents. And their own shots, directed at the rocks still tumbling down the side of the bluff gave Blake a bead on where the insurgents stood. Aiming just behind the bright flashes from their weapons, he got off a quick couple of shots. Each hit its mark, and he heard the satisfying sound of their bodies falling lifeless to the ground.

"Stay low." The voice spoke at his ear again. "They've spotted you. Go to the right and hit the dirt."

Shots from the insurgents ripped up the ground where he had just been. Rolling onto his shoulder, Blake fired another couple of rounds, one passing straight through the chest of one of the men below him, the next shattering another's skull and flinging him backward.

"They're scattering. Bring your aim twenty degrees to the right. Lower—"

He peered into the darkness. "I can't see him."

"Just do it. That's it. Now, fire—"

Another round was squeezed off, followed by the dull sound of it hitting flesh.

One by one, Blake picked off the insurgents, heeding the voice at his ear, diving to one side or sprinting to another spot to avoid their return fire. He was pretty sure that the last one had been their leader—from a distance, he could just make out the figure lying on the ground.

He fired off one more round, to make sure the man was dead. Then the night was silent again. Blake stood up from his hiding spot, then turned and walked back toward the farmhouse.

"It's okay, kid—" Only a single candle was guttering inside; by its light, he saw Adeeb crouching in the corner, staring fearfully up at the Devil standing beside Blake. "Neither of us is going to hurt you." He slung the M16 by its strap over his shoulder. "You're an innocent in all of this, we know that. So stay here, and we'll be out of your hair before you know it."

"No, Blake. That's a mistake." The Devil looked at Adeeb, then turned toward the soldier. "If we leave the boy here, they'll kill him. His friends will put a bullet through his head, thinking he helped you."

Blake knew that the Devil was right. "Then we'll have to take him with us."

"And have him slow us down?" The Devil shook his head. "No. There's a fuel truck outside that's fully loaded. Let him take that instead. Then, if anyone questions him about what happened here, he can say he was off delivering supplies."

Blake nodded. "That makes sense . . ." He gestured to Adeeb. "C'mon, kid. Time for you to hit the road."

Dawn broke over the Afghan hills. By its first pale light, Blake watched the dust cloud of the truck through a paneless window, Adeeb at the wheel and heading for the nearest town.

"Unfortunately—" The Devil was standing behind Blake. "That was the only vehicle. Which means you're going to have to make your own way back to your barracks on foot."

"Don't worry, I'll manage it," said Blake. "I've been stomping all over this goddamned terrain for months."

The Devil came closer. "But even so, it will be a long hike before you get to where you're heading. And the nights out in the open are brutally cold in this part of the world. Call me selfish, but after freeing you, I'd like to make sure that you get home in one piece." The Devil removed his overcoat and extended the garment toward him. "Here—take this. My coat will keep you warm on even the coldest night. And should you need it, its magic will help you in other ways, too."

"Its magic?" Blake set the M16 down. He took hold of the overcoat to examine it. "You're kidding, right?"

"Reach inside its pockets, and you'll see."

Blake did what the Devil said, and drew out a thick, fist-sized wad of paper. It was cash, a roll of large-denomination bills secured with a rubber band.

"Try again—"

The same pocket yielded another roll of bills, even larger than the first.

"All the money you'll ever need. In whatever currency you like. A suitable end, I think, to such an eventful night."

"Wow . . ." There was no way Blake could keep from being impressed. He reached into the overcoat's pockets and pulled out even more. Wad after wad dropped into a pile at his booted feet. "As much as I like?"

"Exactly."

"Whenever I need?"

The Devil nodded and took another step forward to hurry Blake up. "All you have to do is put it on."

Blake ran his hand across the coat's immaculate lapels. It looked as if it would fit him perfectly somehow, even though the Devil was slightly taller than him. The sight of the money at his feet dizzied him.

As the Devil watched, Blake slid his arms into the overcoat's sleeves and pulled its lapels across his chest.

And fell to the ground, scattering the pile of money, as seething pain burned through every fiber of his body. His fingers tore at the front of the coat; it felt as if the garment were on fire, charring the flesh beneath.

He looked down at himself and saw the overcoat darkening with his blood. The fibers of its cloth writhed like headless snakes, burrowing into his flesh with an insatiable hunger. He could feel lacerating, fiery threads digging their way toward his vital organs. His pulse pounded with dizzying force as the reddened tendrils inched through the shivering chambers of his heart, seizing it in a knotlike grip.

An agonized cry broke from his throat. As his eyes rolled back in their sockets, he had a nightmarish glimpse of the overcoat's animate substance rippling and tightening across his raw flesh—

He stumbled backward, barely managing to stay upright. His nails splintered as he fought to rip open the garment. Nothing happened but his own blood welling up into his palms. The overcoat had become one with him, fused to his flayed skin. He couldn't tear it off, no matter how desperately he clawed at it.

Pain overwhelmed him, driving away the last conscious fragment in his skull. He could hear himself screaming, and see the Devil smiling down at him. And then nothing else but darkness . . .

He woke again hours later, only to find that the nightmare had just begun.

The pain from the coat had ebbed, enough to be barely endurable. Blake managed to get to his feet, then stumbled back out of the farmhouse. And found something even worse.

They were still there, arrayed on the ground: the corpses from the firefight in the dark. Eleven of them, each dispatched with a shot from the same M16 he dragged behind himself now. But they weren't the insurgents who had captured him a week ago, and who had been getting ready to transmit his execution over the Internet. He found himself looking down into the blank, lifeless eyes of his own men, all eleven members of the alpha team that he had once led.

He felt the dismay rising in his gut as he stumbled from each splayed-out body to the next, recognizing one face after another. The entire alpha team was there, or what was left of them.

Rescue mission . . .

The realization dawned in his slow, numbed thoughts. The team must have found out where the insurgents had taken him. And had come to save him. But he hadn't been able to see who he had really been firing at, picking them off one by one. The Devil, whispering unseen at his ear, had tricked him.

On the ground, sloping away from the back of the farmhouse, Blake found the last of them. The alpha team's second-in-command; they had all been his sworn companions, but this had been his best friend. The corpse's skull had been ripped open by the M16 round that Blake had placed there, guided by the Devil.

Weeping, Blake gathered his friend's body up to the front of the seething overcoat he bore upon his own frame. And saw from the corner of his eye that the corpse's hand was gripped tight upon a grenade, its pin already pulled and discarded. The grenade dropped from the dead grip and rolled down the slope to the fuel barrels that were stored there. Blake didn't let go of his friend's body, but held it tighter against himself, as though he could somehow shield the dead from what he knew was going to happen next.

The fiery explosion lifted Blake from the ground, tearing the alpha team member's corpse from him. He arced through the air, landing in the smoldering rubble of the farmhouse amidst the walls collapsed by the shock wave from the fuel barrels igniting.

He landed so hard that it amazed him that he was still conscious. As the smoke began to clear, he pushed himself into a sitting position, then saw that a jagged piece of shrapnel, big as his arm, had been torn from one of the fuel drums and lodged in his chest. Its knifelike point had pierced the overcoat and imbedded itself into his heart.

I should be dead . . .

He knew that, even as his trembling fingers seized the metal and yanked it out. Blood gushed from the wound as he threw the red shard away. The blood seeped between his fingers as he clutched his chest and got to his feet.

The alpha team's emergency med kit was in one of the corpse's backpacks. Blake found it, tore the lid open, and pulled out the surgical needle and a pack of sutures. Hunkered on the blackened ground, he bent over himself, driving the needle through the overcoat and into the raw flesh beneath, stitching himself up as best he could.

Dizzied from the pain and his grim labors, Blake staggered over to the farmhouse's water trough. His reflection as he bent over the water was that of a bloodied, grimy scarecrow, his face blackened with dirt and the crusting red from his own wounds and those of his dead team members. When he reached down and splashed the water into his face, it burned like acid, fierce enough to send him reeling backward, gasping in renewed agony.

He realized then that the coat, as full of filth and stinking blood as the rest of him, would never let him cleanse himself of what had happened, of what he had done to his comrades and friends.

Yet there was still one more gift. One more trick that the Devil sent him. Searching about in his dead team members' backpacks, for an MRE or anything else to get into his empty stomach, he came across the comm officer's radio gear. He couldn't get the shortwave transmitter working, but managed to pick up an English-language broadcast signal. He squatted down and listened, comforted by hearing another living being's voice.

The comfort didn't last long. A news report told him of an explosion in the nearest town; a fuel truck, that witnesses described as being driven by a teenage boy, had gone off near the marketplace, killing the young driver and some 350 bystanders.

Adeeb . . .

He knew immediately who it had been. A remote-control detonator, its button in an elegantly manicured hand. That was why the Devil had pretended to be so solicitous of the boy's safety, and what would become of him. Now Blake realized what had been the Devil's plan all along. And how Blake had helped bring it about, just as the Devil had wanted. That was why the Devil's showing up at the farmhouse had been so well-timed, ensuring that Adeeb would be able to unwittingly deliver the truck bomb to its target. If the Devil hadn't been able to use Blake to eliminate the rest of his alpha team, they would have either shot Adeeb or taken him prisoner. The truck and its hidden explosives would have still been sitting outside the farmhouse, unused. All of the Devil's talk about how the natives of his city were so important to him—all just lies. Rescuing Blake had just been the means to a fiery end . . .

He picked up the M16 and silenced the radio, blowing the device to bits. Then he collapsed onto the ground, the last of his strength gone.

With the truth out, the overcoat began to tighten itself upon his body, the heavy, grime-blackened cloth constricting over his bones. Its collar took a stranglehold on his throat, and he clawed at it, unable to breathe. His vision blurred, and he felt like his soul was being enveloped in a shroud of hopeless despair.

As he lay upon the ground, he knew that the overcoat was feeding upon something more than his raw flesh and blood.

It wanted him to die. But yet still be alive.

The overcoat feasted upon his guilt and misery. Which would last longer than the mere scraps and rags of his body. Those things were eternal. They were what his soul was made of now.

But then, as the darkness seemed poised to bury him beneath its weight forever, his fingertips caught hold of the chain around his neck. He pulled out his military ID dog tags, his dirt-encrusted fist gripping tight about the bits of stamped metal. A last memory broke open inside him. The vow he had made so long ago with his fallen comrades.

Avenge us . . . avenge our deaths . . .

That was enough. He pulled a tortured breath into his lungs, and felt the darkness retreating, a little more with each slow heartbeat.

He rolled onto his side, then scrabbled onto his knees, then one after the other, managed to get to his feet. The overcoat still burned his flesh, but he didn't try to tear it off. He knew he couldn't. It was with him forever now.

There was still something left of him. Something from before, that the overcoat hadn't consumed yet. He didn't even know what it was . . .

Not yet. He dimly wondered if he would ever find out.

But it would have to do for now.

It was all he had.

He started walking, slowly, painfully. He wasn't able to see the dimming horizon ahead of him. All he saw was the Devil's sulphurous blue eyes, and that mocking smile. One way or another, however long it took, he'd catch up with that sick bastard.

And make him pay . . .

He opened his eyes. Turning his head on the surgical table, he saw the veterinarian at the sink, peeling off the latex gloves and washing his hands.

"Finished?"

The vet glanced over his shoulder at Blake, then nodded. "As much as it can be."

"Thanks . . ." He raised a hand and rubbed his face, still bearded and dirt-encrusted. "Probably a good thing I wasn't here for most of it."

"I wish I could have said the same for me." The vet got a hand under Blake's arm and helped him sit up. "I've never seen anything like that before . . ." His eyes were already shadowed with fearful memory. "And I don't want to again."

Blake swung his legs over the side of the table. He stood up, holding onto the edge to steady himself.

"There's a mirror over there." The vet pointed. "Take a look."

Legs stiff from being on the table for so long, Blake plodded over to the other side of the room. The mirror on top of the cabinet was large enough for him to need both hands to pick it up. Holding the glass at arm's length, he examined the job that the vet had done. The stitches through the coat were even and precise, as good as any that a tailor could have done. And far better than the clumsy repairs that he had done himself all the previous times that the coat had been torn open during his long journey home.

With a black-nailed fingertip, Blake prodded at his chest beneath the coat. He could feel where the stitches entered his flesh and came back out. The coat was still black and stiff with dirt and dried blood, but at least he no longer appeared as if he were physically coming apart. There were no fresh drops of red spattering the floor beneath the coat's hem.

He set the mirror back down. "We even?"

"You've paid enough," said the vet. "I just want you out of here."

He followed the vet to the building's front door. On the way, Blake halted and looked over at the cages full of animals. "What about them?"

The vet shrugged. "I got more tests to run. These are what I run 'em on."

Blake looked at the ragged, sad-eyed creatures. They were just like him. Trapped in an existence that was neither life nor death, with nothing to fill their days but pain and misery. He knew what it was like to be in a cage, with no way out.

There had been no one to help him. But for these—

"Here—" Blake dug into the overcoat's pocket, and tossed the vet another rubber-banded wad of money. "Tests are over. They all passed."

The vet looked at the cash, his greedy eyes growing wider.

"Still not enough?" Blake tossed over another wad, then another. So many that they started tumbling down to the vet's feet. "Tell your bosses that you had a break-in or something. Then find yourself another job. If I come back this way, I don't want to see the lights on in this place. You got it?"

The vet could barely look across the top of the green mound held against his chest. "Okay. You got a deal. Hell, with this much, I'll never have to work again!"

Blake pushed open the door and headed for the alleyway. A few moments later, he was almost knocked off his feet by the rush of dogs streaming past him, their joyous yaps and howls bouncing off the nearby buildings. A couple of the older and partly crippled ones looked back at him for a moment, then hobbled after the others racing into the rain-washed streets and freedom.

6.

He dreamt, and remembered. For Nathaniel, there was no difference now.

In that darkened room, the one inside his own head, he could see a seven-year-old boy. From high above, drifting through the starless dark of unconsciousness, he looked down and saw the child, sleeping on a threadbare sofa, one of the torn cushions bunched up under his head for a pillow. Across the night-filled window, tattered curtains sagged from a rod with rusting screws pulling from the wall at either end. The child shivered, thin arms hugging himself tight; there was nothing but dead ashes in the fireplace. On the mantel above, a photo of the boy's mother was draped with a black mourning ribbon; tucked in a corner of the cheap gilt frame was a three-sentence obituary, a yellowing scrap from a newspaper dated six months earlier.

Nathaniel felt himself falling toward the child, the child that he had been so long ago, in that other life. In his dreaming, he spread his arms out as he fell; he might have been an angel about to bestow a kiss upon the unlined brow below him. But when he opened his eyes, there was no more falling. He lay curled up on the sofa, not dreaming of the child he had been. He was that child once more.

I remember, thought Nathaniel. *I remember . . .*

Something had woken him up. The clanking noise of an empty bottle being knocked over and rolling across the floor's bare wooden planks. The little boy raised his head and looked over to the sagging easy chair that held his unshaven father. Who was snoring, with the wet sloppy sound that drunks make when they pass out. More empty bottles, some of them knocked over and some of them still upright, surrounded the chair.

With his knuckles, the boy rubbed the sleep from his eyes. With the fire out, the house was cold enough to raise goose bumps under his shirt. But he didn't want to climb the stairs to his room and crawl under the flea-ridden blankets. What if his dad woke up, and no one was there? The house empty and silent, and all the bottles empty? He was afraid of what his dad might do then, in that dark moment.

Suddenly, his father's eyes popped open wide, hands clawing deep into the chair's worn-through arms.

"Dad!" Nathaniel jumped up in shock. "What's wrong?"

His father didn't seem to hear him, but went right on staring into the space before him. In terror, the drunk heaved himself up from the chair, scooped Nathaniel from the couch, and held him out by the arms, like a human shield.

And now he could see what his father had been staring at. There was somebody else in the room with them, though the door was still locked and bolted. A pale, expressionless figure gazed over Nathaniel's head. A hand with no fingernails, so bloodless that it looked as if it might have been formed from candle wax, reached out toward his father's chest. He squirmed around and watched as a ball of light began to glow beneath his father's rib cage.

"Wait!" his father cried out. "I know what you want—I know it's time—but don't take me, please! Take someone else. Take *him*!"

Death's fingers drew the soul closer and closer to the surface. "I do not make bargains, and I do not take substitutes." The voice was flat and without emotion. "No one can escape their fate. It is pointless to try."

"But . . . I swear he's worth it!" His dad's face was luminous with panicky sweat. His coward's hands pushed Nathaniel closer to the pallid, waxen figure before them. "Take a look at him, if you don't believe me. He's weird! He always has been. Just like his damned mother was, before she died. Look!"

Death's unhurried gaze moved down to Nathaniel. A blank moment, then he frowned as though puzzled. "You can . . . see me?"

Nathaniel managed to give a single slow nod.

"But . . . how?" Death tilted his head, studying the small figure before him. "Only those who are about to die can see me. But it's not yet your time."

"I told you! I told you he was weird!" Nathaniel's father squeezed his son's arms tighter. "I've always known it—ever since he was a baby—"

"This should be impossible . . ."

"Exactly! So, his soul must be worth enough, right? Enough to let me go?"

"Perhaps . . ." Death leaned down, peering into Nathaniel's eyes. "Perhaps it is worth a great deal more . . ."

"What do you mean?"

Death laid a cold thumb on Nathaniel's eyelid and pulled it open wider. "He can see me, your son. But I can't see him . . . No matter how deep I look, I cannot see the moment of his death. And I should be able to see that with all human beings."

A wavering smile appeared on his father's face. "And that's good, right?"

"That is impossible to say . . ." The waxen figure let go of the father's glowing soul, and allowed it to sink back into his chest. "There is a darkness in this boy that I have never seen before. A darkness almost as deep . . . as my own." He looked back to the father. "I cannot deny that my curiosity has been aroused. Give him to me, and I will do what you ask. I shall grant you two more years in which to drink yourself to death."

"Make it five," said his father. "Or better yet—ten."

Death considered it for a moment, his pallid face as still as a corpse. "Very well. Ten years. But only because the boy is so unique."

His father let go of Nathaniel, and sank back into the arm-chair.

Death laid his hand upon Nathaniel's shoulder, ready to claim his prize. Nathaniel felt the cold of that touch creep down inside him, toward his heart. It made him shiver, but not from the ice that entered his veins.

"Come with me, child . . ." Death increased his grip, and the night's winds caressed him. Without knowing how, Nathaniel felt himself falling silently through the fabric of space. "It is time, I think, for us to learn who you really are . . ."

The rain woke him.

Or perhaps it didn't—

Nathaniel was as accustomed to its sound as anyone in the city. The unrelenting downpour was constant. The beating of the rain against the window was louder than usual, though. He knew that meant there was a storm coming. A big one, that would lash the empty streets and send rivers down the overflowing gutters. But even that shouldn't have been enough to drag him back into consciousness—not as exhausted as he had been. It must've been something inside him, some dark memory, or a dream of the world's hidden things, that had done it.

His eyes were closed, but he knew where he was. He reached out with one hand and felt the edges of the rough, splintery bed frame, barely big enough to hold him.

The musty smell of damp stones touched his nostrils with each breath he pulled in. The old groundskeeper's cottage, here in the middle of the city's oldest cemetery, was as much home to him as anywhere he had ever known. It had been since the night that Death had brought him here.

"Are you awake, Nathaniel?" The words were spoken in the calm, dispassionate voice that had become so familiar. "Can you hear me?"

He opened his eyes. And saw Death's face, bloodlessly pale, looking down at him.

"How long . . . how long have I been out?"

"Several hours." Death sat on a rickety wooden chair beside the bed. "I let you sleep in the hope that you would recover your strength."

Nathaniel pushed himself up from the thin, creaking mattress. "Don't know if it worked yet . . . I feel like someone hit me with a baseball bat."

Death reached out and touched Nathaniel's chest with a waxen fingertip. "The pain you felt, was it here?"

Nathaniel winced. "Right there. And it still hurts like hell."

"Then it is . . . as I feared . . ." Death turned and gazed out at the drizzling rain. The window was cracked open just enough to let a chill breeze slide into the room. "I must admit that I feel responsible for what has happened to you. More than anyone else, I should have seen it coming. I knew that the realm in which I exist was never meant for mortals such as yourself. No human being was ever intended to witness what happens when I remove a person's soul. But when I came across you . . . and looked inside you . . . somehow I thought an exception had been made." He turned back to Nathaniel. "You were able to learn my magic, and control the darkness as I alone had done before. That led me to believe that everything was different where you were concerned. And that I was no longer alone in this grey universe." No expression of regret showed on Death's face; he might have been enumerating the last few leaves on the branches of a winter tree. "But I see now that I was wrong."

Unease touched Nathaniel's heart. "Why? What's happening to me?"

Death pointed to Nathaniel's chest again. "The divine pins

that hold the soul inside a human being are exceedingly difficult to break," he said. "When they are snapped apart to release a soul, it creates a powerful shock wave across the whole of the realm in which I exist. It seems now that your exposure to such shocks has damaged you. So much so that they have weakened the pins that hold your own soul in place. You must have been feeling this pain for many years, Nathaniel. It was a mistake not to tell me about it earlier."

"I know . . ." He looked down at his chest. But despite the pain, he couldn't see any obvious bruise or injury. "I feel stupid now. And I'm sorry."

"When did it begin?" Death seemed unperturbed by the confession. "Did it start with the first soul you saw harvested? The morning after I brought you here?"

Nathaniel nodded. "But at the time, I didn't know whether it was pain or grief that I was feeling." The memory moved like a dark current through his thoughts. "When you turned over that first body on the sidewalk, I expected it to be a stranger. But then I saw that it was him . . . my father. . . ." He gazed silently in front of himself for a moment, remembering. "I suppose the shock of it was so strong that it hid the pain. Otherwise, you would have seen it from the start."

"I should have warned you first, about what was coming," mused Death, remembering the moment, too. "I am aware of that now. But it took time for me to learn what human beings need. As well you know . . ."

Nathaniel glanced over to the small iron fireplace in the corner. It had been months before Death had thought of putting it there for him, to keep his new apprentice warm.

But at least he thought about it eventually, he thought. *At least he cared . . .*

"I suppose—" Nathaniel's memory returned to that morning, and the sight of his father's smashed-up body in the rain. "It was no surprise to you, because you already knew it would happen. You knew he wouldn't survive those ten years, even as you gave them to him."

"I saw it, yes," said Death. "But granting them to him made it easier for me to take you away, to where your powers could be better understood. When he awoke, and realized what his cowardice had done to you, he was unable to survive the shame of it. As soon as he was sober again, he threw himself from the rooftop. And although I make it a point to never judge those whose souls I harvest, I cannot say, in his case, that I disapproved of his decision."

Nathaniel tried to force the image of his father's broken body away again, and raised his hand back to his chest. "And after that . . . Well, the pain just kept on coming. It grew worse with every reaping round you took me on. But I kept it secret from you because I was afraid."

"Afraid?"

"I thought that if you knew about it, you'd think that I was too weak to stay with you. But by then, this cottage . . . and you . . . had become the only place that had ever felt like home."

He looked over to Death's cold eyes, waiting for a response. When none came, he pulled back the sheets and sat up.

"So anyway . . . Now that we know what's wrong with me, how do we cure it?" he asked. "How do we get rid of it, this pain?"

For a moment, Death sounded almost kind. "Nathaniel, there is no cure."

"What?"

"If there were, I would have given you the remedy already. But the damage that has been done to you is irreversible."

"You're joking—"

"You know I am incapable of such a thing. Each time you witnessed a soul being harvested, the damage to the pins around your own soul grew progressively worse. The damage is now so far gone that it is potentially fatal. I fear that if you witness the harvesting of even one more soul, it will kill you."

Nathaniel felt stunned. "But . . . The reaping rounds . . . They're all I have . . . If you take them away from me, what would I be?" Nathaniel could hardly gather his breath. A black gulf seemed to appear before him, into which he might fall and never be seen again. "Being there at the end, it's my entire existence. I help people to pass over to the other side. That's what I do . . ."

"Not anymore." Death's voice remained level. "The truth is often hard to bear, Nathaniel. But it is still the truth. That is why—for your own good—I cannot allow you to accompany me any longer when I harvest souls. That part of your existence is over. But it does not mean you can't still help me in other ways. . . ." From inside his long coat, Death took out a parchment scroll. "You still know what it is, I presume?"

"Of course I do." Nathaniel watched Death unroll the document. His head was still spinning from the shock, making it difficult to focus. "We use it all the time. It's the Chart of Deaths. It tells us who's marked down to die each day, and where to find them."

"Precisely so." Death ran a waxen fingertip across the rough parchment. "But today, an anomaly has appeared upon it—concerning this city, and the deaths that are set to take place in it between now and dawn. As to what it means, I do not yet know. But as to what it is . . . you should see that for yourself."

Death held the scroll before his apprentice's eyes. Nathaniel leaned forward, peering at the symbols upon it, marked in jet-black ink.

"I don't understand . . ." He pushed his other concerns away and tried to make sense of what he was seeing. "These marks . . . they represent the deaths that are to come, I know. But how can they be increasing in that way?" The inked symbols in front of him were multiplying even as he watched them, as though an invisible pensman were writing them out. "You always told me that every death follows a plan that was written down at the start of Time. If that's right, then why haven't these deaths been there on the chart all along? Why are they only appearing now? And why are there so many of them?"

The question puzzled Death as well. "So many deaths in one place is normally an indication of a momentous event," he said. "But as you point out, those are always marked down in advance. The deaths appearing here seem to have developed a momentum of their own, separate from the rest of history. And if you look closely, you will even see markings here that you have never seen before. Although the majority of them are humans symbols, there are many others appearing now that have the symbols of . . . something else."

"Is that even possible?"

"Apparently, it is."

"Look—" Nathaniel saw something else appear. "What's that?"

At the top of the scroll, as though holding pride of place above all else inscribed on it, a fresh symbol suddenly appeared that was far larger than all the rest. . . .

"What does it mean?" asked Nathaniel. "Who does it stand for?"

"If I only knew." Death peered at the ink as the lines grew stronger. "I have never seen it before. Nevertheless, I fear that it is of some importance." He slowly nodded, musing. "It seems old. Ancient. From a time that precedes even myself."

"So . . . what are we gonna do about all of this?"

"That is the question I have been pondering, while you slept." Death rolled up the scroll again. "As far as I can see, we only have one option left to us. We must discover what these deaths all mean."

"And how do we do that?"

"By dividing our resources. I will collect the souls of the dead, and study my charts and records here in detail. And you . . ." Death nodded toward the cracked window. "You will go out into the living world and search for the cause of this anomaly. You will learn as much as possible about why, and how, it is taking place."

"You mean . . . you want me to go out there *on my own*?"

"It is the safest place for you now, I fear. The shocks that come from harvesting a soul will not strike you there."

"But—" Unease touched Nathaniel's heart. "I haven't been into the living world on my own for ten years. Are you sure you can trust me with that?"

"I do not see why not. You are old enough. And certainly, your powers are second only to mine. The only thing you need to remember is to remain impartial when you search for the answers. We are merely the instruments of Fate, Nathaniel, not its masters."

"I know . . ." The feeling inside him had deepened into something like dread. "That was the first thing you taught me, when I arrived here."

"Then make sure you do not forget it, as you face the temptations of a life outside." Death stood up and moved to the center of the cottage's shadowed space. "Despite your humanity, you belong to the realm of the dead, Nathaniel. You left the living world long ago, and I therefore forbid you to do anything that might influence events today, one way or another. What is right or wrong in the universe is beyond our understanding. That is why we carry off the souls from both sides of the battlefield, and deliver up for judgment both saints and sinners alike."

Nathaniel stood up from the rickety bed and began buttoning up his shirt. "Don't worry. I won't do anything stupid." He found his jacket at the foot of the bed and slipped it on. "And when I'm back, I want to discuss what we're going to do about this again. . . ." He laid his hand back on his chest. "Because having no cure . . . That's just not good enough."

He started moving toward the cottage door.

"There is one more thing, Nathaniel, before you leave—"

He stopped, and looked back over his shoulder.

"As you know," said Death, "what makes you so unique is the fact that I cannot see your fate." He gazed at his apprentice, looking far beyond the surface of his eyes. "Although I have tried over the last ten years to penetrate that darkness inside you, I have never received even the slightest glimpse of your death. Because of that, I advise you to be careful when you step out into the living world."

"Careful?" Nathaniel's eyes narrowed as he regarded his master. "Careful of what?"

"Of everything you encounter. Something extraordinary is about to take place today. I do not know what it is yet, but I can already sense it. And so it is possible, I believe, that once you have followed this trail of death that is unfolding, you may eventually find your own death waiting at the end of it. . . ."

The warning chilled Nathaniel. It took a moment before he could say anything in response.

"Well, at least then—" he said finally. "You'll have the surprise of harvesting a soul you actually know."

7.

With the corpse at his feet, Hank took the little memo book from his pocket. He pulled the pencil stub from the spiral binding and carefully drew a single line, slanting upward from left to right.

There were only lines like that scrawled in the book. No words, no numbers. Just lines in bunches of five. The one he had just drawn completed another bundle. As the blood puddled around his boot soles, Hank counted them up, and did the math in his head. Six bunches of five; that tallied up to an even thirty. Or two dozen, and a half dozen on top: that was how many people he'd killed since he'd taken on this latest job.

He supposed that eventually—maybe soon—he'd lose count. But for right now, it seemed like a good idea to keep track of what he was doing. Otherwise, with scum like the ones he'd been taking out—who'd remember them?

The pelting rain sent dark rivers coursing through the city's streets. Under the ragged awning of a boarded-up storefront, Hank slid the pencil and memo book back into his pocket. He'd seen a lot of storms pound the city, but this was the worst that he could remember. The heavy thunderhead clouds pressed down so close to the earth, he felt as if he could reach up and brush his fingertips along their sodden bulk.

Bad as it was, it didn't matter to him, at least as far as his job was concerned. For something like this, the streets were always dark and disagreeable. The things he looked for always hid themselves in the grimiest dead-end alleys and unlit cellars. Nothing for it but to put his head down and keep lumbering forward, letting nothing stop him.

Turning up the collar of his jacket, Hank peered out through the rivulets draining from the awning's tattered fringes. He was just able to perceive a knot of people in the distance watching from the other side of street. Just ordinary types, the ones who lived in this district's shabby tenements, keeping their heads down and trying to stay out of trouble. He knew that none of them were about to call the cops; around here, somebody getting beat to death on the sidewalk was such a regular occurrence that it was hardly worth noticing.

But oddly, these people did. This time.

As Hank looked over at them, they started clapping, one by one. Applauding him and what he had just done. It couldn't have been for style points—he hadn't pulled any fancy moves, just knocking the wind out of the punk with a boulder-sized fist to the gut, then snapping his neck with a clenched forearm. Hank figured that these people must have really disliked the guy; maybe he'd been some loan shark's leg-breaking enforcer, or just a bullying hard-ass. Either way, they seemed to appreciate Hank having eliminated the creep.

He nodded toward the group. Given the generally loathsome nature of the criminals, psychopaths, and pumped-up thugs that he'd been systematically removing from the city's population, maybe the real surprise was that he didn't get this kind of reaction more often. He turned his massive frame away from them, and headed toward the next appointment he had made for himself.

Which was a Chinese restaurant. Its neighborhood wasn't much better, but at least there were a few neon signs sizzling and crackling overhead, their lurid electric colors shimmering in the wet gutters. Most of them were for cheap bars; every commercial block in the city had at least two establishments like that. But he was looking for the *hanzi* ideographs that spelled out The Dragon's Talon. He found them, at last, at the end of the block.

Hank stood outside the entrance, with its elaborate red-lacquered screens, and looked at the windows above. No sign for the martial arts school that operated up there. And no need for one; anybody who was looking for it would know where it was. He could hear the faint thump of training blows, fists pulled back just enough to keep bones from being broken, and the louder clang of *dao* sabres against each other.

"Where do you think you're going, big man?"

One of the Chinese bouncers at the restaurant's door stopped him with a hand flat against his chest. All three of the men, in their bow-tied tuxedos, might have been a head shorter than him, but shoulder-to-shoulder behind a red velvet rope they looked like more than enough to keep most people out.

"Inside." Hank pointed past them. "I got business there."

"No, you don't—" The lead bouncer spotted the bloodstains spattered across the front of Hank's jacket and trousers that the rain hadn't been able to wash away. "Turn around—" The bouncer readied himself, hands tightening into poised fists. "And keep on walking."

"I don't think so."

The other men drew back a half step from him, reaching for the lead-weighted saps that tugged down the sides of their coats.

"You're making a big mistake, pal." With a sideways tilt of his head, the lead bouncer signaled to the man on his left. That one brought a short truncheon swinging toward Hank's skull.

He ducked his head, evading the blow. At the same time, he brought two fingers straight into his attacker's eyes, dropping him, howling and blinded, to the ground.

The others jumped in, one trying to grapple his arms around Hank's chest, while the lead bouncer jabbed a spiked set of steel knuckles toward his face. The metal points raked Hank's forearm as he brought his knee up hard into the first one's groin. Before the lead bouncer could set up for another shot at him, Hank had picked up one of the rope stands and swung it like a club across both their heads.

One was knocked out cold, the side of his head now concave and matted red. But the lead bouncer managed to get up onto his hands and knees, head lowered toward a pool of his own blood. Hank reached down and picked him up by his neck and leather belt, then swung about and hurled him through the restaurant's open doorway.

The bouncer lay on his back in the restaurant's foyer, stunned beyond any further movement. Hank stepped over his body and looked around at the startled customers inside.

The place was done up in the usual over-the-top style, with

enough polished lacquer and yellow gilt to ornament an emperor's barge from the Han dynasty. One whole wall was taken up with an expensive saltwater aquarium tank, its wavering blue glow turning the closest tables spectral. Lionfish as big as terriers drifted back and forth, fanning out their lethal spines.

"Dinner's over—" Dragging the rope stand along with him, Hank surveyed the restaurant's guests. "I'd advise you to get the hell out of here, if you don't wanna get hurt."

The expense-account businessmen to whom the place catered hurriedly got to their feet, pulling their sleek companions with them. Within moments, there was a panicky stampede toward the door, the waiters and jabbering kitchen staff on the heels of the patrons.

"I'm here for the Mountain Master—" Hank stepped back to let the rush shove its way past him. "Where is he?"

The answer came soon enough.

A couple of tables had been overturned, spilling wineglasses and laden plates across the gold-tiled floor. In the emptied room's silence, he could hear footsteps tromping down the steps at the back. Voices shouted in guttural Mandarin as triad fighters from the martial arts school spotted him. Spangles of light glistened from the blades of the *kwan do* upraised at the rear of the pack. In a wavelike surge, they rushed toward him.

Twenty of them. They might have stood a chance of at least surviving a few minutes if he hadn't been warmed up from taking out the bouncers at the door. Looking across their heads, Hank could see another figure halfway down the stairs, watching the battle. That was the one he had come for—but that meeting would have to wait.

The rope stand came apart after he had flattened a couple of the men with it, the blood-spattered pole separating from the base. Hank tossed it aside and grabbed whatever came to hand; in a restaurant, there were plenty of things to be used as weapons. From the waiters' station, he snatched a handful of ivory chopsticks. Clutched in one fist, they served to break open two more foreheads before being reduced to splinters. Grabbing a chair, he blocked a razor-sharp halberd swinging down toward his neck; with its legs, he pinned another triad member against the wall, then slammed its top edge into the man's throat.

Hank tossed the broken chair aside, letting the corpse slide to the floor. The restaurant was silent again as he swung his gaze over to the stairs.

"You . . . fight well." Each word tightened the livid scar running diagonally across the Mountain Master's face, from one corner of his brow to the side of his chin. Coarse, dark hair, cut ragged by the blade of a fighting knife, dangled close to the jutting edges of his cheekbones. "Better . . . than men I trained." His eyes, set deep in his broad, heavy face, darkened with anger. "But now . . . you are mine."

Hank braced himself as the man's embroidered robes spread like wings, the hulking but unnaturally lithe figure launching a flying kick toward him. The blow struck his chest hard enough to stagger him backward, but he managed to remain upright. He could feel the shock roll through his lungs and heart, then down his spine and legs, like lightning coursing through a grounded rod.

The Mountain Master leapt back. His eyes widened as he

studied Hank. "Should be dead now . . ." He sounded puzzled. "Why . . . aren't you?"

Hank spat out the wad of blood that had risen in his throat. "I guess . . . I'm just too dumb to die." He reached out and grabbed the back of the man's neck, his weight bearing him down to the floor.

The point of the Mountain Master's knee slammed into Hank's midsection, hard enough to send a shock wave up through his guts. His heart went silent for a beat, then started up again as he hammered his fist against the man's densely scarred ear.

With blood leaking from his face, the Mountain Master rolled onto one side, bracing himself against the floor so he could launch a sweeping kick across Hank's legs. His shins would have been crushed if he hadn't leapt back onto his hip. That gave the Mountain Master a split-second opening, in which he launched himself horizontally toward his opponent, fingers hooked into claws—

That was the Mountain Master's fatal error. His nails scraped across Hank's face, but not before his arm shot out and caught the Mountain Master's exposed throat. He clenched his fist, squeezing harder until he could hear the sound, like wet twigs trodden upon in a forest, of the other's hyoid bones cracking and splitting. Hank let go, and the Mountain Master's head lolled to one side.

The man was still breathing. Hank could tell from the bubbles of blood at one corner of the Mountain Master's lips. He reached down and gathered the man's weight up against his own chest, then carried him over to the fish tank against the wall. Salt water sloshed over the edge of the glass as he dropped the

Mountain Master into the tank. The lionfish circled in agitation through the reddening water near the man's face. After a few seconds, bubbles stopped rising from his mouth and nose, and his lifeless eyes stared past the ornamental coral.

Hank steadied himself against the wall, regaining his own breath. That had been a rough one; he knew he'd be pissing blood later. But still . . . no fear.

He searched the entire building, including the martial arts school upstairs and the scullery rooms behind the kitchen, to make sure there was no one left to jump him. He ended his search at a smaller, private meeting room, with a separate entrance onto the alley behind the restaurant. The dimly lit space was bisected by an elaborately carved rosewood screen reaching to the ceiling. Stepping cautiously around the side of the screen, Hank found a shrine dedicated to Guan Yu, the red-faced warrior god. Two statues of the furious deity stood on either side of a high-backed chair, its arms formed into arch-backed dragons. He knew this was where the late Mountain Master had sat when issuing orders to his followers on the other side of the grill, his guttural voice even sterner and more forbidding when his face was hidden.

Hank froze, hearing the door open. Quick footsteps entered from the alley beyond the meeting room. He stepped farther back, hiding himself behind the carved grillwork.

"Master! You've got to help me!"

The image of a young woman was just visible to him as she prostrated herself on the other side of the grill. By its tapered wooden handle, she picked up the brass ceremonial bell there and rang it.

He peered closer toward the openings carved in the wood. He could see the woman clearly now. A strange feeling moved inside his chest, one that he had never felt before.

"Master—please . . ."

He grunted in acknowledgment, knowing that if he spoke, his voice would give him away.

The deception worked; she did not know the Mountain Master had been killed only a few moments earlier.

"I don't know if you remember me, master?" She raised her tear-wet face. Chinese and beautiful. "But I'm Ling—I studied here. At your school."

He grunted once more.

The woman's desperation overwhelmed her. Through the grill, Hank could see her trembling, as though her agonies of remorse and fear were like the storm lashing the roof of the building hard enough to batter the structure from its foundation.

"Please . . ." There were words inside her that she could no longer hold back. She reached out and touched the grill with her fingertips. "There's no one I can turn to now but you and the triad."

He made no sound at all. He didn't need to.

In a hushed whisper, the woman began her story . . .

Her parents had other ambitions for her.

Yes, their child excelled at the deadly skills taught at the Mountain Master's school. So much so, that the master's intent was to someday make her an instructor, her authority second only to his. An honor, perhaps—but how did that put money in one's pockets?

No, she would be a lawyer, just as her parents had decided years earlier. Better their child should apply her sharply honed killer's instinct in a courtroom, rather than in some alley dueling with other schools' star pupils.

Such was the plan she was bound by familial duty to accept.

"All our savings," her father told her. He reached across the bare kitchen table and took her hands in his, squeezing them tightly. "All that your mother and I have scraped together. Penny by penny—for you, princess. And more besides."

From a much worn and handled envelope, her father extracted a sheaf of moneylenders' contracts. The numbers that Ling could see written on the small square notes appalled her.

"Yes—" He nodded when he saw his daughter's widened eyes. "The interest alone is almost more than we can pay. But we aren't worried." Her father waved a contemptuous hand at the stack of paper. "When you are a successful lawyer, with rich clients—then it will all have been worth it."

But there was one flaw in her parents' scheme, and Ling was the first to know it. However incandescent her star had shown under the Mountain Master's tutelage, in the fierce study of blows and counterblows, lightning evasions and whirling kicks to an opponent's throat, at the university, in the private school of law that her parents enrolled her into, that light was rather dimmer.

Perhaps her heart was still at her previous master's school. She had given it there, from the time she had been a little pigtailed girl, and it could not easily be returned to her. *Or else,* she dismally thought, gazing at the impenetrable language of torts and complaints in the foot-thick tomes before her, *or else I'm just no good at this stuff.* Whatever the reason, there was not enough money in the world, let alone her family's purse, to buy her the grades she needed to pass her courses. She was, in fact, the thinnest hair away from flunking out. And no money-back guarantee had been granted with her tuition payment. All that her parents had spent, and all that they owed to the pitiless loan sharks, would be wasted when she crept back in shame to them . . .

"I can help you."

Startled, Ling looked up from the wooden rack of hymnals in front of her. She had escaped to the university's empty chapel for a little while, to try and find an answer to her dilemma. She glanced beside her and saw a dwarfish figure standing in the chapel's aisle.

"Who . . . who are you?"

"Name's aren't important," answered the dwarf. "Let's just say that I'm someone who can help you with your problem. For a price . . ."

"I . . . don't know what you mean. What problem—"

"Oh, come on," said the dwarf, dismissing her pretense. "I've been watching you for weeks. I know you're having trouble with your classes. And I know your parents are in deep debt. But believe me, killing yourself is no answer for you. Even if it looks like that now."

She glared at him. Barely taller than her waist, the figure was further deformed by the hump that bowed his back into a lopsided arc. Wiry brown hair covered his angled shoulders. The tailored three-piece suit appeared oddly elegant on one so misshapen, the skin of his hands and neck covered with septic boils and scarlet eczema.

"Do you really believe yourself to be the first young lady to find herself sinking beneath the weight of the law?" The dwarf rubbed his scabby chin with a spiderlike hand. "I've known hundreds of people like you in my time. And usually, I'm the only one who can ease their fear." He displayed a yellow-toothed smile as he slipped into the pew beside her. "So long as they're willing to give me what I require."

She found herself repulsed by the hideous figure. But stayed there all the same. "What kind of help . . . are you talking about?"

"The kind that doesn't unfairly prejudice people, simply because they have no brains or talent." The dwarf tapped the edge of the pew with a yellow fingertip. "I can give you the answers to all your exam questions in advance. And believe me, with my help, you'll pass your bar exam at the head of your class. Then you'll be a fully fledged lawyer. Just like your parents dream of."

"And . . . the price?" She turned her nose up involuntarily, fearing it would be something physical.

The dwarf saw the expression of disgust on her face, and almost hissed at it. "It's not your body that I want, but something else," he said in a sharp, insulted tone. "I look at you as an investment. I won't ask anything of you straight away. But be aware, by shaking my hand, you agree to pay me whatever I ask for when the day arrives. Though rest assured . . . By that time you'll be a big success, and you'll be able to afford it easily."

An apprehensive shiver ran through Ling's body. The thought of doing any kind of deal with him made her uneasy. But faced with the prospect of shame or suicide, she knew she didn't have an option.

Sensing her acceptance, the dwarf extended his scabby hand toward her. "You're making the right decision," he said drily. "After this, your success will be sealed."

She took his disgusting hand and shook it. And just as he'd promised, there was no looking back. . . .

Thanks to the dwarf's help, Ling passed her exams at the top of her class. Her mother wept, and Ling almost crushed her father with a hug when she laid the ribboned diploma on the kitchen table. A year later, as her career took off, her parents sent her postcards from the Bermuda cruise she'd sent them on. The year after that, she accepted a prestigious position in the city DA's office.

Five years passed, five years of success and its concomitant rewards. And in that time, she didn't hear a single word from the hideous dwarf. In the end, she even began to hope that he might have died or forgotten her. And that the debt she owed him would never have to be repaid.

It turned out to be a vain hope.

There had been time for a boyfriend by then—and a little more. Following a brief fling with one of her fellow lawyers, who soon took up a job oversees with a new wife, Ling found out that she was pregnant. She didn't even bother to write and tell him what had happened—she was making enough money on her own to take care of everything.

Her aging parents were unhappy about the absence of a wedding ring on Ling's hand—but overjoyed by the birth of their grandchild, a beautiful baby girl she named Ren-Lei. Before her maternity leave from the DA's office ended, Ling engaged a nanny for her daughter, a skilled young woman named Anna, hired from the most highly recommended household personnel agency in the city. Anna's salary was a major expense for Ling, but clearly worth it; the woman's professionalism was obvious, and she seemed to adore the baby who had been placed in her charge. Ling wasn't even sure why she took the precaution of installing a hidden video camera in Ren-Lei's nursery, its tiny wide-angle lens hidden in the stuffed belly of a decorative teddy bear, up on the highest of the room's toy shelves.

With every concern taken care of, Ling returned to her office with the district attorney, immersing herself once again in all the subpoenaed grand jury investigations that had stacked up while she had been gone. She might have preferred to have been at home taking care of Ren-Lei herself, but a lifestyle such as the one she had created for the two of them, and for the baby's grandparents, did not come cheap. There were bills to pay. But as long as Ren-Lei thrived in Anna's care, then all the little family's days passed happily enough. . . .

Until this morning. When Ling woke up and went into the nursery, and found the crib empty—and a note on top of the rumpled pink blanket. The roughly scrawled words read, *Your debt's paid—I've taken what's mine*. There was no signature at the bottom of the note, just a star-shaped symbol, crudely drawn by the same angry hand:

Frantic, Ling pulled the hidden video camera down from the shelf, the other toys scattering around the floor. On the LCD screen that the teddy bear opened to reveal, Ling watched as her trusted nanny escorted an ugly little man into the room. The digits in the corner showed that it all had taken place after midnight, when Ling had been sound asleep in her bedroom. The horrid figure that she remembered from five years ago had been too short to reach into the crib. Instead, Anna took the baby and placed it in his arms, then dropped the note he gave her onto the blanket. They left together, the nursery now empty and silent.

A flood of memories surged through Ling's mind. Weeks before, when she had watched the nanny settling the baby down for a nap, Anna's long hair had swept down over one shoulder, leaving the back of her neck exposed. Right at the nape, a tattoo no bigger than the woman's thumb, in plain blue-black ink—and exactly the same symbol as the one on the bottom of the note.

"I couldn't go to the authorities." Kneeling on the other side of the carved grillwork, Ling kept her head bowed. It was obvious she still believed she was talking to the Mountain Master. "By then, I'd seen the same symbol on the DA's ring as well. And on an amulet around the police chief's neck. The dwarf must have people working for him all over this city. People he's helped, who owe him favors."

Concealed from her sight, Hank gave a monosyllabic grunt.

Ling raised her face, damp with tears. "I went back to my office, master. And I did everything I could to find the dwarf myself. I've been through every file I can lay my hands on, trying to find out who he is. But it's like he doesn't even exist. I haven't found any clues about him anywhere. Not a name, or an address, or anything else, despite how weird he looks."

Hank gave another grunt, affirming that he understood all that she had told him. He remembered the dwarf in the limousine. *It has to be the same guy . . .*

"Master, you and the triad are the only ones I can turn to now. I'll give you whatever you ask for. But you have to help me! For the sake of Ren-Lei!" She laid her hand on the grillwork, a fraction of an inch from Hank's face. "I'm so frightened for her. And I know . . . I know it's all my fault . . ."

He felt as though his heart were breaking. Something more than the woman's beauty captivated him.

"I will help you." Hank couldn't stop himself from speaking aloud. "I'll kill the dwarf for you, and bring your baby back." He put his own hand against the grillwork, one fingertip just able to touch hers through the perforated metal. "I swear—"

She leapt back, crouched as though to strike, the fury in her eyes showing past her upraised fists. "You're not the master!"

His voice had betrayed him.

"Who are you? Show yourself!"

Hank stood up and stepped out from behind the grillwork. The woman's eyes widened as she beheld his towering form.

"I'm a friend," he said simply. "You don't know me yet . . . but it's true. I can help you . . . Listen to me, and I'll—"

"There's blood. All over you." Her eyes widened, as though she were struck with a sudden realization. Ling ran to the door leading to the restaurant, opened it, and beheld the silenced wreckage beyond. She stared at the shattered tables and chairs, and the lifeless bodies, red pooling across the tiles. "You killed them . . . all of them . . ." That was when she spotted the Mountain Master, his corpse floating in the aquarium tank in the distance, sightless eyes gazing through the glass at her.

"The master . . ." Her hate-filled gaze turned back toward him. "You killed him . . . you killed my only hope."

Hank shook his head. "No. Like I said, I can help you, too . . ."

"And why should I trust you?" She looked at his reddened hands. "A murderer. A killer. That's all you are." Her eyes locked on his. "Now . . . now there's no one . . ."

She turned and ran. All he could do was reach, trembling, toward the empty space where she had been. He heard the back door slam open, then her racing footsteps disappear into the lightless silence.

"Wait—" Hank knew he had to go after her. To protect her. With a deity's stern regard, Guan Yu watched as he pushed aside a stack of chairs and headed for the alley, too. He collided with the garbage cans, knocking them over onto the wet cobblestones. "Don't go—" He ran after the woman, barely visible through the slanting rain.

"You blew it." Nathaniel's voice was filled with contempt. "What the hell were you thinking?"

He stood near the carved screen. Invisible to them, he had been able to watch everything, hear everything, that had gone on between the woman and the hit man.

Through the room's doorway, he caught sight of himself in one of the restaurant's mirrors that had been left unshattered by the battle with the Mountain Master's students. He could see the expression of concern on his face's reflection. "These people don't mean anything to you," he told himself. It was the rule that Death, his own master, would have quoted to him, if that pale, emotionless entity had been there. "Don't get involved."

It was a good rule—the best rule—and a person didn't need millennia of cold experience to know it.

He picked up one of the chairs and set it upright. He sat down, folding his arms across the back of the chair. Tired—for the last few hours, he had been following the trail of death through the city, just as his master had instructed him to do. Given what had just gone down here with that seven-foot-tall killing machine, he figured he had pretty much found the epicenter of the night's fatalities. Just observing—he had arrived at the restaurant while the fight had been in full swing—had worn him out. It seemed ironic to have returned at last to the world of the living, only to see that many people get iced.

But there had been more to it than that. It had been listening to the woman's story; that had taken something out of him as well. Her name was Ling; he knew that much about her. And her baby had been taken from her. That was the story she had told, through her anguished tears, to the giant hit man. Ren-Lei; probably a cute kid, if she took after her mother. Nathaniel figured the baby probably did. A sad story, but he had heard ones just as sad before. His life so far had been full of sad stories.

But this one had hit him hard for some reason. He laid his chin down on his arms and thought about it. At last, it came to him. *She's looking for her baby,* thought Nathaniel. *She'll go on searching, forever. She'll never stop.* That's what his own mother would have done—he knew it, he absolutely knew it—if she had still been alive when his drunken father had given him to Death. She would have come and found him. No matter what it took.

He got up from the chair and went over to the shrine. He looked down and saw the little drops of water, dark on the tiles below the screen. Those were her tears, he knew. He knelt down and touched a fingertip to one. Then he touched his chest. The pain was still there. It would never go away.

"You really are an idiot," he softly told himself. But if the injury he had sustained, the weakening of the sacred pins that held his own soul inside himself, made it impossible to help anyone whom fate had drawn to his master's world, the realm of the dead . . .

Then maybe he should help someone here. In the realm of the living.

He stood up. He closed his eyes as he brought his wet fingertip to his mouth.

And tasted the salt of a mother's tears.

8.

The Devil stood at the window of the office tower, gazing down at the garden below.

His thoughts moved with a slow, vicious solemnity. At that moment, if all of the city's humanity had but a single throat, he would have seized it in his sharply nailed fist and squeezed until the last bubble of red had burst.

There were the usual supplicants cluttering up the lobby—but it wasn't their whining and begging that had turned his dark meditations even more bloody-minded than before. Desperate people were always scrabbling for his attention, as if he cared about their petty little lives and how badly they wanted him to let them out of the contracts they all had once been so eager to sign. He would deal with the humanity yammering at his elbows when he felt like it. Right now, he needed time to ponder all that was happening at the foot of his glistening tower.

His gaze turned even more incendiary as he contemplated the distant garden. Even as the rain continued pelting down, the peach tree stood in full bloom, the wet blossoms scattered throughout the lush green of its leaves. The sight infuriated him, as it had since the moment when the tree had been struck by lightning. His anger mounted higher as he suddenly realized that this must be what it felt like to be concerned about the passage of time. Human beings feared the approach of some final day, when payment for all their bargains came due; a page ripped from a calendar, or even the ticking of the clock upon a mantelpiece, must send their hearts racing with terror. A sensation like that had been unknown to him through all the millennia of his existence on earth. Yet nevertheless, here he was, brooding about what even the next few hours might bring.

Other creatures seemed happier, though. *Idiots*— He seethed with disdain when he spotted them. A dozen or so of the city's residents, tending the garden. As if their pleasure in doing so was protection enough from the rain. Simple souls, even by human standards, who had not been so foolish as to let their greed and vanity entice them into diabolic contracts. Happy enough to be there, pulling up the garden square's dead, sodden weeds, clearing away the undergrowth that had tangled around the once-dead peach tree, doing what was within their meager, mortal powers to transform this small portion of the world into something pleasant and enjoyable. The Devil despised them—and soon enough, he would take their wishes and dreams and crumple them like scrap paper inside his fists.

Dreams—and something that infuriated him even more. Even from here, he could see hope in the people's eyes, especially those lifted in adoration toward the tree's branches. Some stood there in amazed witness of the miracle happening before them;

others knelt down and scooped up the wet dirt from the base of the trunk, rubbing it over themselves as though it were a sovereign charm against evil.

Even as the Devil watched, more people streamed into the garden square, bearing candle-lit lanterns and lengths of colored ribbon to hang amidst the glossy green leaves. Bit by bit, the tree was becoming the shrine that the dead lunatic had envisioned.

Darting past the worshipper's legs, a couple of children tossed a rubber ball back and forth, while their parents troweled the wet dirt at the side of the garden and planted a row of daylilies. The ball got away from the kids, and bounced off the back of a man sweeping up the discarded plastic bags and other rubbish cluttering the square. From his vantage point high above, the Devil watched in revulsion as the man cheerfully accepted the parents' apology. Leaning on the handle of his rake, the man went on chatting with the others, all of them laughing and looking each other straight in the eye.

"That's not good," the Devil muttered to himself. It wouldn't have been too long ago that even a trivial incident such as that would have ended with the father and the other man first trading snarled insults at each other, then blows. And for the city's residents to look each other in the face, instead of slinking past each other, eyes averted, the way they used to . . . nothing else could have indicated so clearly how the gears of Time had begun meshing and turning. Instead of being frozen in the eternal ice of abandoned hopes.

Eyes narrowing, he shook his head. If little things like that were happening—it meant that other, bigger things were as well.

That enraged him a lot more than just people being so sickeningly *nice* to each other.

They're out there somewhere, he thought. The three heroes that he had dispatched so many assassins to find and eliminate. And still no sign of them, let alone their corpses laid out on the street for him to approve. He had expected far better results—especially from that last one the dwarf had recruited, the giant killing machine named Hank.

And what if his hirelings failed to find the heroes? Then what? In the workings of Time, there were even more things to be confronted. Such as those three heroes, whoever and wherever they might be, assembling that great army of which prophecy had spoken. An invincible army, with the heroes as its generals, leading its ranks as they marched toward the Devil's headquarters.

He nodded slowly to himself. That would be interesting, if and when such a moment ever came. He would have to be ready for it.

Below, the children went on playing around the peach tree. A breeze rustled the branches; a blossom drifted down through the raindrops. A little girl gazed up at it in rapturous amazement. Just as though she had never seen anything as beautiful before.

9.

Beneath the roof of the groundskeeper's cottage, the drumming of the rain filled the wood-paneled office. By the light of a guttering candle, Nathaniel fitted the ornate brass key into the desk's lock. It took an effort to turn, the workings reluctantly grinding against each other.

He pulled the drawer open and began sorting through the age-yellowed papers. At the bottom, he found what he was looking for: a bigger key, cruder and more ancient in appearance, like something that might have been catalogued in a museum of medieval antiquities. When he took the key out, it filled both hands.

Got it. As quietly as possible, Nathaniel slid the drawer shut again. *Now for the real show . . .*

Peering out the little oculus window at the end of the attic, he looked for any sign of Death returning. Through the glass, so old that it wavered and rippled like an ocean tide pool, all he saw was the sheets of rain battering the tombstones. His master was away, collecting souls. That was convenient for Nathaniel, since it afforded the opportunity to sneak back here into Death's home and take care of business for himself.

He knew he had to be careful, though. If Death returned and found out what he was doing, there wouldn't be a master-apprentice relationship between them anymore. There might not even be an apprentice, or at least not a living one. No telling what Death might do to him—the commandment for him to stay away from the Lights of Life had been so sternly delivered, and so often repeated, that he knew he was risking Death's wrath just by having the key in his hand. His master had taken him there only once, back when his training had first begun, then had forbade him from ever returning on his own.

Closing the attic office door behind himself, Nathaniel started down the spiral staircase that wound through all the stories of the cottage. In the cobwebbed mirrors, the candle flame wavered like a tiny ghost. With each tread, the iron stairs groaned, the slight noise vanishing into the shadowed rooms. By the time he reached the basement, he was dizzy from going through one descending circle after another.

Gnarled tree roots, thick as a man's legs, had long ago broken through the old stone walls. Rats scurried into the crevices, then regarded Nathaniel with their spark-bright eyes as he cautiously made his way through the low-ceilinged space. He squeezed his way past ranks of sagging bookshelves, crammed tight with leather-bound volumes. The archives of all the world's deaths—he knew that if he touched any of the books' ridged spines, an unbidden glimpse would open within his thoughts, of the dying moments inscribed within.

The bookshelves extended without seeming end, stretching away in a labyrinth of darkened corridors. Nathaniel's destination lay elsewhere—he kept one hand in front of himself until he felt the mottled surface of an iron door. Setting the candle on the ground, he pushed the key into the hole. It took both hands to turn, the rust of ages sifting down to the bolted sill.

Nathaniel let go of the key and pushed the chamber door inward with his shoulder. A draft extinguished the candle, but he could still see. A shimmering glow poured out from the doorway, lengthening his shadow out behind him.

He stepped into the chamber. The space seemed to reach for miles, as though it were a tunnel that might run beneath the oceans and emerge on the other side of the world. Waist-high stone pedestals filled the immense chamber. On top of each was a glass vessel like an antique oil-lamp cover, wide at the sealed base, then tapering to a narrow outlet at the top. Inside each glass, a small light floated. Billions of them, flickering inside the clear shapes, some larger than others, some brighter.

He knew what the lights were. Death had told him all about them, as part of his apprenticeship in the fatal arts. He could hear his master's unemotional voice: *Each light is the essence of a human being's life. The smallest belong to the newly born, the largest and brightest to those in their prime, the ones fading as though their fuel were almost exhausted—those belong to the aged and infirm, about to die. And when the light is extinguished, that person is no more.* But for each light that dies, Death had told him, another light immediately springs to life, replacing the one before inside the glass vessel. In that way, the balance between life and death was always maintained.

There was no turning back after having come this far in

breaking Death's stern commandment. Nathaniel pushed the chamber door shut. It hadn't been idle curiosity that had brought him here; he had a job to do.

A clear vision held in his mind, of the spell to be performed. Death had shown him that once, too, when he had been in the chamber of lights with his master. But he had never attempted this on his own. And if he failed at it . . . that thought he pushed away.

He sat down on the chamber's floor, letting the glow from the Lights of Life play above his head. Closing his eyes, he let his thoughts slow, then still, then cease. Emptiness, first within, then slowly beyond the limits of his being.

Without looking, he knew that another light had entered the chamber. A radiance formed around Nathaniel's body and expanded outward, like a full moon spreading a silvery haze across gathering clouds. The light flowed wider and wider, filling the space from floor to arched ceiling and rolling down its endless length. As each glass was touched by the glow, a vaporous figure shone above it. Human images, revealing what each living person on earth was doing at that exact moment in time. Laughing, shouting, praying, fighting, caught in passion or mired in sleep; reflections of the images swirled inside Nathaniel, as though he himself were now as translucent as glass. He held the world in his unmoving awareness, experiencing the thoughts and fears and dreams and desires of all who lived. . . .

It was too much to know. Death could withstand such enormity, but for any mortal mind—

Nathaniel felt a trickle of blood drop from his nostril. The halves of his skull felt as though they were about to be forced apart from within.

A sharper pain lanced across his heart. The pins, already weakened, holding in his soul—those began to tremble, a moment away from bursting into splinters. He laid his hand upon his chest, pressing tight, as though he could keep everything there from breaking apart.

You've gone too far. He knew he wouldn't be able to keep this up. *Pull back—*

At the far end of the chamber, the edge of the radiance began to fade. The pain lessened inside him at the same time as he regathered his strength. Above the glass vessels on their pedestals, the tiny human figures faded away. But not all of them— Nathaniel opened his eyes and looked around. The vessels closest to him still had the moving forms floating above them. Those were the spirits of the city, the people in the streets and buildings immediately around him. *That's what I need,* he told himself. The rest of the world would have to take care of itself for the time being. What he was looking for, needed to find, was right here.

He got to his feet and began looking along the rows of glowing vessels. Any with an image of an adult human being above it, he ignored. He was looking for a child. An infant.

At last, he found it. Nathaniel bent down, carefully studying what one of the carved pedestals held. A tiny spark inside the glass, and the form of a baby, hardly more than a couple of months old, drifting above it.

He knew the child's name. *Ren-Lei* . . .

And more than that. With his master, he had reaped so many

souls, in so many districts, that he had picked up a smattering of every tongue spoken in the world.

Humanity. That was what the child's name meant. In Mandarin. The ancestral language of its mother.

The child was crying, its face contorted with uncomprehending fear. Nathaniel's heart trembled in sympathy.

Setting his hands on either side of the glass, he concentrated all of the spell's energy into that space. The spark burned brighter as his own soul joined with it.

Faintly at first, then completely, he was no longer looking at the tiny human image floating above the glass. He now saw through the infant's eyes. His breath rushed from him in a gasp as he realized where Ren-Lei was being kept, where she had been taken. He recognized the place visible around the child. Death had taken him there, more than once. And each time, he had dreaded going. An evil, dangerous place, where no innocent soul should be.

I was right, thought Nathaniel. *To do this*. The conviction formed solid in him that disobeying his master's commandment had been necessary. To save this child . . . and more as well. He didn't care if it was the child's fate, or destiny, or whatever grand words Death used. No one, least of all an innocent baby, should suffer in such a way.

He let the spell fade. What the child saw, he no longer saw. Nathaniel found himself once more inside his own body, gazing at the glass vessel on the pedestal, and the small, bright spark it held. He drew his hands away . . .

Something happened. Another image appeared above the glass, faintly superimposed above the infant's. He leaned closer to the pedestal, trying to make out what he saw there.

It was his own face.

Nathaniel drew back, startled. That was something he hadn't expected. As he watched, he could see the two images fusing together—not into one thing, but one fate. The realization slowly dawned inside him. Somehow he and the infant Ren-Lei were tied together—not just now, but in the future as well.

He let the energy dissipate. The conjoined image disappeared from above the glass. Turning his head, he saw the chamber darken around him, the radiance that had filled it now pulling back into his core.

From the corner of his eye, he saw one glass vessel different from the others. The spark inside was high and strong, the brightest of all those around him. Or it would have been, if there hadn't been a shadow hanging over it, like a shroud.

But worse than that. As Nathaniel watched, he saw that the patch of darkness was somehow a living thing itself, one that had seized upon the light below it. As an owl might swoop down and sink its talons into a mouse skittering through a night forest, squeezing out the small creature's breath. Some evil aspect of this shadow's nature gave it the power to extinguish the light inside the glass vessel, smothering it until the dim, obscured glow could hardly be seen at all.

He had never seen such a thing before, and Death had never told him of it. Nathaniel bent down to take a closer look at the vessel's contents. His eyes narrowed in puzzlement as he discerned something else about the light—

Half of it was gone. Underneath the shadow, the light seemed to have been split down the middle, from top to bottom, and one side surgically removed.

A shiver ran down Nathaniel's spine. The glowing specter both fascinated and appalled him. Nothing in his training as Death's apprentice had prepared him for such a sight. Some great evil had struck the bearer of that hideously impaired soul. The broken light inside the glass vessel could mean only one thing—that there was someone out there in the city whose essence had been riven the same way.

Nathaniel both pitied and feared that creature, whoever—or whatever—it might be. *How can it survive like that?* He could only wonder. Someone with only half a soul, and that part hidden by this encroaching shadow. A human being like that could know only suffering and grief. The pain was beyond Nathaniel's comprehension. It would be a mercy, he knew, to reap the remainder of that agonized soul, drag it from the body that was its prison, and entomb it here in this dark chamber.

But who was it? Whose partial soul floated inside the glass vessel, struggling endlessly with the black shroud that sought to consume it? He didn't even know the man's name.

Not yet . . .

There was still a little bit of the spell's force left inside him. Nathaniel touched his fingertips to the darkened glass, and let his consciousness flow inside it. A human image formed above the vessel. He peered close at the small form. It seemed to be a beggar, with dirty, matted hair. And the equally filthy rags in which the figure appeared to be clothed—Nathaniel could see that those were actually what had once been a long overcoat, now held together by stitches, as though it had been patiently mended over and over. But somehow the garment held the figure in torment; the beggar's grime-darkened fingers clawed at the coat, but couldn't pull it from his body.

That's the shroud, realized Nathaniel. The one around the light, seeking to smother it out. Woven from pure evil, by hands that hated all living things, and sought their destruction. Even now, the shroud was trying to keep the soul inside the vessel from fighting against all the cruel attacks that had left it split in two, a fatally wounded thing. But the beggar's soul, even in its crippled state, still possessed an indomitable will, not just to survive . . . but to triumph.

Nathaniel pushed harder, entering into the man's mind and seeing through his eyes, as he had done with the infant Ren-Lei.

Blake—that was the man's name. A flood of memories, all that Blake remembered, swept over Nathaniel's own thoughts. He saw caves in Afghanistan, an abandoned farmhouse, a boy who had hardly been more than a child . . . Adeeb; that was the boy's name . . .

The memories ended in gunfire and explosions, ashes upon the smoke-tinged air and blood seeping into the ground. The soldier's blood—for that was what he had been back then, and not the abomination he was now—and the blood of his comrades. The ones that he, in his delusions, had killed. The ones for whom he grieved, as he grieved for the boy Adeeb, of whom no trace had been left. No trace but memory.

Nathaniel let the spell fade away again. He pulled his fingertips away from the shrouded glass vessel. He had found out what he needed to know.

This soldier, Blake—the man was here in the city, right now, sealed in the garment that was attempting to kill him. Blood and filth, pain and despair—but still moving forward, driven by nothing but his own will, and those memories that would never fade away.

I can use him. This former soldier had come back to the city for a reason. To kill someone; Nathaniel had been able to discern that much while his spirit had been joined with Blake's. *And I can help him,* Nathaniel realized. There were things they could accomplish together . . . that might save them both.

He picked up the key from the chamber's floor. Too much time had gone by already; he'd have to hurry, to get the key back where it belonged before Death returned. And then he would have to head back out onto the city's streets—

To find the soldier.

10.

He had already saved her a couple of times. And she didn't even know.

Hank crouched at the edge of one of the city's rooftops, watching Ling as she ran through the dark streets below. The Guan Yu shrine from which she had fled, into the alley at the back of The Dragon's Talon restaurant, was located next to one of the city's worst districts. The pelting rain hid him as he followed her. He knew he had to keep her in sight—he wouldn't have entered this zone without readying himself for a fight with some vicious bastard, or a whole pack of knife-wielding punks, at every corner. A beautiful young woman on her own would be easy prey for that kind. But Ling, blinded by her own tears, grieving for her stolen baby, obviously didn't care what happened to her right now.

That was why he didn't want her to know that he was following her, and was making sure that she didn't get killed. She was running from him, as much as all the other bad things that had happened to her, a whole cascade of horrors from the moment she had discovered her baby Ren-Lei missing. If he caught up with her now, there would be no way of talking to her, of convincing her that he wanted to help. And if he told Ling that he loved her, just from those few moments of watching her through the grill-work of the Guan Yu shrine—what would she do, other than try to plunge a furious knife into his heart? *Just wait,* he told himself again. *That's all you can do now.*

Or perhaps a little more. One of the alleys behind him held a stack of unconscious bodies, one of the gangs that he had spotted stalking her. He had made short work of them, blocking their slashing razors with his forearm, then driving his boulder-like fist into their faces, one after another. He had used one of their shirts to wipe the blood and snot from his knuckles, then climbed back up the nearest fire escape in order to keep track of Ling.

A pair of loping predators, working the alleys with a chain strung between them, had actually been more of a threat. Hank had encountered them before, and knew the nasty way they worked, and what little was left of their prey when they were done. Those two he hadn't let live, but instead had pinned them to the ground with his boots, while pulling the sharp-edged chain tight around their throats. If Ling had heard anything behind her, their last gasping struggles for breath, she might have thought it nothing more than the wind scraping bare tree branches across an alley wall. . . .

He could hear something going on below. He ran across the rooftop to which he had just leapt, and looked down.

In districts such as this, the troubles just never seemed to end. During the few seconds in which Ling had been out of his sight, another pack had caught her in their midst. They'd have her pinned to the ground in seconds if he didn't hurry—

Or not. As he swung down to the fire escape's bottom level, he saw that Ling was already taking care of business, despite the tears that streamed down her face. Two of the pack were already splayed facedown on the pavement. A third flew backward, his face imploded into a red mess by the impact of Ling's roundhouse kick. Before that one hit the ground, the rest of the pack had wisely taken to their heels, fleeing down the nearest alleyway.

She wasn't aware of him standing behind her. That gave Hank the opportunity to admire her fighting prowess as one of the fallen punks got to his knees and lunged at her with an open clasp knife. She dodged the blade's glistening point, then used her attacker's shoulder as a pivot point, cartwheeling above him, and brought her whole weight, knees first, down onto his spine. The knife skittered out of his lifeless hand.

"Why," she spoke low and fierce, "are you following me?"

Ling had seen him there, silhouetted in the mouth of the opposite alley. She didn't wait for him to answer, but instead put her head down and charged. Her small fist came at his chin like the point of a spear as she leapt straight toward him. The impact numbed his forearm as he parried the blow, but before he could react, her other fist caught the corner of his brow. He could feel his brain slam against the inside of his skull, blurring the rapid sequence of kicks and punches that followed.

Nearly blinded, all Hank could do was throw his arms wide and grab the woman in a bear hug, lifting her off her feet and squeezing her tight to his chest. There was no way that she could hurt him; the difference in their size made the combat like that of a field mouse desperately hurling itself against a stone mountain. He was more concerned that in her fury, she might actually break her own wrists as her futile blows struck against his chest.

Caught in the straitjacket of his massive arms, she howled and fought to break free—

Her struggles ceased as quickly as her attack had been launched. Hank blinked and tried to focus his gaze, feeling rather than seeing her go limp in his arms. For a second, he wondered if it was a feint, a maneuver to lure him off his guard. Then enough of his vision returned for him to see her head lolling back, her empty eyes turned toward the dark, grey clouds obscuring the sky.

Ling burst into sobs, her despair-wracked body contorting in his grasp. He sank down to the pavement, still holding her tightly. She laid her face upon his shoulder, letting her tears stream down the front of his jacket.

"It's okay . . ." Hank leaned back against the alley wall. The ground was strewn with the city's garbage and rubbish, the rain scouring it toward the overflowing gutters. He rocked the woman back and forth, stroking her dark hair with one hand. "Don't worry . . . everything's gonna be all right . . ."

"No . . . it's not . . ." Her voice was a wailing moan. "She's gone . . . my baby . . . and it's all my fault—"

"Don't say that—"

"But it's true. I'm her mother . . . I was supposed to watch out for her . . ."

"Okay, now look." Hank gripped her shoulders and held her in front of himself. "They stole her. The dwarf and that bitch of a nanny, Anna. They're the ones who did it. They're the ones who are responsible. Not you. You can't blame yourself for what monsters like that do."

She went on crying, turning her face away from him in shame.

"I'm going to help you," said Hank. "I'm going to find your baby."

"But . . ." She looked up at him. "But how . . . ?"

He didn't want to tell her that he knew the dwarf. Not until he was absolutely sure that there was no mistake. "There was a note," he said after a moment. "You said there was a note that was left in Ren-Lei's crib. Do you still have it?"

"Yes—" Ling nodded quickly. She reached inside her jacket and pulled out a scrap of paper. "I kept it—it's right here—"

"Great." Hank took it from her. Holding it by one corner, he turned it so that the scrawl of words was revealed by the yellow glow from the nearest unbroken streetlamp. The rain blurred the ink, but left the words still legible. Just as Ling had recited them, when she had thought she was telling her story to the Mountain Master. He could imagine the dwarf's mocking voice as he read it. At the bottom of the note was the symbol she had described.

He had seen it before. It took him a few seconds to dredge up the memory, then it flashed complete inside his head.

It is *him. The symbol was on the ring he wore.*

Ling peered anxiously into his face. "What do you see?"

He still couldn't tell her. Given everything that was going down, it could be too dangerous for Ling to know.

"Gotta think about it." Hank folded the note and stuck it in his shirt pocket. "There might be something."

His decision had already been made. As the sheets of rain

from the approaching storm lashed against his back, he helped Ling to her feet. The lawyer who had hired him—that was who he needed to find. And if that bastard didn't help him . . .

Well—he rubbed the knuckles of his fist—he'd just have to take it up with the guy at the top.

11.

Some things are easier than others.

Blake already knew that. But trudging through the city's rain-soaked streets, pushing past the sodden rubbish spilling from the alleyways, the truth of that adage weighed even more heavily in his thoughts. His boots splashed through a gutter, its drain clogged by old newspapers and the empty-eyed carcass of a dead cat. *And I still haven't figured out a way,* he thought angrily, *to find the Devil.*

Problem was, there didn't seem to be any difficulty in encountering all the rest of the city's criminals—and getting into fights with them—but none of them seemed to lead to the guy at the top. He was supposed to live in one of the big downtown towers—the whole tower, not just one floor. But if that were true, Blake hadn't been able to discover which one. He had prowled around on those wide, ill-lit streets with no results other than a crick in his neck from staring up at the grimy façades lining them—no amount of rain ever seemed to be able to wash the soot and smoke from the towers. Not to mention the hard glares from the security guards peering out from the buildings' lobbies. He would have had no problem taking care of those sag-bellied rent-a-cop types if any of them had been stupid enough to try and chase him away, but if enough regular police were called in to overpower him, finding himself in a precinct station's holding tank would have seriously impaired the search for his quarry. So, he had gone back to the city's shabbier districts, looking for any connection, any break that might lead him to the Devil's back door.

And hadn't found any. *You'd think,* he grumbled to himself, *that some of these bastards would at least know where their paychecks come from.*

He stopped in the middle of an unlit intersection. To the left and in front of him, there wasn't anything other than more run-down tenements, with rain trickling down the concrete steps to the watering holes in their basements. When Blake turned his head to the right, though, he saw a church.

There had never been many of those in the city, especially in districts like this. Over the centuries, only a few had managed to attract even a meager following. But when those faithful had died off, their meeting places had been boarded up or torn down, either all at once with a bulldozer or bit by bit, starting with the lead being stripped from the roofs by recycling scavengers. The derelict churches slowly crumbled into ruins, mice scurrying through the empty pews, silverfish breeding in the pages of the rain-soaked hymnals.

This one, crammed in between a rubble-filled vacant lot and a shuttered brewery, looked similarly neglected—its steeple tilted a few degrees to one side, as if it were about to topple over completely—but there was at least some light seeping through its stained-glass windows. Faint splotches of yellow and blue glistened on the wet street in front of the church's doors.

Blake stood staring at the apparition for a long minute, as if wondering what it meant. At last, he turned and headed toward the steep-roofed building. If nothing else, this was something he hadn't tried yet.

In the covered porch at the entrance, a statue of the archangel Michael stood above the stone font. Covered in years of dust and pigeon droppings, the stern-looking figure drove a double-bladed spear into the horned Devil writhing at his feet. Blake nodded in approval, figuring that was how wars against the forces of evil were supposed to end. He grasped the door's ornate brass handle and pulled.

Inside, he closed the tall wooden door behind himself and looked around. His breath clouded before him—the church's interior wasn't any warmer than the streets outside. A pair of flickering candles on the altar cast the only illumination across the empty pews.

"Can I help you?"

He saw then the priest watching him, from the aisle at the side, where the front pew ended.

"Maybe—" Blake walked slowly down the church's nave, toward the altar. "I'm looking for something—"

"There's a soup kitchen around back." The priest stepped in front of him. "You can get a hot meal there." The age-lined face above the plain white collar showed a gentle smile. "I don't have much else to offer you, other than that. There's nothing here of any value."

Blake knew that churches, in this city, always had plenty of robberies and pilfering from the poor box. He didn't blame the priest for showing some signs of wariness toward someone as ragged and dirty as him.

"That's not what I meant," he said. "I need another sort of help."

"Oh . . . Well, if it's a personal problem you have, let's talk about it." He gestured toward the pew's bench. "Sit down. Tell me what's troubling you."

Blake squeezed into the pew, leaving room for the priest to sit down beside him. "It's difficult . . . ," he said. "But here's the deal. I'm looking for the Devil. I need to find him."

"The Devil!" A frown appeared on the priest's face. "Why would you want to find someone like that? That's how people lose their souls."

"I want to find him . . ." Blake rested his grimy hands on his knees. "Because I want to kill him. For all the pain he's caused the world."

"And . . . that would be worth doing, I suppose . . . if it were possible. But I'm afraid it isn't. Evil exists—that's the fallen state that mankind is cursed with. And as long as we're that way, then the Devil exists as well. You'd be better off to forget this ambition of yours. You want to defeat the Devil? Fine—you do that through prayer. And through love. You might not believe it yet, but those are the weapons that God gave to us. Pick them up and use them, as He told us to."

"I wish it were that easy." He looked down at the stitches in the overcoat he wore. "And maybe if I were smarter, I'd take your advice. But I'm not, and I can't. So, I'll just ask you this: do you know where the Devil lives?"

"Other than in the hearts of men?" The priest shook his head. "No . . . I don't. Nobody does."

"But he lives here in this city. I know that."

"But those are just tales. Legends . . ." The priest gave a shrug. "Maybe they're true, maybe not."

"I just need an address, that's all."

"But who could give you one? The only people who might have it are those poor fools who bartered their souls to him. And they're all too much in his debt to betray him."

"Because they're scared of him." A current of anger moved inside Blake. "Everybody in this crummy town is. Including you. Hell, the Devil could be living in the building right next door, you could've seen him going in and out—and you still wouldn't say a word."

"That's a little harsh," said the priest. "You should understand—people need to be careful."

"Yeah, well, the only problem with being careful is, that's how the Devil stays in power. That's how he runs this place. He's got his boot on everyone's throat in this city—and everybody pretends like he doesn't even exist. Like somehow, if they don't talk about him, things won't get worse." Blake's matted dreadlocks brushed his shoulders as he shook his head in disgust. "As if that were even possible."

The priest said nothing.

"Okay." Blake stood up. "Thanks for your help. I mean that."

The priest followed him along the nave as he headed for the church's door. "If there's ever anything else . . ."

He stopped and looked back at the priest, then nodded. "There might be," he said. "Someday." He pushed open the door and stepped out into the chill night.

"Please—" The priest called after him. "I understand what you're trying to do. But it's not too late to reconsider. Violence won't solve anything—"

Blake paid no attention to the other man. He found himself again looking at the statue of the archangel Michael. *A soldier,* he suddenly realized. *Like me.* That's what the angel was. With shield and armor, fighting the great enemy. The same thing that he was trying to fight—he could almost hear Michael urging him on, a comrade in the struggle.

But there was a difference between the two of them; he could see that as well. The archangel had a spear, a magnificent thing with flaming blades at either end, burning with the fires of Heaven. *But what do I have?* Nothing but his own bare hands, begrimed with dirt and dried blood. For armor he had only the Devil's own overcoat, encasing him in its evil and despair.

He lowered his eyes, catching sight of his reflection in the stone font. A disgusting image, with its long, matted hair and hideous face. How was something as degraded and loathsome as that supposed to fight the Devil? Weaponless and alone, with no comrades but those that marched silently through his guilt-wracked memories.

But he had no choice, he knew, except to continue. He turned and stepped toward the dark street, ready to continue his search. He halted, realizing that something strange had just happened.

Glancing over his shoulder, Blake saw that the font's water still held his reflection, as though he had not turned away at all. His shadow still fell across the font's base.

He looked inside the church and saw the priest caught in mid-stride, one hand reaching out, his mouth open with the last word he had spoken. Pulse accelerating, Blake turned back toward the street and saw a handful of scattered passersby, each frozen in place, as though he were looking at a photograph of the scene. Even the slanting streaks of rain were stopped in their descent, hanging in the air like dirty streamers.

His thoughts raced in sudden panic. *What the hell . . . ?*

"We need to talk, Blake."

The words caught him by surprise. Bracing for an attack, he scanned the area and saw one figure standing in the middle of the street, looking straight at him. A kid, maybe seventeen or eighteen years old, hair weirdly undampened by the rain, though he stood in the middle of it with the collar of his black leather jacket turned up.

"Don't freak out." The kid raised a hand to gesture at the street around him. "I stopped Time so we could have some privacy. It won't hurt you. And neither will I."

Blake glared at the kid, ready for anything. "Who the hell are you?"

"My name's Nathaniel." He walked toward the church. "You don't know me—but I know you. I know about the cage you were locked in, the deaths of your men, and the boy who blew up the market. I know that the Devil tricked you. And I know that you came back here for revenge."

"Maybe . . ." Blake's expression grew heavy and dark. "You know too much."

"Maybe I do." The kid smiled widely, and hopped up onto the church's porch. "But I'm on your side. I know about that coat you're wearing, too, and what the Devil tried to do when he put you in it. But most importantly of all, Blake, I know that despite the way you feel, you're a very lucky man."

"*Lucky* . . ." Blake felt his eyes narrowing. "Is this some kind of joke?"

"I wish it were," said the kid. "But where souls are concerned, I'm deadly serious. I may work for a different master, but I'm aware of the laws that govern what the Devil can do. And those laws have saved you, Blake. Up to a point . . ." The kid raised a finger, pointing out through the motionless rain. "Remember back in Afghanistan? If the Devil had been there for *you* instead of the boy that night, your soul would have been completely lost the moment you agreed to accept his help. But instead, he just used you as an instrument. You were the tool for him. Not the prize itself. So, since you never shook his hand or consciously did what he wanted of you, he was only able to take away half your soul, instead of the whole thing."

Blake's glower deepened. "Half my soul?"

"And what's worse, because he sidetracked Purgatory that way, he was able to take that lost half away with him, straight down to Hell. Without any kind of trial. That's left you changed, Blake. Forever. It turned you into what we call a wraith."

Blake eyed the kid. "A what?"

"A wraith." Nathaniel took another step into the porch. "Have you ever wondered why it is you can't die?"

"Every day."

"Well, it's because you're half dead already. Half dead, and half alive, and you will be for the rest of time unless you find a way to change it. It's an evil curse, and the Devil uses it to stop the people he's tricked from ever coming after him. You're not the first one he's done it to. And you won't be the last. But what makes you special, Blake, is the fact that you've managed to fight it—even though I can sense the evil of that coat from here."

Blake wondered if he could trust the kid. Popping out of nowhere, knowing all kinds of stuff. He looked back to the scene outside. *The Kid's stopped Time, but I'm still moving. If he'd wanted to, he could have hurt me. And those things he just said . . . Somehow they ring true . . .*

Blake narrowed his gaze. "So you're saying that the Devil has taken half of my soul to Hell?"

Nathaniel nodded. "It's burning down there even as we speak—screaming in agony with the rest of those voices you can hear. And as for the half that's left behind . . . It's locked inside the coat you're wearing. The only reason the coat hasn't suffocated you yet is because your soul is too strong for it. Even though there's only half of it left over, your soul is still bright enough to resist the shroud. That makes you something special, Blake. It makes you unique. Like me."

Blake ran his hand slowly along the front of the stitched-up overcoat. *A shroud . . . Yeah, that sounds about right. . . .*

"And that thing is alive, too," explained Nathaniel. "It's been created directly from the Devil's own evil. A work of genius, really. But so cruel . . ." He eyed the garment warily, disgusted and fascinated at the same time. "You don't think that I could maybe . . . touch it, do you?"

"I wouldn't . . ." warned Blake.

Too late. Nathaniel's fingertips grazed the overcoat's blood-crusted lapel for only a second. But that was enough to send a visible shock wave convulsing through the kid's body. His spine arched, head thrown back, teeth clenching as his eyes flooded with darkness. Looking down at himself, Blake could see the coat's stiff, grimy fabric seething with its own hideous animation, the hairlike tendrils coiling around Nathaniel's fingertips, seeking to feed upon him. The skin of his hand paled white, as though his soul were being consumed as well.

With a muted cry, Nathaniel jerked his hand away. The desperate motion took the last of his strength. He fell backward, the overcoat's grasp upon him broken.

Blake looked down at the figure writhing on the church's porch. Until the kid was still at last. Either dead, or freed.

After a few seconds, he saw Nathaniel's chest slowly lifting with one slow breath after another. He reached down, carefully taking the kid's hand and drawing him up onto his feet.

"Damn!" Nathaniel swayed unsteadily, fighting to keep his balance. He shook his hand, as though it had been burned. His eyes widened as he stared at Blake. "That's . . ."

"What?" Blake leaned toward the trembling figure in front of him. "Did you see something?"

"Too much." Nathaniel slowly shook his head. "I saw . . . visions. Terrible things. It was like . . . like I was looking directly into his heart." His eyes locked on to Blake's again. "How do you . . . *endure* it?"

Blake didn't answer. *To be honest,* he thought, *I don't even know myself . . .*

He looked Nathaniel in the eye again. "Why are you here?"

"I'm here—" Nathaniel's voice was still shaking from the shock of what he'd seen. "Because I need your help. There's someone I need to save. A kidnapped baby. Her name is Ren-Lei. And considering where she's being kept, I'm not sure if my powers are enough to save her on my own. I can do some cool stuff, I know. But if it comes to a fight, I'd prefer to have someone by my side who has some experience."

Blake acknowledged the compliment. "And this baby, you know who's taken her?"

"Yeah, I do. So if you agree, I can take us there without a problem." He paused. "And in return for saving her, I promise to do something for you, too."

Blake eyed him more closely. "Like what?"

"Like helping you find the man you're looking for."

"The Devil?"

Nathaniel nodded. "Help me save Ren-Lei, and I'll bring you face to face with him before the end of the night."

It's a trick, thought Blake. *It has to be. There's no other way I could get such a lucky break.* Except—

He had no other choice. He was no closer to finding the Devil now than when he had started out. And if he didn't—

Then he would be like this, forever. Locked in the coat's dark, consuming embrace. A wraith, a thing with only half a soul.

"All right . . . I'll give it a shot." Blake narrowed his gaze and glanced back to his own grim reflection in the font's stilled water. "But tell me one thing, before we start. This half of my soul that the Devil has stolen. Would it return me to how I was before? Could it turn me back again, into something normal?"

"I think so . . . ," said Nathaniel. "But I guess it all depends."

"On what?"

Nathaniel raised a hand to restart Time. The figures outside began to walk again, going about their business. He watched them for a moment, then turned back to the man beside him.

"On whether or not you can get the Devil to hand it over."

12.

The blossoms had already fled from the tree. Leaving behind on the green-decked branches small shapes that seemed to swell larger even as the people in the garden looked at them. The peach tree's fruit ripened and grew heavier, their juices sweetening with life, the rain coursing across their bright yellow curves.

From the office tower's window far above, the Devil scowled fiercely down at the crowd. Their mere presence, even at this distance, infuriated him. If he could, he would have stretched down his arm and gathered them all into his fist, squeezing the lifeblood from their mangled bodies.

Below, the garden square was now a thing of beauty, its stones swept clean, lush grass trimmed, borders thick with flowers. The mingled scents rose on the air, seeping into the tower's air-conditioning vents and nauseating him with traces of approaching spring. Even worse, the once-abandoned square was now filled with humanity.

He had sent the building guards to chase them away, but to no avail. They just returned, as though summoned by the welcoming reach of the peach tree's branches. The crowds had gotten so large that they had begun spilling into the streets around the base of the office tower, like some happy contagion.

"Don't these people have jobs?" muttered the Devil. They should have all been crouched over sewing machines in sweat-shops lit by sickly fluorescent lights, or scavenging toxic metals from discarded circuit boards, out in the landfill dumps that surrounded the city. Anything productive and degrading, rather than down there, savoring the simple pleasures of existence.

The rage inside the Devil mounted, as though its flames might kindle every fiber of his being. Bad enough that the people in the garden square were happy—some of them were more than that. He could see their faces glowing with reverence, as though they had come here on a pilgrimage, to witness a miracle happening in a sacred shrine. Some of the people in the garden square even had lit candles, sheltering the small flames from the wind with their cupped hands. The sight served to increase the Devil's nauseated disgust—he could feel his scowl tightening on his face, like a Japanese *Oni* mask.

He went on brooding in the office's silence. A few minutes later, he heard the outer lobby door open again. Maybe his secretary had forgotten something and come back for it.

"I beg your pardon, sir." A female voice spoke at his office door. "I don't wish to intrude—but there's someone here to see you."

He didn't bother to turn around to see. "Throw him out in the lobby with the others."

"No, sir. It's . . . someone else."

The Devil glanced over his shoulder. The witch—cheaply

attractive in a sleek pencil-skirted business suit, her overdone mascara and eye shadow stark against her dead-white skin—shrank back from his gaze. As she did, a seven-foot-tall, sullen-looking giant brushed by her in the doorway.

"Who are you?" The Devil glared at him.

"My name is Hank." The giant gazed straight back. "I really wanted to speak to your lawyer. But he said he was busy. He sent me to you instead."

The Devil tilted his head back, surveying the man's bulk. "Oh, yes. The one with no fear." He gave an ugly smile. "Quite an impressive number of kills you've had today, Hank. But so far, the three you were sent to find are still not dead."

"That's why I'm here," said Hank. "I wanted you to know that they're not as easy to find as your little guy thought. There are so many dirtbags in this crappy town that it could take me a week to find the right ones."

"I don't have a week."

"I know."

The Devil mulled the problem over for a moment, then gestured toward the chair on the other side of his desk. "Looks like I'll have to speed things up somehow. Take a seat."

As Hank struggled to squeeze himself into the chair, the witch cowered back against the open door, her eyes fastened with avid devotion upon her master.

"I think . . . I have something that will help you." The Devil crossed the office and pressed a four-digit code into a keypad on the side wall. The wall slid open, revealing a cabinet of solid magnesium that reached to the alcove's ceiling. When the Devil laid his hand flat upon the surface of the cabinet, magical symbols began to glow there, turning from dull red to blazing yellow-white, as though heated by their own inner fire.

Hank looked at the desk in front of him, and saw the same twisting symbols imbedded in the black stone. The central symbol on both the desk and the cabinet was larger than the others. In both cases, it was a majestic, eight-pointed star.

On the front of the cabinet, that glowing, central symbol separated into two equal halves as the cabinet doors clicked open. Inside it hung a dismantled suit of armor, larger than anything even the giant hit man might have worn. An equally massive shield and sword were at the armor's side, all of them constructed of the same gleaming magnesium. On the breastplate of the armor was the star-shaped symbol again, placed right above the wearer's heart.

"There was a great war . . ." Dark meditations tinged the Devil's voice. "Long before the advent of humanity. This is the armor I wore in the final battle." Pride and bitterness sounded in his words. "Before I was imprisoned inside this . . . *pathetic* body."

He turned toward Hank, his gaze locking straight into the hit man's eyes. "There were three who fought me, fierce in their righteousness. Michael, Gabriel, and Raphael, and their wings were such as to cast this world into shadow. They were the ones—I'm sure of it—who planted the tree in my garden centuries ago. That's why I've never been able to destroy it, no matter how often I've tried. It just stands there. Year after year. In expectation of the day when Fate will bring me face-to-face with the three warriors who are prophesied to be my greatest mortal adversaries."

Hank gazed at the armor and nodded thoughtfully, digesting

everything he'd just heard. "I think I get it now . . . Your lawyer refused to tell me who I was working for. But I should have guessed."

The Devil scrutinized the hit man's reaction. "And now that you know it, does it make a difference?"

Hank mulled it over for a second, then shrugged. "Why should it?" he said without the slightest hint of intimidation. "Man or Devil, makes no difference to me."

The Devil gave a satisfied nod, and turned back to the cabinet. From inside it, he took out a dagger and what appeared to be a crystal flask. "If it was archangel magic that planted the tree and brought those three together, then it's about time I countered their tricks with some archangel magic of my own." He laid them both on the desk. "Magnesium, of course—" He pointed to the dagger. "And this—" He held up the flask. "Solid diamond. To hollow it required arts beyond human craftsmanship."

As Hank watched, the Devil drew out the flask's glistening, translucent stopper. At the same moment, the dagger's blade burst into flame, as if the weapon somehow knew that its power was now required.

"Only a weapon forged in Heaven," said the Devil, "can pierce an archangel's skin." He took the burning dagger by its handle and raised it before Hank's gaze. "And once such a weapon is alight, only shield and armor of magnesium can turn aside its blow. Armor—" He pointed toward the open cabinet. "Such as that."

Hank nodded at the dagger in the Devil's hand, its blade sheathed in flames. "So, the knife . . . Is that what you're going to give me?"

The Devil shook his head. "No. I'm going to give you something even more powerful. Something that will allow you to recognize instantly those who have the desire, and above all, the *ability* to do me harm."

The Devil put the burning edge of the dagger against his other palm, and cut deep into his own flesh. He clenched the wounded hand into a fist, then laid down the dagger and picked up the diamond flask. He held his fist above the flask's opening, but instead of a trickle of red blood, a fiery magmalike substance filled the vessel, drop by incandescent drop.

When the flask was full, it looked as if a solar flare had been captured within it. The Devil replaced the stopper, then held the flask toward Hank. "Take it."

Hank warily eyed the radiant object. "What am I supposed to do with it?"

"It's simple," said the Devil. "When the blood is exposed to anyone who intends to attack me, it will react."

He watched carefully as Hank took the flask. The burning substance remained quiescent inside the hollowed diamond. He nodded in satisfaction, assured that the giant hit man was no immediate threat.

Hank carefully stowed the diamond flask inside his jacket, extinguishing for the moment its fiery light.

The Devil walked over to the opposite wall and punched in the key code. The metal cabinet disappeared as the false wall closed. "So—" He gestured with his hand to dismiss Hank. "You have what you came for. Leave me, and get back to your job. I wish to be alone now to—"

To his surprise, the giant hit man raised a finger. "One question first, if that's okay."

Hank worked his huge bulk free from the chair, then brushed past the Devil and strode to the office window. He opened his mouth wide and exhaled on the glass, fogging a hand-sized patch. One blunt fingertip touched the glass and drew the symbol.

"What the hell does *this* mean?" Hank looked back at the Devil. "I've been seeing it all day. And now I find it here, too, on the desk and on that armor."

The Devil's gaze narrowed. "I'm not used to having people disobey me. Luckily for you, I know it's your pantaphobia that's to blame—which is still something that I need."

Hank didn't care. "And the symbol?"

"Very well—" The Devil humored the giant, and held his own hand an inch away from the eight-pointed star that Hank had drawn, as though admiring it. The symbol suddenly burst into flame, etching itself into the glass.

"In short, it is me . . . ," he said. "Or more accurately . . . it is God's name for me. My crest. My truest, simplest symbol. At its purest, it is a symbolic representation of the primordial quasar that I formed on the first day of creation, from which all subsequent stars were born. But it is also the flag that my army fought under in Heaven. That is why those who serve me bear this mark."

Hank nodded. "So, the little guy. If he has this on his ring, it means that he's more than just your lawyer, right? It means that he's part of something bigger. Something . . . bad."

The Devil tilted his head to one side, studying Hank with narrowed eyes. "You could say that, yes. If you wanted to. But—" He began to grow suspicious. "Why do you need to know so much about him? I sense that you're keeping something from me. Is that true?"

Hank shrugged. "Why would I do anything like that?"

"Possibly . . . ," said the Devil, "because you are not quite as stupid as you look."

Before Hank could move away again, the Devil reached out and laid his hand on Hank's brow to read his thoughts.

"I see a woman . . . and a child . . ." The Devil closed his eyes and pressed his hand tighter against the other's forehead. "I see an obligation . . . and hatred, too . . . for the man I call my greatest friend . . ." The Devil opened his eyes and removed his hand. He looked at Hank with scorn. "I was wrong. You *are* a fool."

"Why—" Hank saw no point in denying it now. The Devil knew why he was there, so he threw off the charade. "Because I care for someone?"

"No. Because you meddle in things that don't concern you. And meddling like this will only get you killed." He fixed Hank with his sulphur-blue eyes, as if staring down a rogue bull. "At any other time, I'd let you go ahead with it and destroy yourself. But I still need you, so I'll give you a warning that I expect you to heed." He lowered his voice to a threatening whisper. "The man who took that child has the ability to kill you as soon as look at you, even with your great size and strength. On top of that, he is under my own personal protection, so any move against him is a move against me."

"And Ren-Lei?" demanded Hank. "What about her?"

The Devil regarded him with contempt. "Forget her. If she isn't already dead, she soon will be. So just get back to the job I'm paying you for, and stop wasting any more time."

Hank could feel his knuckles going white with frustration and anger. "But . . . who is this damned dwarf anyway? Why does he do such terrible things?"

"Because I allow him to, that's why!" Sadistic pleasure mixed with pride in the Devil's voice. "He is my Lieutenant, my second-in-command. He has been my closest ally ever since the war in Heaven. But after he fell to earth with me, he was not bound by the same rules of behavior that I was. I am forbidden to pass on the sins of a parent to its child. But he is hampered by no such distinction. Therefore, when someone seeks advancement through him—and enters into a contract by shaking his hand—he takes the child of those he's dealt with as his payment, just as I might take a person's soul. Then, down in his lair, he consumes the bodies and drinks the blood of those babies—as an affront to the senile God who cast me out and crushed my followers beneath His heel."

Silence filled the office, hard and oppressive. After a moment, the witch spoke in a small voice from the open door: "I think it's time for you to leave."

The Devil dismissed Hank with another wave of his hand. "And this time, do as you're told." He crossed back to his desk and swiveled his chair around so that he could gaze out at the low-lying storm clouds roiling across the city. "For both your own sake and mine, forget my Lieutenant—and find me those three opponents that I need."

Hank glanced at where the burning symbol had eaten into the windowpane. "Sure," he said. "I'll get back to finding them straight away. With this glowing blood of yours, it'll be a breeze."

Another empty moment passed, then Hank turned and followed the witch out of the office.

13.

The back door of the town house creaked open an inch with a single push from Hank's palm. He had already torn the rust-corroded padlock and hasp from the rotting wood and tossed them aside. Peering inside, he saw nothing but darkness and dust.

He'd had to shove his way through two separate crowds just to get to this doorstep. The first had been right inside the lobby of the Devil's office. After finding out that the Devil's lawyer wasn't just some kind of weird sicko, but something worse, he'd pushed his way through the mass of supplicants, clutching their file folders and manila envelopes stuffed with photographs and testimonials. Lining up like that to beg the Devil for an extension on their contracts, they had reminded Hank of the densely packed cattle at the city's slaughter yard. Those poor beasts had no more chance of rescue than these two-legged ones. But at least there in the lobby, with the stench of their anxious sweat clotting sickeningly in his nostrils, he'd found the answer that he needed so badly.

"If you're looking for the dwarf, I can help you. . . ." The woman in the middle of the crush looked like a high-up executive from some multinational fashion firm. An older woman, who still would have been striking, if not for the anguish that had consumed her face. "I only have a week to go before my contract's up, and that bastard is going to screw me, I know." She kept her voice down so that the witches wouldn't hear. "Someone over by the door heard you discussing his Lieutenant. Believe me, we all know him. And we all hate him as much as you do."

"But do you know——" Hank lowered his voice, too, and bent down so that none of the witches could see him. "Where I can find him? The big boss said he had a lair. But where is it?"

"Across the square." The woman squeezed his arm. The thought of revenge, from anyone, seemed to excite her. "There's an old town house there. One of the oldest in the city. It's boarded up now, but I saw him enter it once."

Hank got out of there as quickly as possible once he had the information. But picking his way through that mass of humanity, with its mingled atmosphere of despair and desperation, had been weirdly easier than escaping the second crowd he'd had to push through. That had been when he had gotten down to street level, and the crowded garden square. The people were still packed into the space, despite the pounding rain that continually threatened to extinguish the uplifted candles. Shouldering his way among them, he had barely glimpsed from the corner of his eye how large the swelling fruit on the pear tree had become.

Those people, the ones in the garden——their sense of hope was real. Something that had always been in short supply in this city. But somehow it had risen among them, as though the tree's roots had broken open a wellspring below the cracked pavement.

The excitement was palpable among the crowd, brighter in its crackling electricity than the streaks of lighting that stitched the dark clouds hanging above their heads. A few of the murmuring voices broke into louder, wordless, enraptured cries. Hank passed by others, speaking unabashedly to anyone who would listen, heedless of consequence—their words spoke of revolution, hated despots being overthrown, new days dawning. They turned from one another and cast tightly smiling glances at the tower next to the garden, as if they could already envision it crumbling apart, a vertical chasm tearing it from top to bottom.

Just enough light slid in from the back door for Hank to make out the interior's dim outlines. The woman in the Devil's waiting room had told him that the town house was one of the oldest buildings in the city, and it smelled like it, too, the enclosed air rank with mold and mildew. As Hank's vision adjusted, he could discern a bit more. From what he could tell, the town house hadn't been lived in before it had been boarded up and left derelict. The wood floors were bare, the carpets still rolled up along the baseboards, with customs duty tags hanging from their raw jute bindings. The chandeliers were still bagged in canvas, like enormous, grey bats sleeping above stacked and shrouded furniture.

It's some kind of a con job, thought Hank as he looked about himself. *Like a false front.* Somebody, a long time ago, had set it all up to convey the impression that the town house had been inhabited. But the decanters on the grime-shrouded tables had never been unstopped and filled, and the wicks of the candles in the tarnish-blackened candelabras had been left unlit, no fires ever kindled in the empty fireplaces. The town house's only residents were the spiders who had draped the cornices with their dust-thickened cobwebs.

He fashioned a torch from a chair leg, its splintered end wrapped with a tattered sofa cushion. Once the fabric had been set ablaze, he stepped farther into the town house's shuttered rooms. Sleek rats pattered away at his steps.

Passing through what had evidently been intended to be a sitting room and a parlor, he found himself in the town house's library. Most of the mahogany shelves were bare, the volumes intended for them still piled up on the floor. A draft fluttered the torch's flame; he peered closer at the nearest bookcase and spotted a thin opening along one end. He managed to dig his fingertips into the space, then pulled. The bookcase pivoted, revealing a hidden passageway.

Stepping cautiously forward, he followed the passage to the chamber at its end. That room's dimensions were of a perfect square, the walls bare and unadorned. Each of the four walls showed a doorway leading to another part of the town house. At the room's center, a rickety staircase stretched downward. Leaning in with the torch, Hank was unable to see the bottom of the spiraling steps. The stairs might have been a mineshaft to the center of the earth.

He squeezed past the side of the bookcase and set his foot on the first of the steps; it groaned beneath his weight. But he heard something else as well. Looking back over his shoulder, he saw shadows approaching one of the other open doorways, human figures silhouetted by the dim light behind them. Two men stepped into the room.

They stared at him in surprise equal to his own. One of them looked like some kind of beggar, with long, matted dreadlocks trailing to the shoulders of a filthy, stitched-together overcoat; the other was younger, no more than a teenager, wearing a black leather jacket.

He raised the torch higher, so he could get a better look at the pair. He figured the grime-encrusted one was just some poor homeless bastard; the city was full of them. "If you're looking for some place to sleep, I'd advise going somewhere else. This place is—"

Suddenly, he felt the heat of something burning in his own coat pocket. Puzzled, he reached in with his other hand and pulled out the diamond flask that the Devil had given him. The thick, magmalike fluid in the vessel now churned and bubbled, as though boiling in fury.

The beggar stepped closer, circling around the staircase toward him. As he did so, the flask in Hank's grasp exploded. The bright, searing fluid spattered across his chest like molten iron.

He's one of them— Hank's eyes widened as he looked at the filthy specter before him. One of the three that he had been recruited to find; one of those men that the dwarf had said could harm Hank, and bring him fear. Shards of the diamond flask were still clenched in his fist, the sharp edges protruding from between his fingers like a multibladed weapon. He dove toward the beggar, his arm sweeping in a level arc to bring the shards across the man's throat.

With an upraised forearm, Blake blocked Hank's attack. The impact snapped into Hank's chest, a shock wave as solid as though he had struck a wall of granite. With his greater mass and the speed of his rushing leap, he should have been able to barrel over the beggar, flattening the dirt-encrusted figure onto the floor. Instead, the beggar had vaulted over him, eluding Hank's blow like a seagull spiraling above an ocean's crashing wave. He felt one of the beggar's black-grimed hands seize him by the throat; still in midair, the beggar thrust his arms straight, toppling Hank backward.

Hank's shoulder brushed the edge of the central stairwell as he sensed himself falling into the opening. He caught a vertiginous glimpse of the spiraling stairs beneath him, with nothing but darkness at their bottom. Just before he collided with the staircase's curving rail, he rolled to one side, his knee catching the beggar under the chin with enough force to throw him against one of the chamber's walls. The stench of the grimy overcoat filled Hank's nostrils as the beggar lithely rebounded, leaping forward in a low, horizontal arc. The fingertips of one of Blake's hands touched the floor for a split second, enabling him to pivot his entire body around with even greater speed. His muddy boot caught Hank straight on the side of his head, hard enough to blur his vision. All he could do was blindly grapple the other man around the waist as he toppled backward. Both men landed entwined on the steps of the staircase, their combined force splintering the wooden treads beneath them.

Pounding a fist into the beggar's chin, Hank felt the staircase begin to disintegrate. Scraps of ancient plaster spotted his face as the bolts that held the central support to the ceiling were yanked free. The rail pulled loose from the steps and swung about, beating into the walls of the narrow space. Any of the blows he landed would have knocked another man unconscious, but instead Hank found himself gasping for breath as the other's knee slammed into his gut.

This bastard should be out of it—

The single thought lit up the inside of Hank's head, like a match dropped down a well. Adrenaline surged through his veins, not just from the stress of the fight, but from the realization that he had found at last who he had been looking for. What he had been promised. The butt of the beggar's palm slammed under the corner of Hank's jaw, blocking his carotid artery, pulsing stars and grey fog welling up in his skull. *This is the one,* he told himself. His heart sped, pushed by something he had never felt before. The one he couldn't beat, the one who could beat him, could kill him, anything was possible now, everything . . .

He managed to shove the beggar's hand away from his throat, a sudden tide of his own heated blood washing through his brain. The staircase yawed sickeningly in the darkness, more of its splintered fragments, broken steps, and rail segments pelting across his face and the beggar's shoulders.

His knuckles ached and leaked blood as he tried to pound more blows into the face of his opponent. But his fist swept through empty air more times than it hit flesh, the beggar ducking and weaving as though he could see every strike before it was launched. He managed to connect a few times, leaving the beggar's matted hair and beard glistening with red, the skin beneath scraped raw by Hank's knuckles. But for every blow he landed, as their bodies crashed through section after section of the staircase, the beggar came back with a quicker flurry, blinding and dizzying him.

Can't beat him to death—he's too fast—

There had to be another way, some weakness, an opening. Hank sucked his breath in through clenched teeth, his fragmented thoughts flailing from one side of his skull to the other.

Then he saw it. The corner of one elbow had dug under the lapel of the beggar's filthy overcoat, ripping apart the neat stitches and peeling back the crusted fabric. Revealed underneath wasn't skin and dirt, but raw flesh and shimmering lungs, as though all that held the beggar together was the spidered cage of his ribs.

That's how—

Wood splinters and ancient dust bellowed around Hank as his weight, combined with the beggar's, shattered another section of stairs, his back plummeting through the broken pieces. Desperate, he didn't block the beggar's next punch, but let it crack like a boulder against his cheek as he plunged his own hand through the bloodied skin and into the beggar's wet, red chest. His fingers clawed past the pulsing fist of the heart, straining to reach the spinal column behind. He knew instinctively that that was the only way to defeat him, to snap the linked bones and the nerve fibers they held—

Just as Hank's fingertips grazed the vertebrae, his hand and forearm went numb. Rearing his head back, he could see the bloodied edges of the beggar's overcoat seizing tight upon his arm, like a pit bull furiously clamping its jaws upon another beast's neck. Panic, never experienced before, erupted inside Hank; he futilely struggled to pull his captured hand free. It felt as though the combined force of the coat and the beggar's raw flesh were about to snap his forearm like a bundle of dry twigs.

Suddenly, a harder blow hammered up through Hank's back

and shoulders, leaving him stunned and without breath. Dizzied, he was just able to perceive that he and the beggar had struck the solid stone floor at the base of the disintegrating staircase. A cloud of dust rose around them, obscuring the nearby walls. Broken segments of wood cascaded across his face and upraised forearm—that was when he realized the force of the impact had dazed the beggar as well, enough that his arm had yanked free from the grisly trap in which it had been caught.

Hank staggered to his feet. Through the dust roiling around him and the blood streaming across his eyes, he could barely discern the beggar splayed on his back amidst the staircase's wreckage, slowly shaking his head. Hank knew he had only seconds before the beggar regained enough consciousness to launch another leaping attack upon him.

They seemed to have landed in a cellar chamber with an arched stone ceiling only a couple of inches above Hank's head. He looked around and spotted a section of the stairs' railing that was long and straight enough to use as a spear, one end broken sharp. Snatching up the wood segment, he raised it above his head in both hands, bracing himself to plunge its point into the beggar's chest.

The beggar's vision cleared enough for him to see Hank rearing above him. Just as he raised his hand in a futile effort to ward off the blow—

A baby cried.

They both heard it. The thin, wailing sound echoed from the chamber's curved walls. Hank turned his head, as did the beggar, both looking toward the limits of the dark, from where the crying came.

"Ren-Lei . . ."

Hank said the child's name aloud. At the exact same time that another voice called out.

He looked down at the filth-encrusted beggar. Who stared up at him in equal astonishment. It was his voice that had also spoken the child's name.

14.

The sounds of the fighting had gone on for a long time.

Holding on to what was left of the stair rail, Nathaniel peered down into the darkness. When Blake and the gargantuan hit man, fists pummeling each other, had tumbled into the space, the first thing their combined impact had broken away, with a screech of rusted metal, had been the staircase's vertical support. That had started the complete disintegration of the stairs, every piece of the steps and the curved rail snapping free of the rest, as Blake and the giant Hank had struck them shoulder-first or with the straining muscles of their backs. Nathaniel had instinctively reached to grab Blake's arm, to try and pull him back to the room, but it had been too late. The two battlers had already fallen beyond rescue, their conjoined descent barely slowed by the wreckage splintering around them.

There was silence now, though.

"Blake!" He cupped his other hand to the side of his mouth and shouted. "You there?"

No answer came. He wasn't surprised. If the fall hadn't killed Blake, or stunned him into unconsciousness, then he would likely have succumbed to Hank's greater strength and mass. The question now was whether either one of them was still alive.

Only one way to find out, he knew. The staircase spiraling downward might be gone now, but that wasn't going to stop him from investigating. Nathaniel pulled his hand back and folded his arms across his chest. He closed his eyes, letting the darkness from below seep inside him, extinguishing his thoughts . . .

The baby's cry had stopped. For a moment, there was silence in the close-ceilinged stone chamber. Then both men heard a name called out from far in the distance above them.

Blake . . .

Too faint to leave an echo; Hank turned his bruised head and gazed up the shaft that had held the staircase, its wreckage now scattered about the chamber's floor. He supposed it was the kid who had shouted, way up in the abandoned town house above. The teenager who had been wearing a tailored black leather jacket, neatly contrasting with the grimy figure of the beggar he had accompanied.

"Is that your name?" Hank looked over at the other man. The dust cloud roiling about them was still so thick that he could barely make out the matted hair dangling before the beggar's unwashed face. "That what they call you?"

"Yeah . . ." The beggar pushed himself back into a sitting position and laid his arms across his knees. Blood dripped onto the back of his hands from an open gash on his brow. "And who the hell are you?"

"Hank."

"Yeah, well . . ." Blake straightened, drawing in a long breath. "You're one rough bastard, Hank."

"I can be." He gave a nod. "When someone rattles my cage."

He studied the beggar's dust-obscured visage, trying to extract a few more clues from what he could barely see there. Rubbing a hand over one side of his rib cage evoked a pain-filled wince. It felt like an anvil had been dropped on him, more than once. That was the result of the beggar's spinning kicks, which had vaulted through the space between them like cannon shots. He prodded the tender flesh with a fingertip, relishing the pain. That had been the first time he had fought somebody with so much airborne velocity, coming at him from all angles, as though the beggar had been a creature composed of storm winds and lightning rather than earthbound flesh and bone.

The arched chamber's silence settled around them. Hank knew they were both waiting for the same thing. To hear the infant crying again, so they would be able to tell from what direction the sound came.

"That goddamned coat of yours." Hank studied the filthy garment on the other man. "What's the deal with that thing?"

"You don't want to know." Blake's eyes turned to hate-filled slits as he looked down at the red, broken stitches across the overcoat's lapels. "Believe me."

"It's like it's alive or something." His forearm looked as though a wild animal had tried to chew it off. "And you *wear* that thing?"

"I don't have a choice."

Hank wondered what that was supposed to mean. A lot more would have to happen—and a lot more would need to be explained—before he would trust this sonuvabitch, whoever he was. Trusting people was how hit men got killed.

A faint sound broke into his thoughts. Both men's heads snapped up, full alert, as the infant's cry came again from the chamber's distance.

Hank looked over at the other. "Ren-Lei," he said quietly.

"That's right." Blake nodded. "Ren-Lei."

"That's why you came here? To find her?"

"Not just to find her," said Blake. "To save her."

"Okay." He reached a hand down. "Looks like we're on the same job."

The beggar had already sprung to his feet, his movement again preternaturally lithe.

Both men turned, scanning the dust-filled chamber. They could just discern low tunnels branching off in a confusing array.

"That way—" Blake pointed. "That's where it's coming from. That's where she is. I think."

"Maybe." Hank leaned forward, peering into the dark. He turned his head, listening, then nodded. "Yeah, I think you're right." He looked around and spotted a crude torch smoldering in an iron holder fastened to the wall. He tugged the torch free and held it aloft, sending shadows wavering across the rough stone walls. "Let's go."

They headed for the arched tunnel entrance from which the infant's crying came.

Nathaniel opened his eyes. Through the settling clouds of dust, tiny shapes began to take form. White things, some of them smaller than his clenched fist. Others thin and fragile as twigs . . .

He turned slowly about, his skin tightening across his arms and shoulders as he watched the small, dimly perceived objects edge closer to being real. Real enough to touch. He stretched out his hand toward them.

Empty eye sockets gazed back at him. From skulls that he could have held on his palm—he saw now that the walls of the chamber were lined with them. Hundreds . . . thousands . . . beyond count, reaching up to the surface of the world from which he had brought himself. Infants' skulls, broken and gnawed upon, entwined with curving, threadlike ribs. Scarcely larger, femurs and other bones, stacked like kindling, had been split open, the wet marrow sucked out.

Wordless horror overcame Nathaniel. He snatched his hand away, stepping back through the swirling dust. As far as he could . . . anything to get away from the fragile remnants . . .

He collided with the wall behind him. It was bones as well—gazing up over his shoulder, he saw a seeming infinity of them, all the way to the chamber's arched ceiling. In a sudden convulsive rush, he shoved himself away from them. He lost his balance and fell, the wall breaking apart behind him. The minuscule white fragments cracked and scattered in all directions as he landed sprawling in their midst.

Nathaniel looked around in revulsion. It had been a simple matter to transport himself down into this arched stone chamber, lit by flickering torches. Just another one of those tricks his master Death had taught him, to go quickly from place to place when there had been a lot of names on their reaping list. Close his eyes in one place, then open them in the place he wanted to be. As simple as that . . . for one who knew how.

What he hadn't known was where he would find himself. What kind of place . . . what new horror . . .

Holding his arms close to his chest, he forced himself back under control. He had come here for a reason. He had to keep going, no matter what.

Where were the others, though? There was no sign of Blake or the thuggish giant they had stumbled across upstairs. The last sight he'd had of them had been as they had crashed down along the staircase, the fury of their entwined combat ripping the structure to pieces as they fell. But he saw nothing of either one of them now.

Setting his hand down to push himself upright, Nathaniel heard and felt a sickening crunch of tiny bones beneath his palm. He brushed the dry, powdery fragments off on his black jeans. A couple of yards away, the twisted wreckage of the staircase lay heaped about, dust still settling on the broken bits of wood. That must have been where the two fighters had landed, presumably still alive and conscious. Where they had gone from here, and in what condition, was anybody's guess.

Nathaniel got to his feet. He couldn't move without stepping on more infant bones and partial skeletons. Everywhere he looked, he saw the grisly aftermath of a feast that had been going on for centuries, soft tender creatures given over to hideous appetites.

"All right—" He spoke aloud, getting a grip on himself. He had been here on Death's business before, to help his master collect the souls of the slaughtered infants. The sight still turned his stomach. "You just need to keep going." That was what he had decided when he had been able to see through Ren-Lei's eyes, back among the Lights of Life—and had realized that this was the place to which she had been taken. His words drifted in echoes down the chamber. "That's all . . ."

In the distance, he thought he could hear a baby crying. Blake must have headed that way—if he hadn't been killed by that lumbering giant.

The crying came from one of the arched tunnels in front of him. He couldn't tell which one; they were all filled with darkness. *Need a torch*—

His own shadow wavered toward the tunnels; the nearest torch was several yards behind him. Picking his way as best he could across the scattered baby skeletons, he made his way down the chamber and lifted the torch from its iron holder on the curved wall. But when he turned back around, confusion swept across him. For a moment, he couldn't tell whether he had come down the low-ceilinged space to his left, or the seemingly identical one to the right. Both passageways were filled with scattered bones. He could still hear the infant crying, but the thin noise seemed to come from any of the tunnel openings farther away.

Holding the torch above his head, he ran forward, then halted, trying to figure out his next move. The light from the torch was so dim, the overlapping shadows it cast seemed as solid as the chamber's stone walls. Ren-Lei's cry came from the tunnel opening directly before him—but when he stepped that way, the cry sounded from behind. He turned slowly, hoping to discern the noise's source from its echoes.

He wasn't sure, but the crying sounded an infinitesimal bit louder from one tunnel than from the others on either side. He couldn't hesitate any longer; if the crying were to stop, he would be completely lost, with no clue of any sort to follow. *This one or nothing*, he told himself. *Just go.* He held the torch out before himself and headed down the tunnel.

"Hold up—"

Blake laid a restraining hand across the other man's chest.

"What is it?" Hank glanced over at him.

"Take a look around you."

The chamber into which they had fallen, surrounded by the broken debris of the staircase, lay far behind them. Hank brought his gaze around to the walls of the tunnel. Flickering torchlight illumined images painted in black ash and the crusted red of dried blood.

"What the hell is it?" He leaned closer to the wall, squinting as he attempted to make sense of the grotesque scenes.

"Some kind of mural," said Blake. "Like you see in temples."

"Look there." His grimy hand pointed to the wall's closest section. "You see it?"

"Looks like fighting." Hank shrugged. "Some kind of battle."

The mural was filled with interstellar storm clouds and great bolts of lightning, and winged figures tumbling toward the earth below.

Hank remembered the armor up in the Devil's office. "The war in Heaven . . . ," he said. "The one that the Devil lost . . ."

Blake peered closer at the mural, stepping toward another section. He pointed again. "Look—his demons . . ."

Creatures with the faces of men, and the hooves of swine, swarmed among the painted images. Hank could see how the fallen angels had been transformed, as a punishment for their rebellion, with horns where their haloes had been. And more—

brute claws and fangs, scales and bristling fur, tails lashing from their backsides, all walking about on two legs as men did.

"Do you reckon . . . that's what we're up against?"

Blake preferred not to answer. The images were like fragments glimpsed in nightmares, the sooner forgotten upon waking, the better. To think that they might be real . . .

"Let's get this finished," he said. "The sooner we find Ren-Lei, the sooner we can get out of this place."

He headed down the tunnel again. Hank gazed at the hideous mural for a moment longer, then turned and followed after him.

Blue light washed across them as they rounded the final corner in the tunnel.

The tunnel's ceiling had lowered, forcing Hank to move in a crouch, led on by the faint sound of an infant's cry before him. But as he and Blake emerged from the tunnel's mouth, he was able at last to stand upright, as though they had both stepped into a cathedral's vast domed space.

"Look," Blake whispered. "Up ahead—"

Hank turned in the direction to which the other man had pointed. The flickering light given by the torch in his hand was obscured by the fiercer glow from the sulphur burning in a circle of iron braziers. As his vision adjusted, he suddenly spotted a human figure in the center of them, before an altar. Instinctively, his fist clenched and he cocked his arm, readying himself to land the first blow.

Then he saw who it was. The dwarf. The Devil's Lieutenant—

"That's him!" Hank brought his mouth close to Blake's ear. "The one who stole the baby."

The dwarf was still unaware of any intruders, any witnesses

to the ritual he was about to perform. With his hunched back turned toward the men below, he picked something up from the stone platform beside him and held it over his head. An infant, naked and defenseless, its soft skin clutched in the dwarf's withered claws.

"We've got to save her!" whispered Hank. "Let's rush him—"

"No—" Blake gave a quick shake of his head. "Not while he's got her in his hands—"

The sulphurous flames rose higher, casting the central altar into high relief. Both men could now see several ritual objects set out on the pedestal. The magnesium breastplate from the Lieutenant's angelic suit of armor rested on its convex surface, forming a bowl suitable for catching Ren-Lei's blood. Beside it lay the hilt of a broken sword, crafted of the same darkly gleaming metal, the hilt's pommel crusted with dried gore and flecks of bone, thin and fragile as eggshells.

On the wall behind the raised altar, the torchlight caught glints from the rest of the angelic armor that the Lieutenant had worn—when his physical form had been undiminished, and he had fought alongside the other rebellious angels in Heaven. A battle-axe, likewise crafted of magnesium, hung beside the armor's segmented glove.

With eerie calm, the dwarf lowered the baby onto his deformed shoulder, as if cradling her. Then, with his free hand, he picked up the hilt of the broken sword and positioned its butt against the infant's skull, ready to strike.

"Damn!" exclaimed Blake. "He's not going to lay her down. We need to move. Now!"

He sprang forward through the shadows with superhuman speed.

At the same time, an image streaked through Hank's mind of the fight he'd had in the crack house, before the dwarf had hired him. He had needed a weapon then as well, and there had been nothing but a snapped broomstick.

He glanced at the flickering torch in his own hand. Just as before, there was no time to think, no decision to make. His instincts took over, raising the torch and turning its unlit point toward the misshapen figure standing on the altar before him.

The torch flew like a spear from his grasp, trailing sparks and flame. The bright motion caught the dwarf's eye; his gaze turned from the infant. Just in time for the point of the torch's handle to plunge into the center of his brow—

A gasp of shock escaped from the dwarf's mouth as he staggered backward, collapsing against the wall behind him. With a wail of fright, the baby fell. Blake reached the altar and dove forward, catching Ren-Lei in his outstretched hands as his shoulder crashed into the stone pedestal.

"Here!" On his back, Blake quickly held the infant up toward Hank. "Take her—before she touches the coat!"

Hank didn't know what the beggar meant. But as soon as Ren-Lei was in the cradle of his arm, she stopped crying, as though the baby with the wide, innocent eyes had realized that she was safe.

Another sound came into the chamber. A low, guttural moan . . .

They both looked up to the wall and watched as the dwarf

grasped the torch protruding from his brow. The flames played over his hand as his grip tightened; he yanked the torch free and threw it spinning across the temple space. A thick black ichor oozed from the shattered bone, inching down along the curve of one eye socket.

The torch went out when it hit the stone floor, as though trodden upon by an unseen boot heel. In the sulphur-laden braziers, the blue flames dwindled to serpents' tongues.

In a fury, the dwarf's fingertips clawed into the waistcoat of his suit. "How dare you enter this temple!" he screeched. "How dare you disrupt a sacrifice to our dark Lord!" The silken fabric tore to shreds that he cast aside, revealing the naked flesh of his torso. One gnarled hand dug into the seam of the trousers, ripping the cloth from one side to the other, the rags parting from his bandy legs. He stood before them, hideously naked, his sexless groin covered with the same suppurating boils that covered his chest and arms.

But to Blake's and Hank's horror, the transformation continued, the dwarf shedding all human semblance. His inverted fingers dug into his brow, widening the jagged wound left by the torch, tearing open the hollow prosthetic of his head as though it were mere papier-mâché to be discarded along with his waxen ears and nose. The black fluid seeped from the gash torn in the pitted scalp that barely rose above the level of his furiously glaring eyes. He crouched forward, thick saliva dripping from the points of his yellow teeth, the curve of his hunched back splitting open along the knots of his spine. From the wet, sinewed cavity emerged two winglike arms, their muscles gleaming as they arched and tautened above him. His gut expanded, the scabrous flesh finally bursting to reveal a pair of spindly legs, unfolding as a spider might reach toward its prey, their claws raking across the stone edge before them.

What was left of the Lieutenant's face was no longer capable of human words. A piercing screech sounded from the raw, lip-less mouth, as the demon form leapt from the altar, its razored arms slashing toward Hank and the infant he held close to his chest.

Hank turned, sheltering Ren-Lei in his arms. The demon claws slashed across his back, tearing red welts over his shoulder blades. Blake sprung forward and grabbed one of the demon's feet, pull-ing the creature away from Hank and hurling it over the floor of the temple. Howling, the demon crashed into the stone wall, then rebounded in a spinning arc, hands ripping open the front of Blake's blood-encrusted overcoat and staggering him backward.

Still clutching Ren-Lei with one hand, Hank reached up and grabbed the sword hilt that the dwarf had dropped on top of the altar. At the same time, he brought his boot heel into the point where one of the demon's spidery legs joined the swollen body, hard and sharp enough to yank it away from Blake and set it fac-ing him. He rammed the butt of the hilt into one of its eyes, yel-low pus spattering across his wrist.

Screaming in pain, the half-blind creature swept a scything claw toward Hank and the infant in his arms. But Hank had al-ready let go of the sword and brought the magnesium breast-plate down before them as a shield. A trail of sparks followed the claw's point across the metal.

Blake recovered his balance, grabbing the edge of the altar and pulling himself up high enough to grab the battle-axe that hung beside the empty suit of armor. The weapon's double blades burst into flames when he seized its handle, as though it knew it was about to draw blood.

The demon spotted the flames and vaulted upward, hands clawing at Blake to disarm him. The soldier dodged to one side at the base of the altar, bringing his free hand flat against the floor and using it as a pivot to spin himself behind the demon. He brought the battle-axe crashing down upon the deformed head. The blow was so swift that it didn't stop inside the demon's skull, but continued downward through his chest and beyond, slicing its body into two halves, the axe's blade clanging into the stone beneath the bifurcated groin. Each half flopped apart in a spasm of pain and shock; the left side struck one of the braziers, the burning sulphur scattering across the floor.

Both halves of the demon stopped moving at last. The one intact eye dulled, the thick nerve at the center of the exposed cortex writhing like a pink worm, then shivering to quiescence. A thick, black smoke began billowing up from the demon's remains.

"I guess that means the ugly bastard's dead . . ." Blake's matted dreadlocks hung across his face as he leaned forward to look at the baby in the other man's arms. "She all right? Not hurt?"

"Didn't even cry." Hank smiled down at her, then waved a hand before his own face. "How long is this smoke stuff supposed to go on for?" The temple was filling up with black clouds from the demon's corpse, obscuring the light from the braziers and torches. "She's gonna suffocate if we don't get her out of here." He scanned across the dark tunnel openings that ringed the space. "Which way did we come in?"

A second passed before Blake answered. "That one—" He pointed. "I think."

The black smoke followed them as they ran down the tunnel. Hank shielded Ren-Lei's face from it with one of his hands. They halted when they reached a branching point in the maze, gasping for breath as they looked at the arched openings in front of them.

"Now which way?"

"Wait a minute . . ." Blake nodded toward the inky tendrils seeping past them. "The smoke's being drawn that way." He pointed to one of the openings. "It must be being pulled to the surface through that staircase we crashed down. That must be where the tunnel heads to. Come on—"

Hank hurried after the other man. They had only gone a few yards when he heard, rather than saw, Blake colliding with something in his path and falling to the ground.

Holding Ren-Lei against himself, he looked down at two figures sprawled at his feet—Blake and the teenage kid in the black leather jacket, who he had first spotted up in the abandoned town house. "This a friend of yours?"

"Yeah—" Blake got to his feet. "Kind of."

"You okay to move?" He leaned down to peer into the kid's face. "Because we gotta keep going."

"I'm okay." Nathaniel pointed a thumb over his shoulder. "The way out's back there—"

The smoke had already engulfed them again. They ran, with Nathaniel guiding them through the maze's twists and turns. At last, they emerged from the low-ceilinged tunnels, into the open space littered with the debris of the staircase.

Someone else was waiting for them there. Hank clutched Ren-Lei closer to his chest as he saw who it was.

The light from the torch on the wall behind him sent the Devil's clubfooted shadow wavering toward the men and the baby. "How could you . . ." He shook his head, seething with incandescent anger. "How could you believe that you'd be able to walk out of here, without having to pay?"

Blake and Nathaniel stepped in front of Hank, as though they could shield the infant in his arms.

"You have done what not even God dared to do. You have killed the one I trusted more than any other in the universe." The Devil's hard gaze fastened upon them. "But I promise you, his destruction will not go unavenged."

15.

I gave you a direct command." The Devil set his incendiary glare upon Hank. "Was that so hard to understand? I warned you not to come here, and you disobeyed."

As Blake and Nathaniel looked at the figure towering before them, Hank clutched the infant closer to his chest. "It's not that I didn't understand you," he said. "I just didn't care."

The Devil stepped forward, his misshapen foot treading heavy in the chamber's ancient dust. "And how could you all think that I wouldn't find out about this? The existence of all the angels who fell with me is tied so closely to my own that I feel every wound they receive."

Hank brought his forearm across Ren-Lei's face, as though to shield her from the Devil's scrutiny. But he had already spotted the infant. He was still yards away, but he raised his hand toward her, regardless.

"The child will be the first to go. I'll scoop out her brains myself, just to punish her for being born."

Blake strode forward, placing himself midway between his

companions and the Devil. "Before you do that, try taking on a man instead."

The Devil saw the filthy coat, and stared at it in shock. "That mantle . . . It's one of mine . . ." He raised his eyes to Blake's grime-covered face. "And I know you, too . . . We've met before . . ."

"Yeah . . ." Blake gave a single nod. "We have."

"But . . . how can you be here?" The Devil continued to study him, as though he were a piece in a larger, more difficult puzzle. "How can you still walk . . . and speak?" A note of unease sounded in the Devil's voice. "Considering what I took from you, that should be impossible."

"But it isn't—" Nathaniel stepped forward, taking a place next to Blake. "He's too strong to be swallowed by your darkness, Devil. Even though his soul is only half of what it should be, it's still the brightest one I've ever seen."

The Devil swung his hard gaze toward Nathaniel. A dark realization flickered into his eyes. "You . . . I've seen you, too, in the thoughts of the damned. You are the boy who walks with Death."

"That's me."

"And you're saying you have . . . seen this man's soul? Still shining?"

"I have. And because of what I've seen, I'll stand by him now until he gets back what you stole from him."

The Devil gestured to the world above. "Does your master know you're here, acting in this way? As far as I know, you're not supposed to get involved with the living world."

"Things change," said Nathaniel, meeting the Devil's glare.

"I answer to myself now. And because of that, I won't turn back."

The Devil's cold regard moved across the three men in front of him, studying each in turn. "If you could see yourselves. You're like a freak show." His voice was filled with derision. "A giant oaf, a filthy wraith, and a postpubescent goth who's discovered ideals. I find it an obscenity that the three of you should join together in this way. On a quest to save a mere child . . ."

The Devil's words faded to silence. As though slit into his face by an invisible razor, a smile slowly formed.

"Three of you." He nodded. "Of course . . ." One realization sparked another. "I should've seen it already."

To their amazement, the Devil suddenly burst out laughing. His sharp-angled face creased as he tilted his head back, tears leaking from the corners of his squeezed-shut eyes. He had to reach a hand out and balance himself against the nearest wall.

"And just to think, I've always believed that Heaven didn't have a sense of humor!" Having doubled over, he now straightened up, catching his breath. "I've been waiting all this time for three great generals to arrive—at the head of an invincible army. That's what the prophecy has been saying all these years, ever since the tree first appeared." The Devil made a show of wiping his eyes as he shook his head. "But there is no army, other than those idiots up in the garden square. And as for Courage, Self-Sacrifice, and Resolve . . . It's just you three!"

Hank held Ren-Lei higher in his arms, away from the smoke that had started to fill the chamber. "Look, mister. Are you going to step aside and let us leave, or do we have to move you?"

"Move me?" The Devil's laughter faded again. "I'd kill a

thousand of the likes of you before I ever let you pass. You've murdered one of my fallen angels. Part of the fabric of creation. You're going to stay here, and pay for what you've done with your blood and bones." He took another step toward them, watching as all three braced themselves for his attack. "Oh . . . But don't delude yourselves into thinking that I'll dirty my hands with you myself," he said. "The Lieutenant you killed was not only a friend to me, but to the whole legion who fell with me. And they are screaming for revenge as well, scratching to get in at you through these very walls. Or haven't you realized yet just how far below this city you've descended? And how close my Lieutenant's home was to the threshold of my realm?"

The Devil raised both arms, spreading his hands wide above his head. He closed his eyes, and let his fingers curve clawlike, as if pulling some invisible substance out of the thickening air.

Underneath their feet, the stone floor rumbled. The noise seemed to come from the farthest limits of the dark tunnels surrounding the chamber. A shrill keening—faint at first, then louder and louder—cut through the smoke.

Between the Devil's hands, a sphere of churning flame gathered. Sparks shot upward, igniting the torches that lined the chamber's higher reaches. The combined glow reddened the smoke, transforming the space into an outpost of Hell. Nathaniel turned his gaze, appalled once more at the vision revealed, of the tiny interlocked skeletons, shadows flickering in the eye sockets of their broken skulls.

The subterranean groans grew deafening, traveling up into the men's stomachs. Hank looked down at the small form he held, and saw Ren-Lei's eyes flutter open. Her clear-eyed gaze locked upon his for only a moment, then she pressed herself tighter into the shelter of his arms.

Nathaniel leapt back, startled by the jagged fissure that opened before him. The gap widened, dust sifting into its depths as more cracks broke through the chamber's floor. The infant skeletons cascaded from the walls, the bones splintering and snapping in a dry staccato rattle. One small skull rolled against the toe of Nathaniel's boot, and he convulsively kicked it away.

The seismic cracks spread upward through the walls. Rocks tumbled down upon the bones as the vertical fissures spread wider than Hank's massive shoulders. The light from the torches was eclipsed by that from the flames of Hell itself, appearing in the volcanic reaches beyond. Visible through the gaps in the chamber walls, mile-wide craters reached to the horizons of the infernal landscape. Each pit, ringed by razor-sharp boulders, was filled with writhing figures, still human in shape but with their flesh consumed by fire that burned but did not destroy. Sinners, locked in their eternal torment, screamed into each other's pain-blinded faces, seeing nothing but their own damnation, hands of charred bone tearing at any flesh they could reach, no longer able to tell the difference between theirs and another's. Tatters of skin flailed from the tangled, blackened limbs as they clawed toward their prison's rim and were then pulled back by the ones below, over and over, none of them hoping to escape—for in this place, all hope had fled long ago—but all driven mad by the shrieking knowledge that their punishment would never cease, never relent, never be anything but this, world without end.

A black-clouded storm swept over the hellscape, its scorching wind driving the fire across the sinner's naked bodies and into the chamber where the Devil confronted the three men. He stood without moving, the flames curling around his arms and shoulders. The burning light glinted in his eyes as he smiled.

In the distance behind, they could see a horde of demons rushing toward them, hooved feet striking the skulls of the damned, leathery black wings beating the ignited air. Their faces, alight with hideous glee, were shielded by helmets split by the sword blades of the angels who had once defeated them. Broken armor pieces clanked against their chitinous ridged chests as they swung the implements of an ancient armory above their heads, spiked balls on chains catching sparks against notch-bladed spears and scimitars.

"Look out!" Hank shouted the warning through the demons' shrieking cries as the first of them swarmed through the flames surrounding the Devil. Cradling Ren-Lei tighter against his chest, he grabbed Nathaniel's arm and pulled him back out of harm's way.

The snarling creature at the head of the charge swung a hooked pikestaff at Blake's head; he caught the weapon's staff in both hands, straining to throw the demon back against the others coming after it.

Nathaniel shook off the giant hit man's grasp. With the demon horde only a yard away, he braced himself with one leg angled behind him, the forward one bent low. He stretched both hands before himself, palms outward—

And closed his eyes.

The demons shrieked higher, seeing the first of their prey so close, so easy to grab and rip apart.

Then there was silence.

Hank looked over the baby's head, exchanging glances with Blake. The demons stood frozen in place—as did the Devil, still with the thin, cruel smile on his sharp-angled face, where he had been watching from the opposite side of the stone chamber.

"Nathaniel . . ." The pikestaff remained angled in midswing as Blake slowly let go of its shaft and stepped back from it and the immobile demon who wielded it. Both he and Hank stepped to either side of him. "Are you okay?"

A moment passed before Nathaniel responded. He remained in the same outstretched pose, as though pushing against an invisible tide that threatened to engulf them. He nodded slowly, then spoke, eyes still closed: "Get out of here . . . Quick!"

Baffled, Hank looked from him to the stilled demons, then back again. "Did the kid do this?"

"Yeah," said Blake. "But I don't think he can keep it up for long."

"Hurry!" Nathaniel spoke again, a line of sweat beginning to trickle down the corner of his brow. His lips were pressed bloodless. "Get the baby out of here . . . I'll follow when I can."

Leaving Nathaniel behind them, Hank and Blake scrambled up the sloping pile of rubble. At its crest, Blake halted and pointed up the shaft, still lined with the wreckage of the shattered staircase. "I'll go ahead and try out every hold first," he said. "To see if it's secure."

"And I'll follow on with Ren-Lei." Hank gazed upward at the climb ahead of them. "At least there are still a few torches left on the walls, to give us a bit of light."

Holding Ren-Lei in the crook of one arm, Hank followed Blake up the shaft as quickly as he could. By the time he had followed Blake several yards upward, he gave in to the temptation to look back down. He could see the torch-lit chamber, with Nathaniel still poised at one side, hands stretched out in front of himself, holding back the flow of Time and the demons that would be carried on it like a tidal wave when the kid's strength gave out.

Another couple of yards up, he found himself stuck. The next handhold was too far above him to reach while still holding Ren-Lei.

"Hey!" He shouted up to Blake. "Need some help here—"

The soldier looked back down and saw immediately what the problem was. With lightning-quick agility, he lowered himself toward Hank.

"Give her to me." Blake reached down. "I'll hold her until you get your next grip."

"Okay. But be careful—" He drew Ren-Lei away from his chest and held her up toward Blake's outstretched hand.

The infant's eyes widened in fear as the overcoat's blackened sleeve came close to her. She let out a terrified wail, as though the approach of the heavy cloth had scalded her with a searing flame.

Her cry made Hank move even faster. Within seconds, he had climbed farther up the shaft. He reached out one of his massive hands. "Quick—"

As soon as she was back in the giant's grasp, Ren-Lei quieted herself. She cooed up toward Hank's face as she snuggled against his chest.

"She *definitely* likes you," said Blake as he looked down at the mismatched pair below him.

"Just climb, okay . . ."

The bottom of the shaft was a long way down, no more than a smokily glowing dot from this height. With his free hand, Hank dug his nails into the narrow ledge that was all that kept him from falling.

They kept going. Time might have been frozen down below, but Hank could still feel it in the ache of his muscles and the burning of his fingertips, scraped raw by the crevices into which he forced them. Blood trickled down his wrists. Beating the city's armies of thugs to death had been easy work compared to this.

"Okay—" Blake's voice floated back down in the darkness. "I can see it. We're almost there—"

Enough dim torchlight filtered up through the staircase shaft for Hank to just about see the ragged hem of Blake's overcoat. Dust drifted into his face as the other man got an elbow onto the floor of the abandoned town house. Hank stopped in place and watched, head tilted back, as Blake angled his chest over the edge, then scrabbled himself free of the shaft. Lying flat, Blake reached back down.

"Give me your hand—"

Rearing back onto his knees, Blake dragged Hank halfway up into the town house's empty space. Hank got a hand on the floor's edge and with one muscle-straining effort, flopped himself on his back beside the other man, his own legs dangling across the shaft opening. He sat up, arm crossed over his chest, cradling Ren-Lei's small weight.

Less than a minute later, the two men burst from the town house's front door. From its sagging porch, they could see the black silhouette of the Devil's office tower reaching up into the storm clouds.

"Look—" Blake pointed to a crooked finger of lightning that had been caught streaking down from the sky. "The kid still has Time frozen. Even up here."

They hurried toward the garden square at the tower's base. Ren-Lei clapped her small hands together, enjoying the bouncing motion of Hank's lumbering stride.

The crowd surrounding the peach tree was stilled and silent, just as the demonic legions had been, down below the earth's surface. But not for long. Hank pointed to a bee that was hovering near one of the tree's last blossoms. The slow-motion buzz of the insect's wings could be seen. "Damn! Looks like Nathaniel's giving out—"

Blake cocked his head, listening. Below the silence in which the garden was caught, a barely audible vibration could be sensed, moving from the infrasonic to the limit of human hearing. The crowd's mingled breaths and voices signaled Time's coursing approach.

16.

He opened his eyes. That was a mistake.

Past the frozen horde of demons, Nathaniel could see the Devil, cruel smile immobile on that harshly formed visage. *Keep it going,* he told himself. *You can do it.* Inside the bubble of stilled Time into which he had cast the stone chamber, there was no way of telling how many minutes or hours had passed in the world beyond. Maybe Blake and Hank had managed by now to carry the infant to safety, or they might have managed to struggle only a little way up the shaft leading to the surface. If they were still there, and he wasn't able to keep his spell going, the furious, pursuing demons would stir to life again, then swarm up the shaft and annihilate the three human beings, like molten rock surging from the center of the earth.

All Nathaniel could do was hold the spell for as long as he could. Palms thrust out, he gritted his teeth, summoning every resource he possessed. He had already pushed beyond his previous limits, keeping Time frozen for longer than he ever had before. Or so it seemed—all those other times, he had been in the city's night air, sour-smelling as garbage strewn in back alleys, but still freely available to draw down into his lungs. *I'm on the Devil's turf now*, thought Nathaniel. Things might work differently down here, as though Time and gravity and existence itself were weakened and rendered threadbare.

That worry was what had caused him to open his eyes, just to keep from being swallowed up by the darkness inside himself. He could feel the sweat trickling down his forehead, the chamber's heat evaporating it to pure salt before it could reach the corners of his eyes. Just before him, he saw his upraised fingers trembling, the tension from his locked arms spreading through his hands. Farther away, where the walls had opened with a cascade of tiny skeletons, stood his enemy.

The Devil's eyes did not meet his. Instead, he'd had his sulphurous gaze narrowed upon the infant in Hank's arms, as Nathaniel had summoned up the spell to stop Time. The Devil, frozen in place, was still looking a few degrees to the side of him, long after the two men had escaped with Ren-Lei.

Nathaniel's pulse inched forward a beat as he watched the pupils at the center of the Devil's eyes. The small dark spaces suddenly contracted almost to pin-points, as though the mind behind them had finally perceived the other figures' disappearance.

Then the Devil's gaze shifted, agonizingly slow, the way a marksman might carefully adjust the angle of his weapon, bringing a helpless target into the crosshairs of his scope. Until he was finally looking straight into Nathaniel's eyes . . .

An invisible spark passed between the two of them.

He knows, realized Nathaniel. *He knows what I've done.*

A deep basso rumble traveled through the ground, as though the world's tectonic plates were shifting. In the same stilled moment, he saw the Devil's shoulders swell and rise, straining against the burden that weighed him in place.

Like a fragile crystal sphere, the spell began to crack at its edges. At the periphery of his vision, he could see dust sift from the chamber's arched ceiling, and the smoke curl and writhe upon itself. The Devil's gaze tautened to slits, dagger points aimed into the center of his skull. Nathaniel squeezed his hands into trembling fists, desperately holding onto the spell's unraveling cords.

They snapped, and were gone from his grasp. All around him, Time roared back into full motion. The mounting howls of the demons pummeled his hearing, the sudden shock wave dizzying him with the blood bursting at his inner ear, the chamber tilting as he lost his balance. He stumbled backward, as though struck by an invisible tidal wave. He had only a fragmented glimpse of the Devil's eyes widening in delighted triumph as the spell's broken shackles were shrugged off.

His spine struck the floor hard enough to knock the breath from his lungs. Gasping for air, he felt himself borne upward, the chamber's ceiling hurtling toward him. He turned his face to the side and saw that the Devil's legions had grabbed hold of his arms and legs, lifting their prize above their heads, the blades of their archaic weapons clashing sparks over the crests and dents of their helmets. Beyond them, he could just discern the Devil commanding his horned army with an upraised hand, bidding them onward in their maddened rush.

Suddenly, he felt himself torn free of the demons' clawed grasp, as the Devil flung one arm even higher above his head. An unseen force sent Nathaniel hurtling through the chamber's smoke-darkened air.

A searing blast of heat rolled over him from behind. He managed to twist himself onto one side and saw one of the wall's openings rushing toward him.

But nothing could halt his helpless trajectory. The flames roiled upward from the craters beyond as he was pitched into Hell.

"You hear that?"

Blake grabbed Hank's arm, halting him just yards away from the garden square. He brought both their gazes back toward the abandoned town house from which they had fled, carrying Ren-Lei with them.

"What is it?" Hank peered toward the building's dark silhouette. From somewhere below it, a raucous chorus of mingled screams and cries could be heard. "What's going on—"

"Time's started up again." The soldier's dirt-stained face turned even grimmer. "They're coming for us . . ."

Even as he spoke, the town house trembled on its foundations, as though struck by seismic tremors from deep in the earth. Slates snapped and slid from the eaves, exposing the attic's sagging timbers. The demonic war cries swelled loud enough to peel the wooden planks away from the boarded-up windows, the dust-clouded glass shivering in the frames, then bursting into shards glittering through the night's shadows.

The town house's walls bowed outward, as though a slow-motion bomb had been ignited inside. The chimneys crumbled, raining down fragments of brick and mortar. As though it were a toy box's lid, the roof separated from the walls, shoved upward by a billow of smoke laced with churning fire.

Hank pressed Ren-Lei tighter to his chest, covering the other side of her head with his broad hand, keeping the bloodcurdling shrieks from her tiny ears.

Churning flames exploded from the town house's windows and doors, the red tongues separating every piece of the structure. Blackened framing timbers spun end over end before plowing into the dry weeds surrounding the building. Blake shielded his eyes just enough to see the demonic figures spiraling upward in the gout of fire, slashing and jabbing the burning magnesium blades of their weapons in all directions.

Screams rose from the garden square as the people gathered there now saw the armored demons racing toward them, the ones on the ground howling as they ran, those aloft blotting out the night sky with the unfurling of their leathery wings. The adults scooped up the children who had been laughing and playing before Time had stopped, shielding them with their bodies as they huddled against the base of the office tower, or running with them toward the unlit alleys beyond. Their panicked escape was cut off by the shouting, grimacing horde that ran into the streets ahead of them, then turned and swept their weapons like scythes, to drive the people back to the square.

The young witch called Anna stood against the window of the Devil's office. What she saw below sent the cold blood racing through her veins.

In the garden square, all Hell was breaking loose—literally.

She watched as a four-armed demon, short-bladed cuirasses in each fist, carved up a human figure, jabbing and slashing with the weapons. The process was a model of predatory efficiency: in a few seconds, there was nothing but a dismembered carcass at a screaming woman's feet. The witch slowly nodded, enraptured by the sight.

Behind her, Anna could hear the stampede of feet in the office's lobby, as the terrified supplicants scrabbled and clawed for the exit. Perhaps those human fools thought that the vibrations hammering the building were those of an earthquake, and they would be safer beyond the shivering walls. The thought of what would greet them outside brought a crazed smile to her face.

Glints of light played across the window as she gazed down. Those were from the staffs and burning blades striking at the branches of the peach tree in the center of the garden, the demons' wrath mounting with the futility of their attack. Each blow left the tree unharmed, a lightning flash hurtling the assailant onto his back, cursing.

At the top of the surrounding towers, the winged demons had flown up and stationed themselves, crouching and leaning forward to scan the chaos below and search for prey. To the young witch looking up at them they seemed like gargoyles come to life.

As she watched, one unfolded its wings and vaulted out into the night sky. It swooped through a wide parabola between the other towers, its talons seizing at last upon the concrete ledge immediately before the witch's gaze. The creature had the slavering snout of a jackal, eyes inflamed with hunger and cruelty as it peered through the window at her.

The glass burst into razor-edged shards, flying into Anna's face and across the span of the office, as the demon thrust its claws toward her. She was already bleeding before she landed on her back. The tips of the demon's yellow fangs imbedded themselves in her throat—

But only for a moment. The demon drew back, cringing from the starlike emblem tattooed on the back of Anna's neck, revealed when her dark hair had been swept aside.

"Yes . . ." She wiped the tiny drops of blood from under her chin as she knelt before the demon. "We belong . . . to the same master . . ."

With a shriek of frustrated hunger, the demon spun away from the witch and launched itself out the shattered window and into the night sky.

Hank and Blake stood back-to-back, surrounded by carnage.

"Maybe we should run for it—" Hank held Ren-Lei tighter against himself. "Just get her away from here—"

"No." The soldier's grimy overcoat was spattered with fresh blood. "These bastards will come right after us, no matter where we go. They catch us someplace where we can't maneuver, they'll rip us to shreds."

"Then we gotta stay here and fight." Hank lowered his head, peering across the garden square. "They haven't spotted us yet—but they will any second now."

Blake nodded toward the infant in the other man's arms. "What're you going to do about her?"

"I don't know." He looked at the tangled undergrowth behind them. "I can't just hide her somewhere. Even if they don't spot her, she could still get trampled in the fight." He held the baby out toward Blake. "Here—hold her for a second. I got an idea."

Ren-Lei began crying as soon as Blake had her in his hand. Careful to keep the coat's blackened sleeves away from the squalling infant, he watched as Hank ripped off his shirt, then tore it into one long rag. He drew the cloth around his shoulders, knotting an improvised sling at his bared chest. "Put her in there," he ordered Blake, "and make sure it's tight."

Blake tied the loose ends around the other man's waist and shoulder. The baby's tiny form was now snugged motionless against Hank's chest. She whimpered at her confines for a moment, before her eyes opened, gazing up at the giant with complete trust.

"You just take it easy." He tucked his chin down so he could look at her. "We'll get this sorted out—"

As Ren-Lei smiled and made soft cooing sounds, Hank saw a bright spark reflected in her dark eyes. The spark grew swiftly larger at the same time as he heard a shrill, ululating cry from the sky above. He looked up and saw a horrific visage, eyes widened with lethal delight, vipers writhing in its mouth. Clawed fists swung one blade of a double-ended spear toward Hank's skull, flames licking up from its blades. The demon's power dive was so rapid, there was time only to shield Ren-Lei; he crouched over, bent spine toward the creature.

Something hit him from behind, but it wasn't the scything edge of the demon's spear. He fell hard onto his shoulder, still holding the baby to his chest in the sling. At the periphery of his sight, he glimpsed a grime-encrusted figure vaulting above him, one of Blake's hands on his shoulder, the other swinging a shovel that had been left behind by one of the people who had been working in the garden. Sparks shot from the magnesium-forged blade as the shovel connected with it. The shaft of the tool snapped, the shovel's blade hitting the ground yards away. Blake used the splintered shaft for another parrying blow, which sent the spear pinwheeling out of the demon's grasp. Blake's leap carried him high above the demon and, as though it were the point of a lightning bolt, the wooden shaft darted hard between the demon's eyes, driving it stumbling backward, arms flailing.

The demon regained its balance as Blake landed lithely upon his toes with one hand outstretched. Vipers hissed as the demon swept up its spear and swung around one of its fiery blades; it missed Blake's chest by an inch as he darted to one side, the weapon's daggerlike point piercing the wooden shaft. Before the demon could wrest the spear free, Blake snapped the fingertips of his other hand into its throat. The quick impact was enough to bring steaming blood vomiting around the snakeheads; their jeweled eyes went dull, scale-covered bodies dangling limp as Blake jumped back, letting the demon drop at his feet.

Bent over to catch his breath, Blake watched as Hank got to his feet and went over to the corpse. "What the hell are you doing?" Black smoke had started billowing up from the demon's fatal wounds. Hank reached through the fumes to undo the strap of the demon's helmet. "What do you want that for?"

"Got another idea . . ." Fanning the smoke away from Ren-Lei, Hank stepped back with the armor piece. "This kid's going to be as safe as possible." He placed the helmet over the baby like a magnesium turtle shell, running the strap under the linen sling and drawing it tight to hold it in place. "There—now she's a *tank*."

"Get ready—" Blake straightened up. "Here come that sonuvabitch's buddies."

A chorus of guttural shouts struck their ears as four demons charged toward them. The one in front brandished a flaming axe in each of its three arms. Hank ducked under the weapons like a boxer, then spun around with a horizontal kick, impaling the lead demon on the heel of his boot so hard that its bowels exploded and the severed ends of its spine tore through its back. He yanked his foot back, and two of the other demons went sprawling over their leader's still-quivering corpse. As it fell, Hank caught a pair of axes from its lifeless hands. A downward swipe split one horned head into equal halves, while an uppercut slashed through the third demon's neck. He pivoted, ready to dispatch the last of the group, only to see that Blake had already run it through with the spear's fiery blade.

Blake tugged the weapon free and stared down at its bloodied length. "Hold on . . ." He studied the spear's intricately worked shaft. "I've seen this thing somewhere before . . . He was holding one just like it . . . The statue in the church . . ." Amazement sounded in Blake's voice as he held the double-bladed weapon up before his eyes.

"What are you talking about?" Hank stood back-to-back with the soldier as more demons encircled them. Still gripping both axes, Hank glanced away from the assembling horde, looking over his shoulder at his blood-encrusted ally. "What statue?"

"I think . . . this is *his* weapon!" The flames leapt higher from the blades at either end of the spear as Blake cried out. "The spear that Michael fought the Devil with, when he threw him out of Heaven. Somehow . . . it's found its way to me!"

17.

Nathaniel lay amidst the fires of Hell. From beyond its limits, he could hear the Devil shouting furiously at him.

"You idiot!" The Devil's voice snarled with rage. "Did you think a simple trick like that would stop me from getting what I want?"

I don't know, thought Nathaniel. It didn't seem to matter now.

He placed his palms on the rock at his sides and pushed himself up into a sitting position. Enough of his powers still remained to cool the jagged stones. But that still left him trapped in Hell.

When the Devil had thrown him through the gap in the chamber's wall, he'd landed in a small space between the flaming pits, with their gouts of molten magma leaping up toward craggy ceilings writhing with fire, then falling back with a splash of sizzling white sparks. Waves of heat rolled over him, shimmering his vision, as though he had been on the surface of the sun—yet he wasn't consumed, reduced to a flake of black ash. *He's not done with me*—that dreadful realization formed solid at the center of his slowly reassembling thoughts. *There's more to come.*

"Oh, yes . . ." The Devil easily discerned what he was thinking. The clubfooted figure stood before the wall's opening. "There's so much more for you to learn." The scowl on the Devil's face twisted harder. "You can't beat me with Time, you fool. I was there when Time was *created*. It was my own stars and sun that made Time possible, by creating the first night and day. I am not subject to its laws, like humans are. Time is in me, not outside."

Nathaniel tried not to listen. *Pull yourself together,* he commanded. He concentrated on gathering what little remained of his strength, so he would be able to stand and fight again—

It was already too late. He was unable to move from the spot; all he could do was watch, gaze uplifted, as the Devil stepped through the opening into Hell, and strode toward him, the misshapen foot striking heavier than the other.

The Devil reached down and gathered Nathaniel up by the front of his singed leather jacket. Holding him in midair, the Devil brought his cruelly smiling face close to his, then tossed him farther into Hell's confines.

Nathaniel landed sprawling in one of the pits, the impact enough to pulverize the flaming bones of the sinners whose prison it had been. He rolled over onto his knees, the white shards crackling under his hands.

"Hurt me all you like, it still won't save you—" Against the roar of the fiery winds, Nathaniel heard his own voice as he looked up at the Devil. Blood hissed into red steam as it trickled down his face. "Your reign is over," he gasped aloud. "No matter what you do to me—"

"Why? Because of the prophecy?" The Devil sneered down

at him, his eyes aflame. "In case you hadn't noticed, apprentice, that fairy tale is over. There is no prophecy anymore. It's dead."

"I'm not talking about the prophecy—" Nathaniel left one hand against the rocks, pressing the other against the ache in his ribs. "I'm talking about what I've seen with my own eyes." Behind him, the scattered bone fragments slowly began to reassemble into human form, so the eternal torment of the charred sinners could resume.

"Seen?" A frown formed on the Devil's face. "Seen where?"

"On the Chart of Deaths," said Nathaniel. "I didn't know what the symbols meant at first, but I do now. The smaller ones, they're your demons. All marked down for annihilation. And the large one in the middle . . . that one's *you*."

"Enough!" The Devil's rage still seethed as he looked down at Nathaniel. "I fear no scrap of paper from your master's closet—no matter how many symbols rise up in its ink. The only ones who are going to die today are you and your friends. Or have you forgotten that you still need an army to bring about my downfall? But you have no army. The human crowd holding its vigil up there is already being slaughtered. And as far as I can see, there is no other army."

Nathaniel looked into the flames above him. He was able to sense those human deaths as well. His master would be up there, too, he realized. Collecting the souls from that slaughter.

How do I stop it? The words weighed dismally inside his mind. *I saw the scroll . . . I know how it should end . . . But without an army, how can I make it happen?*

"I don't know . . ." Nathaniel struggled to his feet, swaying unsteadily. "How you'll die . . . but you'll be defeated. Even if I have to do it myself."

"Yourself?" The Devil laughed. "With what, your bare hands?" He sneered at him. "Forget it, boy. Whatever power you have is fading in these flames."

"But not my will," said Nathaniel. "And as long as I have that, I can still resist you."

The Devil shook his head. "But the problem is that you *don't* have your will. Not anymore." He pointed to Nathaniel's heart. "Your willpower became mine the moment you crossed over the threshold of my realm."

The Devil spoke no more. He crouched down, then leapt across the space between them, his straining hands outstretched like a tiger's claws. His force struck Nathaniel's shoulders and bore him helpless to the ground. In a moment, he was flat on his back, the Devil kneeling on top of him.

"It's useless to struggle——" The Devil's hand moved down to Nathaniel's chest, then clenched into a fist, as though seizing upon something deep within him. He managed to raise his head, and saw the Devil drawing out a vaporous substance, glimmering as if studded with points of diamonds. The Devil lifted the vapor, displaying it before Nathaniel's eyes. He felt emptier than ever before, like his body had been hollowed of its organs. "This is your willpower. All of it. But not for long . . ."

The Devil stood up, sneering as he regarded the translucent substance in his hand.

"Mine to keep——or destroy." He spread apart his fingers, letting Nathaniel's will rest in his open palm. "Without this, what are you?" The Devil smiled. "What is anyone?"

Unable to move or speak, Nathaniel watched as the Devil threw the glittering vapor into the nearest pit. It sparked, then burst into blue flames, like an igniting gas—

At the same time, a fiery, annihilating wind seemed to scour through all the chambers of Nathaniel's mind. Within the limits of his skull, there was no escape from what was happening to him. He felt something inside, the core of his being, dwindle and weaken, as though bits of his flesh were being carved away by the point of a scalpel-like blade.

His gaze turned toward his own hand, lying flaccid upon the ashen rock. He tried to lift it, merely bring it up an inch into the air—nothing more than that. As he watched, he saw his fingers tremble, as though straining against unseen wisps of spider silk strong enough to bind them in place. He summoned all his determination into the tendons of his hand, ordering them to curl the pale flesh into a fist, fingertips scrabbling through the dust and cinders . . .

Nothing happened. He might as well have been looking at a corpse's hand. A thing that life and desire had abandoned.

The Devil bent down and searched Nathaniel's eyes, then straightened again.

"There, that's better." He nodded, turned, and strode away among the fiery pits.

I can't stay here . . . Nathaniel's will might have been extinguished, but his thoughts continued. He could picture the world above, the storm clouds rolling above the city's darkened streets. *That's where I should be. With them . . . the others . . . fighting . . .*

But it was no use. Words and images flitted by, with no connection to each other, like moths captured inside his emptied skull. He knew what he should do, but could no more accomplish it than he could move his limbs. As though he were an unstrung marionette, he sprawled on the ground, motionless.

This is eternity, he realized. Fear gripped him, though it couldn't move him. *I'll be here like this, forever . . .*

Something moved, at the limit of his vision. A human form, crawling through the flames toward him.

One of the sinners, thought Nathaniel. *Another poor bastard trapped here.* But what could it want from him?

He couldn't raise his head to look. All he could do was wait until the burning, blistered figure was directly above him, its reddened eyes gazing down into his.

The sinner's eyes widened in amazement, as though it were somehow able to recognize Nathaniel from that other world, the one above. In which, long ago, it had been a living thing, a human being like others, not yet damned to eternal pain.

"Nat . . ." The sinner's voice was a harsh, parched croak. "Nat . . . is that you?"

It can't be, thought Nathaniel. *It's impossible.*

One of the sinner's hands, a shriveled relic of blackened bone and skin, trembled as it reached toward Nathaniel's face, stopping a few inches away from touching him. He wanted to close his eyes, to block out the sight of the charred creature above him, but couldn't.

He gazed up into the sinner's ruined face—

And recognized it. Even through all the charnel years that had passed, something remained there. A dark, golden fleck at the pupil of one eye that he remembered from when he had been a child. A child looking up into the face of a drunk who gripped him in his trembling hands—

A flood of memories surged through his brain.

He could see a man, a living one, sending out a boy to buy his booze. He knew the boy he saw was himself—and the man was his father.

As was the burning sinner here, reaching down to stroke his hair—but stopping an inch away from that faint contact. What was left of his father pulled his hand away, knowing that he could no longer even touch his son. The son he had sold to Death, to buy himself a few more years on the surface of the earth. And who, by that cold transaction, had condemned his soul to eternal torment in the fires of Hell.

18.

The smoke hung low over the garden square, thick and choking. Blake gazed across the mounds of demon corpses. The only thing recognizable from before the battle had begun was the peach tree in the center of the garden, the space around it transformed into a hilly deathscape of fanged and clawed creatures, stacked one on top of another, all dead or expiring in their broken armor. But even now, more were coming to the battle, their cries ringing as they climbed out of the abandoned town house's wreckage. The night sky thickened with the tumult of their batlike wings, bright glints flashing from the blades of their weapons, just like on the mural in the labyrinth below.

He looked over to where the giant hit man Hank was visible, towering over the bodies heaped around him. The two of them had been separated during the fight, each slashing and hacking at the demons who came surging straight into their faces, backing up to draw one into a position where its head could be lopped off, diving to the side to avoid a battle-axe swinging down like a crescent guillotine, then lunging upward to spear the attacker through its guts. The action had grown so furious that there'd been no way that either man could keep track of the other; all they could do was keep fighting, trusting that his companion was doing the same somewhere else.

Catching his breath, Blake watched as Hank twisted a demon's head from its neck, tossing the armored head to the side while it still grimaced and snarled at him. If anything, the big guy had an even harder job: his size made him a more obvious target for the demons to attack, plus he had to fight while shielding the infant strapped to his chest. Blake wondered what Ren-Lei's reaction was to all the mayhem happening around her. Snugged inside the helmet they had strapped over her, she might well have simply curled up and gone to sleep, secure in the warmth from her protector's laboring heart.

Blake's exhausted thoughts were interrupted by another shape swooping over his head. Without even seeing what it was, he jabbed up into the air the point of one of the spear's blades, sheathed in white-hot flames. A shrieking curse struck his ear as a many-armed demon dodged the weapon. A half-dozen scimitars, one in each of the creature's fists, swept windmill-like at his head. He managed to parry them with quick, darting thrusts of the spear, but there were too many, coming too fast, for him to get a shot at the breastplate behind them. Blake found himself retreating step-by-step, the spear's staff growing slick with the sweat of his palms.

He heard the heavy impact of Hank's boots through the ground before he glimpsed the other man running toward him, flaming axe upraised. But before Hank could reach the spot, a knot of demons swarmed around him. The foul odor emanating from the exposed intestines that linked all five together, each one's innards looping into the next one's gaping abdomen, filled Blake's nostrils. Through the scimitars that he continued blocking, he could see the demons circling around Hank, the wet mesh of their guts forming a tangled net on all sides.

The demons tightened upon their prey, intestines binding around Hank's ribs. One of them scented more tender prey under the magnesium helmet on the human's chest. The points of its dagger teeth snapped off as it futilely tried to gnaw through the metal.

The damp fecal contents of the demon's guts sizzled as Hank's white-hot axe sliced through them. Each swipe of his weapon left more writhing lengths upon the ground. With the demons now separated from each other, Hank was able to bring the axe straight down upon their heads, splitting each in half, one after the other. In less than a minute, ten bifurcated forms sprawled before him, their guts the only parts still moving, whipping back and forth like blinded worms.

One of the scimitars wielded by Blake's assailant dug its edge into the stone bank at the garden square's edge. He dove on his side to escape the other blades, completing the roll and springing to his feet, out of the demon's reach. Snarling, it struggled to free the caught scimitar; that gave Blake a moment to catch his breath, pulse hammering inside his chest.

At the same moment, he spotted another a pair of winged demons swooping down at Hank. Before they could even swing the swords in their fists, the hit man had scrambled on top of the demons he had just killed. Added to his own height, it gave him the reach he needed to take off the heads of the ones attacking from above, the axe cutting through their necks in one flashing arc.

"Look!" Blake caught the other man's eye. He pointed through the smoke filling the square. "There, behind you!"

Chest spattered with the flying demons' gore, Hank turned and looked over his shoulder. The battle-axe slowly lowered in his grip as he spotted the next apparition to join battle with them.

Striding past the smoke-shrouded branches of the peach tree came the Devil.

The earth shook with each strike of his cloven hoof, now exposed. Its crescent edge shattered the skulls of his fallen soldiers as he strode, heedless of their prostrate forms beneath him. His forelegs were drenched to the knees with their blood. His nails had sharpened to talons as they dug into the front of his shirt. He tore open the white cloth, throwing the tattered rags to either side. Seared across his bared chest, back, and arms were the same emblems that had seethed alight from the desk in his private office, in the tower looming far above the square. The symbols protruded from his skin, like the welts singed in place by a white-hot branding iron. Largest of all was the eight-pointed star in the middle of his chest, above his heart.

The sight so transfixed Blake that the six-armed demon was almost driven from his thoughts. He suddenly heard the whisper of a scimitar blade slicing through the air; he dove to one side, the blade missing his head by a fraction of an inch. Jabbing one of the glaive's points toward the demon, he drove it back.

A light fiercer and harsher than a noonday sun flooded the garden square. Hard-edged shadows sprang around the corpses where they lay. Turning his gaze from his attacker, Blake saw that the Devil had halted in the middle of the square, scanning about for his enemies. It should have been easy for him to spot Hank's massive figure, but his furiously slitted gaze had fallen upon Blake instead. Unable to move, he watched as the Devil gathered a sphere of fiery plasma between his outstretched hands. A single thrusting motion and the fireball shot toward Blake, a glowing trail stretching behind it to the Devil's fingertips.

Hank was able to react. He snatched up one of the creatures he had just killed, and threw the corpse straight at Blake. Its impact knocked him to the ground; sprawled on his back, he saw the fireball streak directly above him, hitting the scimitar-bearing demon instead. Its torso vaporized in a blinding flash of light, the six arms spiraling loose across the corpses mounded nearby.

More demons, weapons clashing overhead, were already rushing toward the spot, as though their commander's appearance in their midst had reignited their fury. Blake got to his feet; dazed, he leaned his weight on the staff of the spear and gazed at the onslaught. They would be on top of him in seconds.

"There's too many of them!" he managed to shout across the corpses to Hank. "We can't fight them all—"

The hit man glanced over at him for only a moment, then turned and braced himself, one hand laid on top of the helmet strapped to his chest, the other raising the axe back behind his shoulder. Ready to swing and slash apart the first demon to reach him, and the one after that, and all the others, for as long as he could. Until he would be buried beneath the mass of their stabbing, clawing fury.

Blake turned away from the grim sight. There was only one person he could think of, one who might be able to save them. A last ally they could call upon. If Death's apprentice was even still alive . . .

19.

There's so much . . . I need . . . to tell you . . ."

The red eyes gazing down at Nathaniel looked as if they had been boiled in pitch. The fires of Hell had charred away the face's skin, leaving a few black, ribbonlike scraps dangling from the exposed muscles and tendons.

"I'm sorry," continued Nathaniel's father. The words came haltingly, past the dry, swollen tongue in what had been his mouth and what was now a cracked, lipless wound. "That's what . . . I wanted to tell you." A tear mingled with the blood seeping from the raw flesh. "I always . . . wanted to tell you."

He heard what his father was saying; he heard the scraped, croaking words. And he even knew what they meant. As he lay motionless on the hot, fissured ground of the Devil's kingdom, he saw past his father kneeling above him, to the surrounding rock-fanged pits. From them, he could hear the mingled whimpers and cries of other tortured souls. Those wordless sounds, human as they were, meant as much to him as what his own father had just said.

Maybe . . . His disconnected thoughts inched slowly through his skull. *Maybe I would've cared . . . a long time ago.* Before the Devil had stolen his will from him. Maybe what his dead and eternally damned father had just told him, those few words, would have meant everything to him. But it took will to listen, to care. To connect. Now, words—even these—were just noise, with no more meaning than that of the fiery winds rolling across Hell's terrain.

"Son . . ." The blackened figure peered more closely at him. "What's happened . . . to you?" Fingers of deracinated bone reached toward Nathaniel's shoulders, halting and trembling a few inches away from him. "Why don't you . . . get up? . . . Why not . . . escape?"

"I . . ." He spoke without emotion, blank as empty air. "I don't know."

A terrible thought seemed to rise up into his father's face. "Nat . . . The Devil . . . Did he . . . touch you? . . . Did he . . . take anything out of you . . . Out of your heart?"

Nathaniel nodded silently.

"Did it look . . . like smoke? Did it . . . sparkle? Like diamonds?"

An even slower nod. "Yes . . . I think so . . . Maybe . . ."

"What . . . did he do with it? Where did . . . it go?"

"He burned it," answered Nathaniel. "It disappeared. Gone . . ."

"That's . . . not good." The bones of his father's hands clenched into white fists. "He took away your will . . . to resist him, Nat . . . . That's . . . what he did to me. To everyone . . . he tempts. But once he has taken our will . . . he does not destroy it. He keeps it safe. Then . . . when our souls are trapped here . . ." One hand pointed to the surrounding fires. "He gives us our willpower back again . . . to mock us . . ." His father's lungs labored visibly with the effort of speaking. "Because here . . . trapped in Hell . . . our willpower can do us no good. It only . . . pains us more . . ."

"You're right . . . I suppose . . ." He didn't know why he bothered to speak, to agree. "It doesn't matter to me. Not anymore . . ."

"But it should!" His father gnashed the black stumps of the teeth in his exposed jaws. "Because it could be different . . . for you, Nat. You're not dead yet . . . and not damned. You could escape from here . . . if you still had your will. I could . . . steal it back for you . . . if it existed. But it's gone . . ."

"Too bad . . ." If he had been capable of wishing, he might have preferred that his father would leave so he could simply gaze up at the fire-blackened crags of Hell's ceiling, forever. "But if it's gone . . . it's gone . . ."

"I have . . . an idea." Nathaniel's father pointed to his own chest, and the shapes sluggishly moving inside its cage. Something brighter sparked there. "I can give you the will . . . that the Devil gave back to me . . . My own will. To replace the one . . . you've lost." The parched voice turned softer. "Then you can go back . . . to the surface world . . . But it won't be easy, Nat . . . And it will hurt you. It will hurt a lot . . ."

"Don't bother . . ." Pain or no pain, it no longer concerned him. "I don't want to go back. Not anymore."

"But if you go back . . . you can fight the Devil . . ."

"No. I can't . . ." Nathaniel shook his head. "It's impossible to win, I see that now. The Devil was right. You need an army to defeat him. And I don't have an army. It doesn't exist . . ."

"That's only what he wants . . . you to think." His father

reached out to shake his son to his senses, but drew back again before his hands could make contact with Nathaniel's skin. "He wants you to believe . . . that everything . . . is hopeless. Just like it is here . . . in Hell. But that's wrong, Nat . . . Fighting for what's right is always worth it . . . And if you need an army . . . raise one yourself. So many people in this world have suffered . . . because of his evil . . . So use them. Show him . . . he's wrong . . ."

No reaction came from Nathaniel. The things his dead father spoke of—they were all just dreams. Damned and sent to Hell for all eternity, the man was still the weak, wishful creature he had been in the world of the living, and without the excuse of alcohol now, which had fueled all his worthless fantasies before. Drink, then dream, until all the bottles were empty, and only the dreams remained. And not even the courage to keep from selling his own son to Death, just to buy more time to drink, and dream. What did it matter? No more now than it had then. It was all just dreams. *Big talk,* thought Nathaniel. *That's all.*

"Nat . . . You have to decide . . ." His father spoke again. "What do you want me to do?"

"I told you . . . I don't care."

"But you *must* care!" said his father. "If I give you my will . . . you can escape . . . Try to force yourself . . . to think . . ."

"I can't . . . I don't want to."

"Then I will . . . decide for you . . . I'll do . . . what is best for you. Like I should have done . . . for you before."

His father had warned him that the process would be painful. Even by the standards of Hell. Nathaniel soon found that his father hadn't lied about that.

The blackened bones of his father's hand seized Nathaniel's

wrist at last, gripping tighter and tighter. His own hand burst into flames at the touch, the scathing fire traveling up his arm, all the way to his shoulder, as though the father's damnation had somehow ignited the living flesh of his son. The absence of will was not enough to shield him from such torment. Nathaniel screamed in agony, shrill and high, like a child whose hand had been forced upon a red-hot stove. He tried to pull his hand free of his father's grasp, but was too weak to do so. All he could do was go on screaming as his father took Nathaniel's hand and placed it upon the charred bones of his chest. Flames leapt out from between his father's ribs and breastbone, fierce and consuming.

Slowly, the transfer began. Just as his father had also promised. The glimmering substance inside his father's chest, brighter than the flames, seeped past the heart's black, hard knot, and out into the open. The shimmering substance hung there for a moment, like a cloud of diamonds, then moved along Nathaniel's burning arm, toward his chest.

Gasping for breath, he dropped his head, and could see the bright mist of his father's will settle at the base of his throat. Its luminance dimmed as it seeped inside his chest, toward the straining pulse of his own heart. A few sparks rested on his bared skin for a moment, then disappeared with the rest.

Hell itself disappeared as Nathaniel closed his eyes. His hand and arm were still aflame, but the agony had been extinguished. All such immaterial concerns had been thrown miles away from him, along with the burning stones and craters of this infernal domain. All he knew was the infinite space inside himself, and the white bolt coursing up his spine and into the center of his consciousness.

He clenched his fists as his father's grip upon his wrist loosened and fell away. The flames that had coursed up his arm faded and died out, leaving his skin scorched and blistered. His muscles tautened, swelling his chest as he drew in one deep breath after another. As he looked down at himself, he could see his heart pumping fresh blood through every tissue, restoring the life that had been slowly ebbing from him.

His father sank down onto his knees, his reddened eyes staring blankly in front of himself. Nathaniel stood upright and looked at the blackened corpse crouching at his feet.

"What . . . happened . . ." Faint words stumbled from the lipless mouth. He looked up at the figure before him. "Nat . . . is that you . . ."

He doesn't even have the will to remember. The sad realization filled Nathaniel. He filed the knowledge away with his other dark memories. All the things that he couldn't forget, that he would have given the world to be able to let go. Just as his father had now been able to. *He doesn't remember, not even what he just gave up.*

"Yes, Dad." He nodded slowly. "It's me."

"There's so much . . . that I wanted to tell you . . ." Confused, disjointed thoughts crawled behind the dead eyes. "I wanted to ask you . . . to forgive me . . . forgive me, Nat . . ."

"It's okay." He reached down again. "I forgive you."

"Do you . . . really . . . ?"

"For everything," said Nathaniel. It was all the absolution he could give. "I forgave you long ago. Before you even died."

It was enough. The fragmented mind behind the other's gaze, which had held nothing but sin and remorse, clouded over. The charred body toppled backward, sprawling without motion, without will, into the flames tormenting his flesh—

But not his mind. Not anymore.

I've given him what he needs, Nathaniel realized. *For the rest of Time . . .* He looked at the corpse, glimpsing the tiny spark of salvation glowing in its eyes. Even in a place such as this charnel inferno, that was enough, for someone who had once been damned, to now find peace.

Nathaniel gave a slow, silent nod, as he understood even more. For his father to be at peace here, in the center of the Devil's domain—that was a victory. *I can't take him from here,* thought Nathaniel. *But I can leave him here with his dignity. That will be our triumph . . .*

From far away, at the earth's surface, he could hear his own name being spoken. Someone was calling for him, in greatest need. He turned and walked away, across the flames and toward his fate.

20.

The fire had torn open the sleeve of his leather jacket. Past the burnt edges, he could see his skin, burned by the flames that had traveled up his arm as his father's will had been transferred to him. That pain had been many times worse, unendurable, but it had ended. This was the pain of his own flesh, throbbing with each pulse of the blood beneath, each flexing of the muscles and tendons.

I'm lucky, thought Nathaniel. *To feel that—*

He scanned across the stone chamber, beneath the dark shaft leading up to the earth's surface. Once he had stepped out of this domain, beyond the flames and smoke of Hell, the gaps that had broken open in the walls had closed, their jagged edges grinding toward each other like the movement of boulders in an earthquake, sealing off the infernal vista. The splintered skulls and bones of the murdered infants still lay scattered about the space, grim reminders of the enemies responsible for their deaths.

Touching his own scorched flesh with a fingertip produced an involuntary wince from him. It would be hard to put up much of a fight, with his arm burned like that, once he managed to rejoin

Blake and the hit man Hank. *But then again,* he thought, *that's not the kind of fighting I do.*

He walked underneath the shaft, kicking aside the broken pieces of the spiral staircase that had filled it before. Whatever he was going to do, whatever part he would play in the battle against the Devil, he knew he had to rejoin his comrades as quickly as possible. He closed his eyes, blocking out everything around him, letting his pulse and breath slow . . .

"That's not right." He had opened his eyes as soon as he had completed the spell to transport himself back up to street level. Tilting his head back, he had expected to see the ornately timbered ceiling of the abandoned town house; that was the spot for which he had aimed. Instead, he saw the roiling storm clouds of the night sky, rain pelting down toward his face.

But the town house's floorboards were underfoot. He brought his gaze back down and scanned the area. He could see now that he was surrounded by the ruins of the structure, the walls flattened and pushed outward as though a bomb had gone off in the middle of them. The rubble stretched out in all directions, shards of broken windows glittering across the broken wooden beams. In the distance, the dark silhouette of the Devil's office tower loomed above the garden square at its base. The shrieks and cries of battle assaulted his ears; he could make out the demonic legions rampaging chaotically through the space, their bat-winged counterparts swooping above, slashing at any human beings unfortunate enough to have been trapped below.

That's where they are, Nathaniel realized. He couldn't spot Blake and Hank, but knew they would be in the thick of whatever fighting was going on. *If they're still alive—*

His first instinct was to rush over to the garden square and join in the action, however it was going, whatever he might be able to do. For a combat-hardened soldier such as Blake and a giant hit man like Hank, it might be a battle—but for the other human beings caught there, it was nothing more than slaughter. He could see it from here, the weapons slashing and tearing, their blades wreathed in flame. On every side, the stones were washed with the steaming blood of the innocent. Men and women and children alike, their lifeless bodies tossed to either side by the rampaging demonic horde. That was how the Devil worked, unleashing chaos without regard to those who got swept up in it. Something like that wasn't the Devil's concern; all he wanted was death and pain, in endless supply. And now he was getting it.

Yeah, and what're you going to do about it? Nathaniel clenched his fists at his side, trying to force an answer from his brain. Down in the stone chamber, far below the town house's ruins, he had shoved that question aside, figuring that he would know what to do once he got here. Hank and Blake might be good at killing demons, either by tearing their heads off or running them through with some kind of weapon, but his own talents were a little less crudely physical in nature. *Maybe some kind of spell? But what?* Stopping Time had bought some precious breathing room for them, allowing Hank and Blake to escape from the Devil and reach the surface, but what good would it do now? Even if he got to the square and pulled off the spell—and right now, after the marathon session through which he had put himself down below, his resources along that particular line felt close to exhaustion—he might be able to stop the slaughter for as long as his strength held out, but then what? As soon as the

Time-stopping spell faded away—and it would—then the demons would continue with their orgy of destruction, not even aware that anything else had happened. *A lot of good that would've accomplished*, Nathaniel mused glumly.

As his brain scurried desperately along its unyielding circuit, something his dead and damned father had said popped into his thoughts. *If you need an army . . . you could raise one.* Nathaniel frowned, trying to remember what exactly his father had said. The rest came suddenly: *From all the people who have suffered because of him.*

Perhaps . . . that was possible. For him.

His thoughts slowly began to take shape. Into a realization that had never dawned on him before.

I belong to both worlds now, thought Nathaniel. *To both the living and the dead . . .*

No one else could do what he could. No one else had that power. Everything that had happened to him through the hours of that single day—all that he had seen and done—served to tell him that.

For a moment, it felt as if he were standing on the edge of a great, empty chasm. Yet one that was contained within himself. A dizzying perspective, to know at last that he had become greater than his master.

His powers could work in the realm of the living—and that of the dead. Even his master hadn't understood that. Death had been concerned only with his own plane of existence. Death might be able to walk among the living, but only to reap their souls and send them off to Purgatory to be judged.

I can do more, thought Nathaniel. *To help win this battle*. Perhaps only for a while. Just as he could halt Time, but not end it—

He sensed the chasm inside him filling with awesome possibility. Something of which only his powers were capable. But which might also encompass his own destruction.

Such an undertaking might be possible for him—but it would call upon every resource within his being. It was another kind of spell, one that tore down the barrier between the worlds—and one that he had never attempted before. And worse—one that nobody had ever even contemplated before. The spells his master had taught him had merely helped him do his job of reaping souls. Anything else, he had been sternly instructed to put out of his mind.

Of course, he remembered Death telling him, *it is possible to create new spells. Ones that no one has created before. But* you *cannot do that.*

He had demanded to know why. He had learned all the spells that Death had taught him, mastered them, gathered souls with them. Why couldn't he make a new spell?

Because—Death had patiently spoken—*for you to create a spell, to bring it forth from inside your being, you would first need to be the master of yourself. The spell would need to come from your own innermost certainties and desires. But for that, Nathaniel, you would have to know, at last, exactly who you are. And more . . . You would finally need to decide to which realm of existence you want to belong. To that other world, in which your body exists—or here with me, in this quieter world where the darkness inside you is at home. You would have to choose between life, and pain—and my existence, in which all such human burdens are but a memory that can no longer hurt you.*

His master's words faded from his thoughts.

It had taken him a long time—ten years—to figure out, but

he had made his decision. His choice. The world to which he belonged. The will that his dead father had given him—that had been the last piece he had needed to complete the puzzle. The will that he had lost, that the Devil had stolen from him—that had been a child's will, still immature and ignorant. What he had now inside himself, his father's will, was one that had become mature, through grief and suffering.

And that was what had allowed the great understanding to unveil itself inside him.

Nathaniel gave a slow nod, the realization flooding through him. *I belong to both—the living and the dead.* He was at home here, in the world of those who still breathed, and whose hearts beat in their chests, and who still wanted so much, no matter the pain and cost, no matter how much those desires tormented them. But he would be at home there as well, in that other world, the one he shared with his master Death. *And that means,* he realized, *that any magic I create—it would work there as well as here.* In both realms. A spell for the living and the dead . . .

And that would be enough. Enough to assemble an army. One that could defeat the Devil.

He closed his eyes. He spread his arms, palms outward, feeling the power begin its slow, gathering course, up from the base of his spine.

The effort needed to create the spell, the demand upon his innermost resources, grew in tandem with the power he had summoned up. One would have to be greater than the other, he knew; that was the risk he had undertaken. Once committed to this course, there was no turning back. If there wasn't enough power within him to complete the spell, then it would destroy him.

And pain—that was involved as well. More than he might be able to endure. Nathaniel could feel the pins that held his soul inside him begin to tremble. They were already weakened by all that he had gone through. If they gave way . . . then he would no longer be in the realm of the living. His master's world would claim him forever. He clenched his open hands into fists, gritting his teeth against the agony that spread outward from his heart.

Time crawled, but did not stop. It crept on, agonizingly slow, as both the power and the need swelled inside him.

Then he could hear, beyond the sounds of battle and murder in the garden square, another sound. Other voices, other murmurs and cries, from those just beginning the journey he had already made, from the realm of the dead to the realm of the living.

In all of the city's graveyards, the dismal territories of neglected tombstones falling amidst tangled weeds, every creature—once living, once human—who had suffered because of the Devil's schemes and entrapments, now parted the dank grass above themselves. Their cold, pale hands pushed aside the lids of their pauper coffins, ripped aside the tattered winding-sheets in which they had been buried, and clawed upward through the clay and mud that had stoppered their gaping mouths. Dank soil, mingled with tatters of skin, slipped from the dead's stark faces as they climbed into the starlit world from which they had been banished.

Iron hinges groaned as mausoleums' heavy doors swung open. Those who had been rich and powerful in life, only to be rendered stiff and cold as any starved beggar, left their marble biers and stumbled out into the night. One by one, in the city's morgues, the aluminum drawers slid open, the freshly dead climbing out, shrouded in hospital white and with paper tags looped around each one's toe.

Still standing in the middle of the town house's ruins, Nathaniel turned away from the garden square and opened his eyes to look across the dark streets behind him. He could see now the approach of the army summoned by his spell, one which none had dared assemble before. From all quarters they came, white bone showing where flesh had rotted away; others, more recently interred, might have appeared as though alive except for the cold pallor of their skin and their hollowed eye sockets. Their unblinking gaze revealed no souls within—no spell could return those— but the dim sparks of memory showed instead. Each grim figure remembered the Devil's twisting schemes and malice, suffered while alive, unavenged in death—until this moment, this call to battle. As night-flying insects are drawn toward candle flames, the reanimated corpses trudged on in relentless silence, joining forces with their resurrected brethren in the garden.

The spell had taken a lot out of Nathaniel. He closed his eyes again, drawing in one slow breath after another, knowing that the final battle was about to begin.

21.

The storm woke her.

Even with her eyes closed, the shapes and forms of her dreaming were starkly illuminated by the lightning that leapt beyond the window. She was running in those dreams, both searching and pursued, through alleys so dark and narrow that her shoulders were scraped raw by her passage through windowless buildings, so tall that storm clouds crowned their tops. Suddenly, the crash of thunder struck with force enough to send her stumbling onto her hands and knees, looking up to see the sky transformed into one blinding blue-white expanse . . .

Another jagged stroke of lightning, and Ling's eyes opened wide, the afterimage from her dreams confusingly layered over the harsh-shadowed angles of the room in which she lay. For a moment, it seemed as if the alleys through which she had been running now held her familiar closet door and dresser bureau. That frightened her; fingertips dug into the bedsheets on either side as she gasped for breath.

This is where he brought me, Ling told herself. Back to her apartment, where she would be safe. She pushed aside the blanket that the giant hit man Hank had drawn on top of her. Her shoes lay on the floor, but she was still fully clothed. The clothes she had been wearing when she had run through the city's real alleys and streets, not the ones inside her head; turning her face against her shoulder, she could detect the mingled scent of the city's rain and her own desperation seeping from her pores.

More rain rattled the bedroom's window in its frame. The storm's onslaught grew more intense. From this floor of the apartment building, she could glance out the window and see the hooded streetlights just below, swaying and bobbing in the wet lash of the wind, like the lanterns of ships lost at sea.

He promised me.

Those words remained as Ling's thoughts cleared from weary sleep. That was what Hank had done, out there in one of the city's worst districts, as he had kept her from running away from him. He had sworn he would find Ren-Lei, save her, bring her back. No matter what it took. He must still be out there, searching—or killing, taking the necks of her daughter's captors into his massive fists and snapping them like dry tinder. Whatever it took. A vision came to her, of the giant figure striding relentlessly forward, eyes narrowed in a face set hard against the sheets of icy rain. Shoving open every barred doorway, turning the city upside down to find nothing more than a scared child—

She thought she could almost hear her baby crying, somewhere outside. *That can't be,* Ling told herself. She turned her eyes toward the window, letting the flashes of lightning play across her face. There was something she could hear, past the crack and rumble of thunder. Something human, and terrified.

The screams of her neighbors grew louder. As though they

had seen something outside, beyond all comprehension, unleashing every fear.

Ling scrambled out of the bed and slid open the door to the apartment's balcony. She stepped out and grasped the rail, looking down into the streets below.

She could see them then, the rain drenching the figures stumbling past, rivulets of water coursing down the rotted flesh, the bones visible inside the tattered shrouds. A dead army marched in grievous array through this street, and every other passage that Ling could view from her apartment. She looked to the side and saw the old lady who lived in the unit next door, transfixed on her balcony, screaming past the wrinkled little fist pressed to her mouth, but unable to tear herself away from the horrific sight below.

Something momentous was happening. Ling could see the spot to which the animated corpses were heading: the garden square at the base of one of the city's office towers, its top hidden by the low-hanging storm clouds. Dark smoke rose from the area in front of it, twisting and writhing through the rain's downpour. Even from this distance, with each breath she could taste the fumes on her tongue, cloying and foul.

All of this must have something to do with Ren-Lei; she was sure of it. One way or another, though she couldn't understand exactly how. Maybe the giant hit man's search for the infant had somehow unleashed these grisly forces.

She rushed back inside from the balcony, pausing only to slip on her shoes before running out the apartment's front door. A few moments later, the lobby's elevator slid open. Pulling her jacket tight around herself, Ling pushed open the door to the street.

Far above, the smell of decay and formaldehyde hadn't struck her nostrils. Now it did, bringing bile into her throat. She drew back against the wall of the building, trying to avoid contact with the corpses filling the street. It was impossible; there were so many of them, filling the sidewalks as well as all the space between. Threadbare burial clothes and cold skin brushed against her as she flattened her hands against the wall and turned her face away, trying to hold her breath for as long as possible.

Fighting down her repulsion, Ling pushed herself away from the building and into the midst of the dead army streaming by. Their withered muscles kept them from moving as quickly as she could. She worked her way through their ranks, pressing forward to reach the garden to which their slow, relentless steps were being called.

Ren-Lei. That was all she could think. *Maybe she's there—*

Something on the street's pavement tripped Ling. There was just enough space between her and the corpses ahead that she wound up landing hard on one shoulder, then scrambling quickly onto her back, terrified of being trampled by the dead massed behind. She found herself looking up into the hollow eyes of one of the dead. The corpse regarded her for a moment, then turned and shambled after the rest of the lifeless army.

She managed at last to reach the edge of the garden. The sight she beheld staggered her backward—

Two immense armies were locked in battle. Demons beyond her nightmares flew on claw-tipped batwings, filling the smoke-filled sky above their hideous brethren. Any one of them would have been enough to send a human being, shocked witless, running for a hiding place. Their fanged and tusked faces were lit by the fiery blades of the weapons held in their bloodied claws. Guttural howls broke from their throats, each snarl and cry lusting for the flesh of their victims. Ling cowered backward, her breath seized above her panicked, racing heart.

The other army was even more dismaying. All that she had seen before of the resurrected dead was eclipsed. Now she saw a seemingly endless throng of corpses, their white bones protruding through grey, rotted skin, stumbling forward from all directions. It didn't seem possible that the earth had held so many graves. The dead of centuries past outnumbered the living.

All was chaos inside the garden's confines, the dead locking into combat with the Devil's horde. More smoke billowed up from hideous corpses strewn across the ground. On all sides of the slaughtered demons, the battle surged back and forth, like tidal waves crashing against a rugged coastline's cliffs and rocks. From above, the storm clouds pelted torrential rain, through which the winged demons plunged with blood-reddened swords, or were caught and pulled down, then torn to pieces by lifeless hands.

Her thoughts had been stunned motionless by what she saw. All her hidden nightmares, which thankfully faded upon waking, seemed to have emerged from the confines of her skull. The vision challenged her sanity—it would be easy to let go and fall into madness, rather than believe such things could exist.

But she knew that if she did that, there would be no chance of finding Ren-Lei. As monstrous as the world had become, it was the one through which she had to search, if she wanted to save her child.

As the rain coursed down Ling's face, she fought down the revulsion and horror moving inside of her. If she could just catch sight of Hank—she knew that if he was there, then Ren-Lei must be nearby. But all she could see was the shrieking, hissing demons and the weapons hacking at the dead army swarming relentlessly forward, from all sides of the square.

The storm worsened, its winds howling louder than the battle below, the clouds darkening to pitch-black. Bolts of lightning, larger than any Ling had ever seen, struck sizzling into the ground, each blinding flash silhouetting the demons and corpses that it sent flying through the air. By one such explosion, brighter than a noonday sun, she caught sight of another figure, a black man with matted dreadlocks flying above the shoulders of a grime-encrusted overcoat. Standing upon a mound of lifeless demons, he whirled a double-bladed spear so fast about himself that its edges formed a flaming, lethal helix, slashing apart the demons that hurled themselves toward him. The smoke from their corpses writhed darkly around him, obscuring him for a split second, before being ripped through by another blurring swing of his spear. One demon managed to elude the blades, its claws reaching toward the man's throat, only to be caught by a windmilling kick to its chitin-armored groin. Yanking the spear free from the horned skull he had used as a pivot to launch himself in a flying spin, the man sprang swiftly forward, lifting one flaming blade up through the demon's abdomen, then out through its throat as he pulled the spear's shaft back toward himself. The gutted demon toppled down across the others as the weapon whirled about once more without ceasing.

Another radiant burst, not glaring white like the storm's lightning, but eerily violet in color, caught her eye. She turned and saw a cabal of the Devil's witches, their backs against the entrance to the tower, their hands outstretched before them. Incandescent bolts shot spiraling from their palms, scattering the corpses arrayed before them. But there were too many for even their combined magics to defeat; for every corpse whose limbs were blasted from its torso, more swarmed toward the witches, threatening to engulf them with their sheer numbers.

Past the backs of the dead, Ling spotted a face she recognized. *It's her*—a fierce shock seared her spine as she saw the one who had passed herself off as a simple nanny, the one she had hired to take care of her baby. And the one who instead had given Ren-Lei to the hideous dwarf.

She dove into the thick of the battle, climbing across the heaped bodies of the slaughtered, shoving her way past the demons locked in hand-to-hand combat with the dead, dodging the blades of swords and spears, as she headed for the tower's entrance.

By the time she had crossed the square, the corpses had toppled onto the coven, like a slowly cresting wave. Ling could see nothing but the backs of the dead, flashes of the violet light sliding past their intertwined bodies.

"Get back!" She grabbed the shoulder of the first one she could reach, tugging it from the pile and sending it sprawling behind herself. "Get away from them!"

She managed to claw her way through the dead, pushing each away from the rest. Until she could at last pull free one of the figures trapped beneath them.

Blood trickled from the mouth of the youngest witch, the one who had posed as Ren-Lei's nanny. She glared up at Ling, her neck still marked from the earlier bite of a demon.

"Anna—" Ling gasped out the name, her heart racing as she grabbed the witch's arm and yanked her to her feet. "Where's Ren-Lei?" Desperate, she swung the back of her hand across the witch's face, then again, sending blood spattering across Anna's shoulder. "Tell me or I'll kill you!"

"Let me go!" Anna struggled to free herself from Ling's grasp. "I have to find my master!" A crazed spark appeared in the witch's eyes. "And find a way—to give him more power—"

The corpses had finished off the other witches, leaving their broken bodies on the ground. They turned and stumbled back into the fight, leaving behind the two women.

Before Ling could react, a violet glow coalesced above Anna's hands, then shot outward, striking her full in the face. She staggered backward, then fell.

Anna turned and ran for the tower's entrance. With another blast from her hands, she cleared the corpses of the other witches from the entrance to the tower. The door shattered, its glistening shards raining across the ground. With a last mocking glance at Ling, the witch ran and disappeared into the darkness inside the building.

Ling knew she had no choice. The witch was her best, her only, option to find Ren-Lei at this point. She scrambled to her feet and ran after the other woman.

She found herself in the building's lobby. Anna was already gone. Standing before the elevator doors, she watched as the red numbers mounted upward, finally stopping at the twentieth floor.

She'll be waiting for me, Ling realized, stopping herself before her hand could push the button for the next elevator. *I better be ready. For anything . . .*

She ran over to the lobby's reception desk and ripped out a length of telephone cord. She had learned a lot at the Mountain Master's school; now was the time to use it. A heavy crystal paperweight lay on the desk; she quickly tied a monkey's-fist knot around it, turning the cord into a makeshift rope dart.

With her weapon dangling in one hand, she pressed the elevator button. A few seconds later, she was traveling upward, ready for battle.

22.

The tide was turning. And not the way it was supposed to.

With reddened sweat running down his naked chest, the Devil had mounted to the top of a mound of his slaughtered followers, the better to survey the course of battle. As the rain continued pelting down, flashes of lightning illuminated a dismal scene inside the garden square. He scowled as he watched reanimated corpses, somehow called forth from the city's tombs and graveyards, driving the struggle's outcome. Individually, the dead were easy prey for his legions, bones flying apart with single blows from the demons' weapons, blades severing the rotting flesh and tendons that had held the shambling forms together. But en masse, the sheer numbers of the dead prevailed. Cold, pallid hands dragged flying demons out of the night sky, skeletal fingers ripping apart the leathery wings. As warrior ants in far-off tropical hells could swarm over and bring down creatures hundreds of times their size, so did the moving corpses bury demons beneath their combined weight, until steaming blood spurted across the square's paving stones.

From the Devil's vantage point, the garden now appeared like the dumping grounds of some monstrous charnel house. The dismembered fragments of human remains, already far gone in decay, intertwined with the crushed and broken demons. Thick torrents of smoke churned upward from the demon's bodies, rendering the battle between those who remained even more nightmarishly confused; maddened, the remaining demons struck and slashed blindly in all directions, impaling their own kind as often as they caught one of the walking dead on the points of the weapons. The bodies had mounded so high that clambering over the bloody remains was the only path from one side of the battlefield to the other.

"I grow weaker," the Devil murmured darkly. His legions were so close to him, so much a part of his substance, that the death of each was like a knife-blow to his heart. To watch so many being slaughtered was to suffer a million fatal cuts. But even more infuriating was that he still didn't know how this dead army had been summoned from their graves, and set against him and his followers. To have done so was to have wielded an awesome power— but who in the city possessed the strength to cast such a spell?

The answer came from behind him. A voice shouted: "You wanted an army—"

He whirled about and saw Death's apprentice standing at the base of the mounded corpses.

"So I brought you one." One sleeve of Nathaniel's leather jacket was charred to tatters, revealing the equally blackened skin of his arm.

"How—" The Devil stared at him in shock. "I left you to rot in Hell."

Nathaniel said nothing in response, simply smiled.

He could see the difference in the young man. Even with the injured arm, Nathaniel looked stronger than he had before, as if the powers he held had enlarged his muscles and bones, rendering him taller and more threatening. And not just that: he was no longer a mere boy, Death's youthful apprentice. Something had matured him, turned him into a man. The eyes that gazed upon the Devil showed no fear or hesitation. Fear clenched cold inside the Devil's gut, as if—for the first time—he was looking upon his own certain destruction.

Before he could speak, the cold grasp of the dead seized upon his legs, nearly toppling and dragging him from the top of the grisly mound on which he stood. Distracted by Nathaniel's sudden appearance, the Devil hadn't seen a half dozen of the dead coming up on the other side. A single sweep of his arm sent a churning fireball into their empty-eyed faces, scattering them in all directions.

But he knew he couldn't get rid of the dead army until he had first taken care of Nathaniel. As long as Death's apprentice was alive, his own survival was in question. Nathaniel had been the one who had raised the dead; they would keep coming, wave after wave of them, as long as his magic called them to battle.

The Devil closed his eyes and crossed his arms upon his chest. He summoned his own power, every fiery atom that his body held coalescing one by one with the others. Greater and greater, the scalding flames reached down into his groin and up into his throat. If he held that force a moment longer inside, it would consume him. Instead, the Devil flung his arms wide, unleashing a ball of radiant plasma, expanding wider than his own form, and flying straight at the insolent human standing before him.

The great fireball halted halfway between the Devil and the target at which he had aimed it. It hung there, the churning radiance that played across its curved surface wavering red-tinged shadows across the stacks of dismembered bodies.

Past the glowing sphere, he could see that Nathaniel had raised his good arm, holding his palm outward, halting the plasma in its course.

"How . . ." The Devil glared at him in mingled rage and wonder. "How can you do that . . . ? There is no power on earth that can defeat me."

"Think again . . . ," said Nathaniel. "Because the coldness of death brings an end to everything in time . . ." He gave a slow nod. "Including you."

As the Devil watched, the fireball began to turn to ice. Its surface silvered over with hoarfrost, the radiance gradually dying inside. Its trail of fire, extending back to the Devil, froze as well. His eyes widened as he looked down and saw the ice forming around his hands, trapping them in a thick crystalline casing. But it didn't stop; the ice grew, setting around his wrists and forearms.

The Devil's response edged into panic. He frantically smashed one growing mass of ice against the other, trying to crack them into shattered crystals. A few whitened shards were chipped away, melting into steam as they arced through the fiery air. But the clear, unbroken ice grew larger, even as his attempts to free himself grew more desperate.

Within a few moments, his elbows would be frozen inside the encroaching ice. If he didn't do something soon, find a way to break the spell that Nathaniel had hurled at him, his entire body would be encased motionless inside it. He struggled to break his arms free of the encroaching mass of ice—in vain. It had already grown too heavy, shackling him to the spot. Chest laboring for breath, he threw back his head.

"To my side!" The Devil's voice cried out across the battle-field. He desperately looked about, seeking his followers. "Now!"

A ghastly peace had begun to settle upon the garden square.

The dead and dismembered outnumbered the living. The army of corpses, torn bone from bone by the demons' weapons, lay motionless. The spell that had exhumed them, set them stumbling toward the fight, now seeped away in the rain pooling beneath the fragments of their bodies. Rivulets of blood, once hissing like steam, now clotted upon the shattered skulls and riven breastplates of the Devil's legions.

"Two of these bastards left—" Blake looked over at Hank, standing a few yards away. "And you wouldn't know it, they're the worst."

Hank rested the blade of his axe on the ground, as though he could draw strength from the earth through it, to replace even a little of what had been drained from his muscles. "I haven't enjoyed any of 'em." Behind him, the stack of scaly, armored bodies reached to the height of his head. He rested a hand on the helmet still strapped to his chest, taking a peek inside to make sure that Ren-Lei was still safe. "Let's finish this."

A resolution more easily made than accomplished. The demon that had come vaulting across the mounds of bodies to confront Blake dug the points of its claws into the mouths and eye sockets of the fallen. It had a face only partly human, the lower half formed into the curved, jagged-toothed mandibles of a giant carnivorous insect. Rearing upright, spreading wide its glistening, heavily muscled arms, the demon snarled with fury. The segmented armor of a scorpion tail arched over its back, the hooked stinger wide as a cart wheel and glittering with poison.

Facing Hank at the same time was the largest of all the demons that had burst from the confines of the earth's depths. It towered above him, rearing erect on legs formed of massive, writhing snakes; the blood of its victims tangled the coarse mane of its lion's head, shielded by a magnesium helmet heavier than any that its slaughtered comrades had borne. The creature tilted its head back, emitting a deafening roar, needing no words for its promise of death and retribution.

Blake and Hank drew closer, setting themselves back-to-back as the two demons approached. The giant scorpion lunged forward at Blake, the point of its stinger swooping at his chest. He parried it with the double-bladed spear in his hands, tilting to one side so that the venomed point passed within inches of his face. Its force was still enough that it penetrated Hank's shoulder instead, the curved hook emerging just above his shoulder blade. The black ichor of the stinger's toxin shot into the air and landed in a hissing spatter across the ground.

Blake saw what had happened, and heard the gasp of sudden pain from Hank. The scorpion's claws snapped futilely at Blake as he leapt onto its back. He swung the spear at the unarmored joint between the scorpion's body and its segmented tail. Black ichor spurted from the wound as he severed the tail free. The fierce glare in the humanlike face dulled, then went unfocused and blank as the head lolled forward, the claws flopping to the ground, dead.

Hank had managed to jerk the stinger from his shoulder. Using it as a handle, he swung the severed scorpion tail in a flat arc, bringing its wide end hard into the lion-headed demon's face, staggering it backward. That gave Blake the chance to race across the fallen scorpion's head and bring the spear slashing through the hissing serpents that held the giant lion-headed demon upright. The snakes' scalding blood sprayed in all directions as their amputated lengths writhed upon the ground. Roaring in outraged agony, the demon collapsed upon its knees. Hank set a boot sole on the demon's mane and hacked at its neck with his axe, finally chopping the helmeted head free and sending it rolling into the closest mound of bodies. It came to rest upside down, a fountain of red bubbling up from its opened throat.

"There." Hank sat down heavily. He laid the axe, its blades still wrapped in flame, on the ground beside him. A rare smile formed on his face. "Was that so hard?"

The Devil seethed as he saw what had happened to the last of his followers. Bound by the ice encasing his arms, he had cast his gaze across the battlefield and spotted his other dreaded enemies, the wraith and the giant hit man. The fight between them and the last two demons had resulted in two more smoking figures on the piles of the dead, and the abandonment of his hopes of rescue from the spell which trapped him.

But there was still a chance. Even though slaughtered, the demons still belonged to him, were still part of him.

He summoned up the last reserves of power within himself, calling out—silently this time—across the battlefield. Still wearing its heavy magnesium helmet, the lion's head stirred and rolled an inch away from the corpse mound. It rose into the air, suspended by the Devil's will, then flew above the battlefield, trailing smoke from its slashed throat.

In front of the Devil, Nathaniel turned and saw the demon's head tumbling through the dark sky, above the intertwined corpses. As it approached, faster and faster, it arced toward the ground, striking the flow of ice that extended back to the Devil's fingers. The ice shattered from the blow, sending bright shards in every direction—and freeing the Devil.

The hit man and the soldier saw this, and weapons upraised in their hands, they raced toward the spot.

"You won't escape," Nathaniel told his opponent. "You have no more power—that was the last of it."

Death's apprentice had truly perceived the Devil's weakened state. He stumbled down from the mound of bodies and looked desperately around for any way out. Hank and Blake were impeded by the tangled bodies littering the battlefield, but they would still be upon him in minutes. In the distance, he spotted the ruins of the abandoned town house; he turned and ran toward it, each stroke of his cloven hoof digging into the blood-sodden ground.

He managed to reach the edge of the garden square. But the dead saw him coming. Between the garden and the abandoned town house were a score of corpses, damaged from their battle with the demons, but still animated by the spell that had summoned them from their graves. An arm of bone and tattered, pallid skin reached up and grabbed him, tugging at his knee. He stayed upright, but more skeletal hands were clutching at him, dragging him down. The ones from a little distance away got to their feet and stumbled toward him, reaching out to bring their yellowed bones around his neck.

There were too many of them, and he was too weak. The Devil stumbled and fell, and the dead were on top of him. They knew who he was, even without being able to read the symbols branded upon his bared body. The dead bore him down into their midst, a clawing wave, their hard, fleshless fists pummeling him. With every blow, they exacted payment for their suffering, and the world's.

23.

The elevator doors slid open, and Ling ran out into the huge lobby outside the Devil's office.

With the overhead lights switched off, she could see that the room was empty now. *Careful* . . . Anna was here somewhere; she could feel her presence. *Waiting for me.* Some spell, no doubt, kept her invisible. Ling knew she would have to be careful to keep from falling into the other woman's trap.

She looked around as she stepped cautiously forward. A dim, fiery glow seeped through the room. By its partial light, she could see a frieze of statues lining the walls above her head. The gruesomely carved forms depicted the torments of the damned, sinners writhing in flames, skin flayed into strips, innards torn from their bodies on the prongs of demons' pitchforks.

More red light washed up into Ling's face from below. She looked down and saw that the floor beneath her feet was transparent, crafted of thick, tempered glass. But what was revealed to her was not a carved representation of the Devil's infernal domain, but the actual fires of Hell, churning and roiling far below. She could feel the flames' heat turning the office lobby into a crematory oven.

"I knew you'd come."

The softly spoken words caught Ling by surprise. Before she could react, the witch darted past her. She turned and smiled in pure malice at Ling, then unleashed a spiraling violet bolt from her upraised palms. The magic pulse stunned Ling, dropping her to her knees.

Expecting another blow, she quickly rolled onto her back, a sweep of her arm sending the rope dart toward her assailant. But the weight at the end of the cord shot harmlessly into empty space; the witch had already disappeared again.

Drawing the weight back into her hand, Ling stood upright, warily scanning the office for any sign of the woman. The lurid, shifting light filled the room with disorienting shadows. Their edges sharpened when another streak of violet, stronger than the first, hit her between the shoulder blades, knocking her sprawling across the floor. Without turning around, she sprang to her feet and sent the dart flying behind herself. The weight chipped the plaster of one of the room's walls, but hit nothing else.

The next blow, even more intense, pushed the air from her lungs as it threw her back. The next pulse would have been fatal, if Ling hadn't dodged it by rolling onto her side. The violet radiance seared close by as she sent the rope dart straight toward the source of the bolt. She heard the thud of the weight striking flesh; Anna flickered into visibility as she staggered backward, blood trickling from her brow.

Another throw of the rope dart looped the cord around the witch's neck; Ling yanked her forward, an upraised knee sinking deep into the woman's gut. A quick forearm across the side of Anna's jaw sent her sprawling at Ling's feet. She knelt hard on the witch's back, gathering up the long black hair in one fist and using it to shove the bleeding face against the floor.

Anna screamed in agony as the fires raging beneath seared her face, their heat drawn to the evil inside her. Pain gave her enough desperate strength to throw Ling off. One eye swollen shut by the blistered skin, Anna exchanged a quick flurry of punches with her. Ling dodged and parried the blows, then leaned back to bring a roundhouse kick against the witch's chest, driving her back against the wall.

The sculpted figures of tormented sinners dug into her, as though she had fallen into a nest of thorns. Every direction she writhed and turned, there were more of the stiff, immovable fingers clutching at her limbs. From her own pinioned hands, she fired another round of violet pulses. One caught Ling in the shoulder as she dragged Anna out into the room. Ling quickly bound her wrists with the rope dart's cord and threw her to the floor.

"Now tell me—" She brought her face close to the witch's. "Where's my baby?"

Anna hissed and spat at Ling. "You should be *proud* that she was taken! It's an honor to serve our master, as well as his Lieutenant. I gave my own baby to him of my own free will. And do you really think your mewling brat is fit for anything better than that?"

Ling brought the loose end of the cord around Anna's neck and pulled it tight. She watched the witch struggle for breath, then leaned close to her ear. "Where is my baby?"

"She's . . . down in the garden . . ." The cord was loosened just enough for a few words to be gasped out. "With . . . with the giant . . ."

Hank—that must be who she means. The realization sent Ling's heartbeat racing.

She left the witch on the floor and ran into the Devil's office. The cold wind of the storm and the dying sounds of the battle in the garden square came through the shattered window that filled one entire wall. She stood at its edge, icy rain pelting her face, peering down until she was at last able to spot the figure of the giant hit man who had sworn to save her child.

In the distance below, near the peach tree in the garden's center, Hank jumped down from a pile of smoking corpses, remains of the Devil's legions. A helmet was strapped to his broad chest; from the way he carefully held it in place with one hand, she knew that must be where he was guarding Ren-Lei.

She turned from the window, and had only a momentary glimpse of the witch's glee-filled smile, before one of the lobby's heavy table lamps smashed straight into her face. Blood streaming into her eyes, Ling felt Anna's hands grab her by the throat and throw her sprawling on top of the black lava-stone desk.

"I don't need magic," snarled the witch, "to finish you off." She pressed the largest of the lamp's shards like a dagger against Ling's throat. "But my master requires a sacrifice. Your blood on his altar will give the Devil the power he needs." She pressed the shard's edge down tighter. "Then we'll see who wins this battle . . ."

24.

The army of the dead dragged their prisoner back into the garden.

Blake was the first to spot them coming. He looked up from the torn stitches across the front of his overcoat, now blacker with the blood and grime of battle, red drops from his own torn flesh spattering upon his boots. Through the rain lashing down and the choking billows of smoke, he could discern the shambling silhouettes, collections of bones and decaying flesh in human form, held together and animated by Nathaniel's spell. Two of them grasped the arms of another figure, larger and once stronger, pulling him along between them, across the mud and gore of the battlefield.

He glanced over at Hank beside him, and pointed to the approaching figures. "They got him."

The hit man had loosed the strap holding the demon's helmet to his chest, so he could reach in and tenderly stroke the baby's soft, fine hair. Ren-Lei cooed and laughed at the touch of the massive hand, nearly as large as herself. He brought his gaze up from the baby and looked where Blake had directed him. "Looks like they worked him over pretty good."

A few yards away, Nathaniel stood with head lowered, his burnt and blistered arm dangling at his side. His eyes were half closed, his breath deep and slow as he worked to conserve what little strength he had left. The force that drove the dead's footsteps still emanated from him; when the spell came to an end, they would return to the cold earth from which they had been resurrected.

He looked up, catching sight of the figure that had just been thrown to the base of the garden's peach tree. Slowly, he walked over to where the others stood, surrounding their defeated foe. Something bumped against his forehead as he passed beneath the branches of the peach tree. He glanced up and saw how low they hung, the green-leaved stems laden with ripe fruit, the soft golden skin glistening under trickles of rain. He reached up and touched one with his finger, just enough to set it swaying before his eyes. *The prophecy*, he realized. *It said this would happen. When the time was right . . .*

Another few steps and Nathaniel stood looking down into the Devil's eyes. "You're beaten. You know you are . . ." He spoke quietly. "But there's still a way for you to save yourself, if you agree to do what we say."

Contempt bittered the Devil's words. "I'm not interested in your mercy."

"Maybe not. But you should be interested in staying alive." Nathaniel's burnt arm hung loosely at his side. His comrades, the soldier and the giant hit man, stood close behind. "You're free to go—as long as you swear to leave us in peace from now on. And by 'us,' I mean everyone. No more of your schemes and temptations. Just leave mankind alone, and crawl back into the flames."

One corner of the Devil's mouth curled. "Is that all?"

"No," said Nathaniel. "There's one more thing." He turned and nodded toward Blake. "Free my friend of the shroud you've put him in, and give him back the missing half of his soul. Do that now, and you can live. If not . . ."

"You really are a fool, boy . . ." The Devil dragged himself to his feet, the cloven hoof digging into the blood-drenched ground. "Because you don't understand me, even now." His naked back pressed against the trunk of the peach tree. "Mankind is of no interest to me, and never has been. I haven't acted as I have all these millennia in order to cause you humans pain, but to damage the one who created you. Because for every tear that mankind sheds, God sheds one, too. And His constant pain on your behalf has been my only pleasure."

From the corner of his eye, Nathaniel saw the hit man's fist tighten on the handle of the flaming axe he still carried.

Blake did the same with Saint Michael's spear.

"Victory or defeat, it makes no difference to me," continued the Devil. "All that has ever mattered to me is that I have a chance to make your Creator suffer. So even in this state, I spit on your offer. . . . And curse each of you in turn!" He pointed to Ren-Lei, whose small face could be seen peeking out from the battered helmet. "I curse that puking baby you've saved to a life filled with loneliness and sorrow. And as for you—" He glared up at Hank. "The oaf who holds her . . . My curse to you is that you find that fear you're searching for, and become so crippled by it that it robs you of your strength." He turned his scathing gaze toward Nathaniel. "To you, the boy who brought about my defeat, I curse you with the task of picking up the pieces of the chaos you've caused today. And last of all . . ." The Devil turned finally to Blake. "To you who needs the most from me, I give the least. I curse you to remain the way you are forever. Let your lifeless, deathless misery be my parting gift to the world. And may it darken the life of everyone you encounter. Until they end up hating your stinking, rotting hide as much as I do."

Blake's face set hard as he gazed at his tormentor. He stepped forward, shoving his way past Hank and Nathaniel, bearing the double-bladed spear in his hands.

"Is that all you have to say?" he asked.

The Devil continued to glare at him, but made no more answer.

"Good," said Blake. "Then now it's my turn to give a curse to you . . ."

He raised one of the spear's fire-wreathed blades, ready to drive it forward into the Devil's body.

But before he could complete the move, the Devil threw out his palm toward the coat. As Hank and Nathaniel watched, the blood-encrusted shroud tightened around Blake's body in answer to the Devil's call, pinioning Blake's arm in place.

Blake's shoulders twisted from side to side as he writhed inside the coat. Beneath the tangles of his matted dreadlocks, the veins stood out on his forehead as he gritted his teeth. The Devil raised his arm, and the coat's arm raised itself, too. It tightened itself upon the muscles of his wrist, making it impossible for him to let go of the spear's shaft.

The coat's grime-covered sleeve brought the weapon back upon itself, turning its flaming blade toward Blake's throat. He tried with all his might to fight it off. But the Devil's coat was stronger. Inch by inch, the fiery blade moved closer, its edge burning into his neck.

Blake only had one chance. Beside him on a mound of smoking bodies, he spotted a demon's curved dagger. Before the Devil could realize what he was doing, he grabbed it with his free hand, and sliced three long gashes into his stiffened arm's shoulder, elbow, and wrist.

Blood spattered across the ground in front of him. With his arm now freed from the fabric's constraint, he tossed away the dagger, seized the spear in both hands, and drove its burning point forward into the Devil's chest.

The lunging thrust pierced the eight-pointed star above the Devil's heart. A thick, glowing magmalike substance crept along the spear's shaft as the blade burst out again from between the Devil's shoulder blades, lifting and pinning him to the trunk of the peach tree. Sparks flew from the smooth bark as soon as the Devil's crawling blood touched it—

And the world turned silent.

Across the garden square, the gaze of the living and the bony, hollow eye sockets of the dead turned toward the peach tree. None had ever seen what they now beheld.

The hinge of Time itself stopped, then turned in another direction. One it never had before.

For a moment, the rain pelting through the dark air hung suspended, as though each drop were now a shimmering diamond. Above, the low-hanging storm clouds were touched with a new radiance, the crests of the distant hills about to fall beneath a sun that had never risen before.

Breath held, the living looked around at one another. Seeing the same wordless realization in each other's eyes. All their history, and that of the generations before them, had been nothing but the pain and torment inflicted upon them by the Devil. Now that history had ended—

And a new one had begun.

The rain fell once more, streaming across their uplifted faces. The sodden ground beneath their feet seemed to murmur, as though the earth itself wondered what a world without evil would look like.

Shadowed by the peach tree's glistening branches, the Devil's fiery eyes dimmed, then dulled blank as he hung lifeless from the tree.

25.

The desk cracked in two, the mass of black lava-stone splitting from front to back. On the polished surface beneath Ling's back, the break went right through the middle of the eight-pointed star. She could feel the glowing emblem's heat begin to die away.

At the same time, the tattoo on the back of the witch's neck flared white-hot, as though the ink had been transformed to some incendiary substance. The star emblem, which signaled devotion to the Devil's service, singed the long black hair that fell across it; Anna screamed in pain, dropping the shard of the broken lamp that she had pressed against Ling's throat. She clawed at her own bloodied neck, staggering back from the desk.

"My master!" Anna's cry cut through the air. The unseen force that had ignited her tattoo now grew even more powerful, shaking the building itself, as though it were gripped by an immense, clawed hand.

Unbalanced, the two halves of the lava-stone fell away from each other. Catching herself on her hands and knees, Ling saw the desk's drawers spill open. A large-caliber silver pistol, malevolently shining, tumbled onto the floor in front of her. She scooped it up in both hands and rolled onto her back, aiming the gun at her attacker and squeezing off three quick shots.

Flowers of wet red blossomed across Anna's chest. She fell writhing in the office's doorway. At her back, above her shoulder blades, the eight-pointed star burst into flame. In seconds, her body was wrapped in fire.

Ling felt the floor beneath her tremble, as though, with the Devil's demise, the tower's foundation and even Hell itself were caught in the tremor of an earthquake. A spiderweb of cracks shot through the office's ceiling, plaster raining down upon her. She threw the gun aside and got to her feet, running past the witch's charring corpse and toward the safety of the lobby beyond.

The floor buckled hard enough to throw her against the secretary's desk. On all sides, the carved depictions of Hell's torments toppled into the lobby. Stone fragments skittered across the transparent floor as thick black smoke obscured the ceiling. Tongues of fire leapt upward as the floor broke into pieces.

Arms shielding her head from more falling debris, Ling ran out to the elevators in the hallway. Both sets of steel doors were open, revealing the cables that dangled in the dark, empty shafts, smoke billowing upward from the floors below. At the end of the corridor was the door to the emergency stairway; she yanked it open and started down, her rapid footsteps echoing from the bare steel treads.

Just get out, she commanded herself. *In one piece*. She grabbed the stair rail in one hand and used it to swing herself across the first landing she came to, then down the next flight of steps. Heartbeat racing, gasping for breath, she caught the scent of something burning and spotted a few black tendrils seeping up the stairwell. The emergency lights flickered above her head, striking dismay in her gut. If the electricity went off at the same time that the building filled with smoke, the ventilation system would go down as well; she would choke to death, in the dark, before she could reach the exit at the ground floor.

Another tremor rumbled through the tower, knocking her off her feet and slamming her hard into the corner of the next steel landing. As she steadied herself against the wall, a crack split open beneath her palm; through it, she spotted a flicker of fire, as though the interior of the building's structure had begun consuming itself. The acrid smell of electrical insulation, the sheathing of the cords and wires burning inside the walls, stung her nostrils at the same time that plaster dust sifted down upon her head.

You've got to get to her— She picked herself up and started down the next flight of wobbling stairs. *You've got to get to Ren-Lei—*

The emergency lights went out before she could reach the landing below. At the same time, a section of the exterior wall, stretching taller than her and wider than her hands could reach, broke loose and tumbled into the stairwell. If she had been a few steps farther down, she would have been crushed beneath it. A cold wind rushed across her from outside, and she could see the night sky, heavy storm clouds hanging close above. A bright tinge outlined the churning shapes, as though a thread of sun had managed to penetrate their obscuring bulk.

As she watched, the clouds shifted. At their center appeared an even darker space, a circular gap revealing infinite space beyond. The clouds began to circle it, the rain-heavy masses at the horizon lumbering slowly, the others swirling faster and faster the closer they were to the darkness drawing them to itself. A vortex formed, as though the night sky itself had been turned to a whirlpool. The wind grew more forceful, sweeping across the earth like a tornado. Its spiraling tail reached down through the office towers and toward the tree at the center of the garden below.

In less than a minute, the black clouds were completely drawn away from the sky's edges. The peach tree lit up as it anchored the swirling vortex, as though its very branches were formed from the sun that had been hidden for so long. The glow was so bright, it seemed to eat the darkness itself.

At the world's horizon, the first light of dawn streamed through the jagged hills, touching the remaining clouds with a dark-red radiance. The night's fading stars glinted through the gaps torn through the dwindling storm. Across the city, the towers' rooftops were revealed.

Ling turned her head, gazing up along the exterior wall that had broken open before her. She could see now the unlit windows of the floors above. What was concealed behind them could only be imagined. . . .

The building convulsed again, hard enough that she had to grasp the crumbling edge of the wall segment to keep from tumbling out into the air. Looking down the tower's length, she felt her head swim, dizzied at the sight of how far the ground was below. A fall from this height would be fatal, and there were no handholds on the sleek, glassy surface with which she would be able to climb down. The stairwell was still her only route of escape.

Her eyes had adjusted to the dim light. She could see that she would have to go back up to the top of the stairs behind her so she would be able to scrabble over the collapsed wall section and down to the next landing. She would be in total darkness beyond that point, but the way would be unobstructed, at least until the next tremor sent more debris crashing into the stairwell.

She quickly reached the point where she could clamber across the top of the fallen wall. There was a gap only a couple of feet wide between the wall's edge and the landing's ceiling. Jagged concrete and broken iron rebar scraped at her stomach as she crawled forward—

A hand seized onto her ankle, dragging her back.

Ling rolled onto one side, shoulder pressing against the ceiling. In the darkness, she could just make out Anna's hideously blackened face, glaring red eyes burned lidless by the fire that had engulfed her in the Devil's office. The witch's broken nails dug into Ling's knee as the hissing, snarling specter clawed itself toward her.

She brought up her other leg, far enough to slam her heel sharp into Anna's fire-blistered face. Two hard blows, but the witch still clung to her. In the narrow confines of the space in which she was trapped, Ling realized there was no way to break free of the witch's grasp, to get away from the blackened hand reaching for her throat—

Her fingers sank into burnt flesh as Ling grabbed a blackened arm. She pulled the witch up on top of herself, what was left of her enemy's face pressing against her own. There was just enough space for to bring her knee into the woman's abdomen as she felt broken teeth gnawing at her own throat. Muscles straining with the effort, she yanked Anna's body higher across herself, then turned onto one side and hurled her toward the crumbling gap in the building's exterior wall. The witch's clawlike nails raked across Ling's cheek and the corner of her brow, then the woman tumbled free, falling into the night's cold, empty air.

She dragged herself to the top of the section of the wall and looked out. The witch already appeared the size of a doll, then no larger than a handsbreadth, as she spun cursing and screaming, a black silhouette against the bloodied pavement rushing up from below. A final burst of dull red sparks shot out from her body when she struck the ground. Then she lay motionless, her shattered form contorted out of any human semblance.

Ling panted for breath, gathering her remaining strength before she let herself slip down the angle of the wall segment. She managed to reach the stairs beyond, then started down them, hurrying into the tower's darkness.

26.

The first light of dawn summoned the priest.

It had been a long night. The darkest part of it had been spent by him in the cemetery behind the little church. Rain had soaked his heavy woolen cassock as he had stood among the graves, their tombstones toppled over by the cold, lifeless hands that had clawed up through the sodden earth. Tombs and caskets had been shattered open by the force of that mass resurrection. The grey forms of the dead, some of whom he had recited the funeral service over, had shambled past him, unheeding of his awestruck terror. When the graveyard had finally been emptied, he had watched the corpses joining up with others, all heading to the battle for which they had been summoned. He had known that it was some great climactic struggle that was their destination—the grim set of their jaws and empty eye sockets had told him as much.

Which meant they still needed his prayers, as did the living. Overcome by his own shameful fears, he had hid himself inside the church, kneeling before its altar and praying for his own deliverance. Paralyzed with terror, he had remained motionless there, head bowed, as hours had passed . . .

Now he pushed open the heavy front door of the church and looked out. And saw something that he hadn't beheld before.

Across the city's skyline, a reddish gold radiance sparkled off the buildings' windows. The puddles of water in the streets were just as luminous, reflecting the sun's topmost edge, just breaking over the darkly silhouetted hills in the distance.

The sky was in motion, black clouds swirling into a vortex somewhere above the center of the city. He knew what spot it was—the garden square at the base of one of the tallest and most oppressive-looking office towers. Something had happened to the building; part of it had broken away, and the rest of the exterior walls were blackened with the smoke still drifting upward.

All through the night, as he had prayed unceasingly, he had heard the sounds of frightful battle coming from that direction. Now everything seemed peaceful, there in the distance and throughout the city.

He turned his head and saw others streaming from the tenements and shops all around the church. Fear had kept them inside—and who could blame them?—but now they stepped out into the golden air, looking up and marveling at the transformation that had been wrought, somehow tangible though yet unseen. With hands outstretched at their sides, they stood in the middle of the empty streets and slowly turned about, as though trying to catch the smallest glimpse of the grace that had suddenly been bestowed upon the earth.

It's true, thought the priest. *It has happened. That for which we have waited—*

He realized what he had to do. He turned and rushed back into the church. Within seconds, he was in the little chamber at the base of the steeple, where the bell rope dangled. The space was choked thick with dust and cobwebs, undisturbed for decades. That was how many years it had been since the great iron bell had been rung. He grasped the heavy rope with both hands and pulled. Above him, a joyous noise clanged out—

And others. He could hear them outside the church as he pulled the rope over and over again. All across the city, bells were ringing. Flocks of pigeons scattered from every church steeple, roused from their nests by the hammering sway of the bells bursting from their soft chains of neglect. Other hands pulled the ropes that had gone untouched for so long; other hearts leapt upward as his did, hearing the brazen chorus set the air shimmering through the city's streets.

The sun had risen far enough to send a shaft of light between the city's towers. With the rope still in his hands, he could see the carved stone font bathed by the dawn angling beneath the eave of the church's roof. The statue of the archangel Michael above the font seemed unsoiled and beautiful now, as though the night's driving rain had somehow cleansed it, as no storm ever had before.

The priest let go of the bell rope and walked back out the church's front door. He leaned toward the statue, raising one hand to touch it. As the other bells continued ringing, he saw something he had never noticed before; a look of triumph seemed to play upon the archangel's face. He drove the double-bladed weapon through the serpent writhing at his feet, as if he were already celebrating this triumph over mankind's fallen enemy.

The bells summoned the dead.

Sunlight flooded the city's streets. In the garden square, the dead rose to their feet.

"What's happening?" Hank cradled the helmet with the baby inside against his chest, and watched as on all sides, the battered and broken corpses stood upright, their pallid faces turning to the sky.

He and Blake looked up as well. Above them, the last trailing remnants of the storm clouds streamed down into the tree. The black hole at the sky's center began to grow smaller, as though it were consuming itself.

"It's over," said Nathaniel. He stood quietly nearby, head still lowered. The mingled pealing of the church bells had brought his eyes open, and he had turned his head to one side, listening to them. Now he gazed across the garden square, at the standing dead. "We won."

"Yeah . . ." Blake held the torn, filthy overcoat together with one hand as he brought his gaze down. "This army's mustering out."

The sun had risen high enough to shine past the dark shape of the Devil's office tower, bathing the garden square bright and warm. For only a moment, the faces of the dead army were turned toward its radiance. Then, as the sun's rays touched them, each corpse burst into a fine white dust, scattering upon the breeze.

Hank looked back up. The sky was completely open and un-clouded now. He could feel the tension unlocking in his bones, fatigue seeping through every fiber of his muscles. Glancing over at Blake, he could see the same slow tide moving through the dreadlocked wraith. He had seen Blake dart through the sky like black lightning, faster than his eye could catch, cutting down every foe that had reared before him. Now Blake looked earthbound, caught again by gravity. Merely human once more . . .

"Feeling okay?" he asked quietly.

Blake looked over at him. A second passed, then a corner of the soldier's mouth lifted in a weary smile. "Better than usual . . ."

There were other dead in the square. The sunlight fell upon the lifeless demons, their slashed and hacked carcasses piled in mounds, greasy smoke spiraling from their bloodless wounds. They evaporated in sulphurous explosions when the sun hit them, blue flames shooting from their scaly flesh.

As Hank watched them disappear, he saw their broken, dented armor begin to glow hotter, too, as though the magnesium were about to ignite.

"The helmet!" At the last second, he grabbed hold of the demonic helmet strapped to his chest, yanked it loose, and threw it aside before it could burn Ren-Lei.

At their feet, the abandoned helmet suddenly burst into blue flames, as did all the other demonic weapons cast across the battleground. Blake looked across the garden, watching as the wickedly curved blades and razor-sharp spear points consumed themselves, the flames curling into the sky like cobalt serpents, before disappearing from the mortal world for good.

Bit by bit, every vestige of evil vanished from the garden. Except for one. The Devil's body still hung from the trunk of the peach tree, the double-bladed spear transfixing his symbol-inscribed chest.

As the morning sun rose higher, its angle shifted, the edge of its radiance sweeping across the garden square. Within a few minutes, the roots at the tree's base were illuminated, then the trunk below the Devil's cloven foot; then the light was full upon his lifeless body.

But it didn't burst into sulphurous flame and vanish like the other demon bodies. The spear, too, remained secure, the burning point of one of its blades deeply imbedded in the trunk.

Blake reached out and touched the weapon. "This one isn't evil like the rest of them." His voice was hardly more than a whisper. "You can feel that when you touch it. But I wonder . . . How did it end up in a demon's—"

The ragged soldier jumped back. Before him, the arcane symbols on the Devil's flesh had begun to glow, as though summoned to life by the sun's touch.

"Nathaniel . . ."

"I see it . . ." A sudden fear touched Nathaniel's heart. As though hypnotized by the burning apparition, he peered toward the fiery symbols as they grew bigger.

Hank brought his hand across Ren-Lei's face, to guard her from the burning light. "What's going on?"

The symbols grew even larger and more fiery, slowly revolving on the Devil's skin like some newly malignant galaxy forming. An involuntary shudder ran through Nathaniel as a partial realization formed inside his mind.

"I screwed up . . ." He turned to the others, the certainty coming together inside him. "He made the stars. And that was before Death was born."

Hank glared back at him. "What are you talking about?"

"I'm talking about the sun!" said Nathaniel, pointing up the sky. "It's a star, too, just like the rest of them. It's still a part of him. And now . . . it's reconnecting—"

In a blinding flash, the symbols on the Devil's skin exploded, white-hot sparks flying across the garden square. Nathaniel braced himself and threw his good hand forward, sending an arching wave of ice toward the fire to extinguish it. But it did no good. The glistening fragments melted, then evaporated before they hit the ground.

Before Death was born . . . Before the war in Heaven . . . The sun is bringing his archangel body back to life . . .

The earth trembled beneath the men's feet and the ensuing explosion's shock wave knocked the three of them to the ground. Peering through the glare leaking through their upraised hands, they could see the city's towers leaning away from them, an invisible force surging over the buildings, powerful enough to uproot them from their foundations and fling them toppling into the empty streets.

The glaring light increased, ripping apart the Devil's human shell and casting out Saint Michael's spear. The symbols remained, floating upon a figure made of magma. The burning form grew larger, the limbs and torso expanding until they towered above the three men. The immense body churned with solar plasma like the surface of the sun.

The reborn Devil opened his eyes again, revealing the same sulphurous blue as before. With a roar that shattered the windows in the remaining buildings, he spread the wings at his back, their span wider than the reach of the peach tree's branches behind him. The wings' beating drove a wind strong enough to flatten everything in the space except the tree, still shielded by its own magic, and the Devil's three opponents, crouching on the ground below him.

Blake jumped up and ran to where the spear had landed. Weaponless since his demon axe had burned away, Hank shielded Ren-Lei with his bare hands. At Hank's side, Nathaniel held out his good arm, ready to protect them any way he could.

But the reborn Devil didn't attack.

He glared at them, and at Blake in particular, his new voice rumbling as low as the earthquake that had set the towers trembling at the edge of the square. A string of guttural noises issued from his mouth, more like the clashing of boulders than words. Each syllable seemed weighty as prophecy.

"What did he say?" Blake turned toward Nathaniel. "He said something to me. What?"

The Devil's words, their meaning and the implacable wrath behind them, had left Nathaniel stunned. "He used the language of magic . . ." Nathaniel felt the weight of the dread words settle like stones upon his soul. "If I understood him right, we need to get out of here . . . Now!"

The others heeded his warning. Keeping an eye on their enemy, they backed away for a few yards, then followed Nathaniel's lead by turning and running as fast as they could toward the streets beyond the garden square.

A shadow swept across them, blotting out the sun as the Devil's wings beat with greater power, bearing him aloft. At the mouth of the nearest alley, they halted and gazed upward as the fiery entity dwindled to a speck in the unclouded distance.

Suddenly, the blazing point grew larger as the Devil hurtled back down toward the earth that had spurned him.

"Get back!" Nathaniel pushed against the others' shoulders. "He's going to hit!"

So great was the speed of the Devil's cometlike descent that the words were barely out of Nathaniel's mouth before their enemy's massive body, formed of raging solar plasma and pure enmity, struck the ground, just as it had when he had first been cast from Heaven. The impact tore the garden to dust and splintered rock, jetting upward like a volcano's plume, and exposing a gaping chasm beneath.

The Devil's immense form dove headfirst into the jagged opening. Fire leapt from its depths as a seismic wave sent the ground heaving apart. Leaves trembled around the peach tree's golden fruit as its roots tore free from the earth. More fissures opened around it, the rocks at their edges crumbling away as the tree toppled into the chasm. Only a gaping hole remained where the garden had filled the space before the tower. The foundations of the Devil's office tower were revealed, lit by the magma streaming beneath two enormous magnesium doors, twenty floors beneath the earth's surface.

Hank backed away from the alley's mouth, shielding the infant's face from the choking dust that filled the air. Blake remained standing where he was, gazing in tight-lipped fury at the scene before him.

"What the hell did he say to me?" The soldier turned his angry gaze at Nathaniel.

"It was a challenge . . . ," explained Nathaniel. "Aimed directly at you. He said that if you want the other half of your soul back, you should follow him down to Hell and try to take it from him. He told me to tell you that he'll be waiting for you in the hell-fire . . . for as long as it takes."

Blake turned away, looking back toward the gaping fissures that had torn apart the garden and the city's streets. He nodded slowly. "I understand," he said. "The sonuvabitch wants a re-match."

27.

With the spear in hand, Blake stood at the edge of the chasm, gazing down. The magma below burned as hot as the weapon's double blades. A familiar voice spoke behind him.

"If you're heading down there, I'm going with you."

He turned and saw Hank, with the infant cradled in his arms.

"Thanks for the offer . . ." He looked at Ren-Lei, cooing and gurgling. "But I think you've got other things to take care of now. I'll have to handle this one without you."

"Blake's right . . ." Nathaniel joined the other two men before the chasm, stepping through the dissipating dust and smoke. "The most important thing right now is to get Ren-Lei back to her mother. And after that, I think you should stick around and watch their backs for a while, in case there are still any demons around that we've missed."

Hank mulled it over, and nodded. "Maybe you're right. I didn't bring her through all of this for nothing. And her mother's desperate to see her, I know." He paused, feeling awkward. "So . . . if you're sure you don't need me . . ."

Blake held out his filthy hand to say good-bye. "Stay safe,

friend. It's been an honor fighting with you." He smiled up into the giant's face. "If you ever need my help, just ask."

Hank gripped Blake's hand so tight he almost broke it. "When I see you again, buddy, I want to see you wearing something different, okay? No offense, but right now, you look like an old carpet that's been dragged through a slaughterhouse."

Nathaniel shook Hank's hand, too. Then he stroked the top of Ren-Lei's head to wish her all the best. "Take care, big fella. I'll be in touch."

With a final nod, Hank turned away. But after only a couple of steps, he halted and turned back. "Hey, kid. All that stuff that the Devil said about Ren-Lei's life . . . You don't think there was any truth in it, do you?"

Nathaniel shook his head. "Honestly? I don't. The Devil didn't have enough power left to curse Ren-Lei or any of us."

"Yeah . . . ," Hank said thoughtfully. "That's what I thought, too."

He said no more, but slowly turned away again. Blake and Nathaniel watched him go.

Hank had almost reached the edge of the garden square when he heard a voice calling his name. He glanced over his shoulder and saw Ling running toward him. Behind her was one of the service doors of the office tower, which she had managed to shove open against the weight of the rubble piled against it.

An unfamiliar, wordless confusion filled his thoughts when she stood at last in front of him. Her gaze caught his for only a moment before she looked down to the bundle in his arms, wrapped in his torn shirt, the strips of cloth smudged with blood and dirt. Tears streamed down Ling's face as she stood on tiptoe and gently took her baby. Ren-Lei laughed happily, recognizing her mother.

"You did it." She clutched the baby tight as she looked back up at him. "You found her. You saved her."

She reached up with one hand and laid it against the side of his face. Her touch lasted for only a moment before she drew him down into a kiss.

His knees weakened. He had to wrap both arms around her shoulders to keep from falling. Sheltered between the two of them, Ren-Lei chortled even louder, apparently amused by the strange actions of grown-ups.

Then his thoughts cleared, enough to realize something deep inside. Just like the Devil's curse had foretold, he'd discovered fear, as he'd always sought to do. But not fear for himself—it was fear for the ones he had come to love.

What if something happens? He felt dizzied and appalled just by imagining all the world's unseen hazards. *And I'm not strong enough to protect them?*

He held on to Ling even tighter, as if somehow he could make it impossible to let go. . . .

Nathaniel watched the couple embracing in the distance. If they didn't forget about the baby and crush the poor thing between themselves, everything would be fine. For them, at least.

He turned toward Blake. Before they had spotted the young woman running out of the battered office tower, the soldier had just about been ready to plunge into the chasm in order to knock on the Devil's front door. He saw that Blake was still there, his back to him, silently peering down into the molten depths.

"You know I'm going down there with you, right?" said Nathaniel. "Just give the word, and we'll ring his bell together."

No reply came from Blake. He still stood motionless at the chasm's edge.

"Because I don't feel like giving up on this halfway through, you know what I mean?" He tilted his head to one side, peering at the ragged soldier. "I'm starting to enjoy being my own master. And it feels good, finally making a difference . . ."

He had thought that Blake was preoccupied with his own dark, brooding thoughts. No words, no movement—but he suddenly suspected that something else was going on.

"Blake?" He stepped to the edge of the chasm and leaned slightly forward, so he could look into his face. The soldier didn't seem to even notice him, his gaze fixed on the magma below.

Which wasn't moving, either.

He looked down at the tongues of fire, which had been flickering out of the red-hot stone but were now frozen in place, like a photograph taken of a volcano's interior. He noticed as well that there was no shadow cast at his own feet; it had remained where he had been standing a moment ago.

In the distance, Ling and Hank were also fixed in place, as though they could gaze into each other's eyes without end, not even speaking or breathing. Beyond them, bits of falling rubble hung suspended against the now cloudless sky.

"Hello, Nathaniel . . ."

He turned, and saw the familiar face of Death. His old master.

Death studied him, peering deep into his eyes. "You've changed, Nathaniel . . . It seems that since I saw you last, you have grown into a man."

"I've been through a lot, I guess . . . since the last time you saw me."

"I know." Death gave a single nod. "I have been aware of every step you've taken. And in some strange way, I have been . . . impressed."

Nathaniel turned away and looked out over the battlefield and its wreckage. He didn't want to look back into Death's eyes yet. Not until he'd said what he needed to say. "There's something I need to tell you . . ."

"I can see that."

"It's about my life, and what I want to do with it."

Death watched him without emotion. "Go on."

"I don't . . ." Nathaniel found it difficult to find the right words. "I don't think I can work with you anymore." He turned back, hoping Death would understand. "Since today, I've learned what it's like to help people. Living people, I mean. Not just the dead like it was before. And you know what? I like it. I like the fact that I can change a person's fate. So I intend to go on doing that for other people from now on. I want to set off on my own, and help as many people as I can."

Death's pallid face frowned a little in confusion. "I'm sorry, Nathaniel, but I don't understand. What do you mean, you have changed a person's fate?"

"Ren-Lei . . . we saved her." He glanced over to the unmoving couple in the distance, and the frozen baby giggling between them. "Because of us, she can grow up and live a long, healthy life."

Death's expression didn't change. "Nathaniel, what you have achieved tonight has been impressive, as I said. But if you believe it has made a difference to anything, you are wrong. You saw the Scroll of Deaths yourself. Everything that was marked down upon it has come to pass. All those who were destined to survive have survived. And all those who were due to die have died. Or at least, they will have done, once the problem that your interference has caused has been corrected."

A dark suspicion entered Nathaniel's thoughts. "Corrected?" he said. "In what way?"

Death cast his gaze across the tiny human being in Ling's arms. "With the baby. The one you call Ren-Lei. She was set to die last night in the fallen angels' temple. And die she must. Your interference has merely postponed her death, not cancelled it. Her soul still needs to be harvested. And *that* is why I am here."

"No!" Nathaniel's voice turned taut and fierce. "You can't. Her life's been saved. We fought to save it. Do you have any idea how much blood was shed so she can live?"

"And you believe that matters?" Death's tone remained level and unemotional. "The laws of life and death must be upheld, Nathaniel. The balance must be maintained if the world is to proceed as it should. You know much about the workings of the afterlife, but you do not yet know everything. And if you don't believe that, then come with me, and see for yourself why the child must die."

Nathaniel stood silent for a moment, considering his alternatives. In the end, he saw that he had no choice. "All right, I'll come with you . . ." he said. "But only to see what you mean."

Death held out his waxen hand, ready to lay it on Nathaniel's shoulder. But Nathaniel stopped him before the hand could touch him.

"Hold on—" He motioned to the frozen figure in the filthy overcoat, standing transfixed at the edge of the chasm. "If I go with you, what will happen to Blake? Without my help, will he be okay? Will he beat the Devil, and get what he wants?"

Death looked at the figure. But as soon as he saw the grime-encrusted coat he turned away again, uninterested. "Such a wraith is no longer my concern," he said. "I only deal with those who pass on from life to death—not those who are trapped between the two. However, to ease your human concern, I will tell you this. . . . Whether you help him on his quest or not, it makes no difference. The wraith's fate will remain the same, however you act."

So there's nothing I can do for him. Nathaniel looked again at his friend's black-smudged face and tangled hair. *No matter what I decide . . .*

"Just so." Death had read his thoughts.

"Then show me . . . ," said Nathaniel. "Show me what I need to know." He saw the waxen hand rise up again and lay itself upon his shoulder. "Take me back to your realm one last time."

28.

I've been here before." Nathaniel gazed around at the chamber. "But it seems like a lifetime ago."

Billions of lights extended in all directions around him. The carved pedestals that supported their glass vessels stretched on far beyond the limits of what Nathaniel could see. The ancient, low-ceilinged chamber reached into the distance, seemingly without end. Above him, he could feel the weight of the earth, as if the groundskeeper's cottage, surrounded now by emptied graves and tombs, was at the center of all things.

"Why did you bring me to the Lights of Life?" he asked. "What's here for me to see that I haven't seen before?"

Death walked a few yards down the chamber's length, stopping in front of one of the vessels. "Come," he said. "This is Ren-Lei's light." A cold fingertip touched the side of the glass. "It shines brightly, growing stronger all the time."

"I'm not surprised," said Nathaniel as he joined his former master by the glass. "She's with people now who love her."

"True . . . However, that is not what I'm here to show you. Instead, look there—"

Death pointed to the air above the glass. To the space between the vessel and the low-lying ceiling.

Nathaniel looked to where he pointed, and to his surprise, he saw another, fainter glow hovering in the darkness. It was so tenuous and dim, it looked as if it might disintegrate at any moment.

"What you see there is a soul that is waiting to be born," said Death. "But because of what you've done, it has not yet been able to find a place in which to ignite. Instead, it is fading away into nonexistence, even as we speak."

Nathaniel looked at the glowing cloud with concern. "I see . . ."

"But do you?" asked Death. "I have told you many times, Nathaniel, each soul here is governed by the rules of Fate. The order in which these glasses are emptied and refilled follows a predetermined plan. According to that plan, Ren-Lei's light should no longer be here. But because it still is, you have in turn condemned another soul to die." Death's eyes mirrored the faint cloud of light as he regarded it. His face remained emotionless, but nevertheless firm. "The life you see here is waiting to replace that of the girl you saved. And it will be a fine life, I can tell. It is a life that will achieve many great things in its allotted time. Many people will find happiness because of this life. And many others will be inspired to be better people because of its example. In short, this is a life that will benefit the world and take it forward. It will be a glorious life, like only a handful of others throughout human history. But now, due to you and your selfishness, this extraordinary life is threatened with destruction before it has even been born. And I cannot allow that to happen, Nathaniel. No matter how much you beg me."

Death made a move to lift Ren-Lei's glass, ready to extinguish her light by force. But before he could, Nathaniel stopped him.

"Wait—" He put his one good hand on the glass, too, and gently pressed it back in place. "If that light above is destined for great things, how do you know the same isn't true of Ren-Lei's? Maybe . . . maybe Fate *wanted* her to be saved. So that she could do the world some good as well."

"If that had been the case, then her light would have been provided with a different glass."

"But . . . isn't that still possible?" Nathaniel looked across the chamber at the countless glass covers. "What about all those other people who were killed tonight? They must have left some empty vessels behind them. So if the light above her needs Ren-Lei's glass, then why not move her into one of theirs?"

"Into another vessel . . ." A look of amazed wonder appeared in Death's gaze. "Only you, Nathaniel, could ask such a question." He turned away, casting his eyes over the billions of flickering lights. "It is an intriguing thought. And yes . . . perhaps her light could be moved into another glass, if one was empty." He shook his head and turned back. "But there is no such glass. All the others were filled the moment the lights inside them died. Search this chamber as you wish. There is not an empty vessel to be found."

For a moment, Nathaniel made no reply. A realization, still faint as the unborn soul hovering above Ren-Lei's, had begun to form inside him.

My face . . . An image returned to him, from the last time he was in this chamber. *That was why I saw my face here, above her light.* He knew now that he had glimpsed something which had been hidden from his former master.

"Tell me something," he spoke at last. "You've always said that you can't see my fate. That it's closed to you. Is that still true?"

Death gazed into his eyes, and nodded. "It is."

"So . . . if you don't know when my death's going to happen . . ." The words came slowly as he worked out the possibility that he had glimpsed. "Then that must mean that no other light has been planned into the system to take over my glass when I'm gone."

"What you say . . . is true." Death's gaze rested upon him, trying to work out what he was thinking. "The uncertainty about your death has meant that no light has been put aside to replace yours. Your glass will remain empty when you die."

"Then there's the answer!" It was all clear to Nathaniel now. He'd come this far. Now he had no choice but to follow his chosen journey to the end. "Let me die instead of Ren-Lei, and then transfer her light into the place I leave behind. Because that's possible, isn't it? You could do something like that, without it doing her any harm?"

"I suppose—" Death's gaze shifted as he mulled it over. "It could be done . . . If I permitted it."

"And let's say that was the case—how long would she be able to stay there, after she's moved into it?"

"That is . . . impossible to say." Death had trouble keeping up. "She would have the right to stay there until a new soul could be worked into the plan to replace her. But because of the complexity of that, I cannot say for certain how many decades, or even centuries it would take."

Nathaniel smiled, amused at the notion of little Ren-Lei living so long. "And what about her health? Could you guarantee me that she'd stay fit and strong, and never suffer from a single day's illness in that time, no matter how long she lived?"

Death slowly nodded. "If I wished it, it would be so."

Nathaniel drew in a deep breath. *So it's clear* . . . He gazed down at his burnt arm. It was still a charred mess, yellowish serum weeping past the burns' blackened edges. *But that doesn't matter now. Nothing does* . . . He brought his eyes back up to his old master's face.

"Then please . . . ," he said. "As a parting gift to me, do me this one small favor, and let me die in Ren-Lei's place. Keep her Light of Life safe for me, and look after her for all the years of her life. Then the two of them can both exist together. Both Ren-Lei, and that other soul that's hanging in the air above her. And who knows?" he smiled. "With them both alive like that, at the same time and place, maybe they'll even meet each other one day, and make the world a better place together."

Death frowned, perplexed. A note of incomprehension and even envy filled his voice. "And . . . you would really be willing to do such a thing? You would be willing to sacrifice yourself for someone you don't even know?"

"I have to," said Nathaniel. "There's no other way."

"But . . . aren't you afraid of your death, like others are?"

Nathaniel gazed down at Ren-Lei's light before answering. "Why should I be afraid of it?" he said. "So long as I know that the good it brings will live on after me when I'm gone.

Because . . . you know . . . I think death loses its importance . . . if you can see that it's happening for a reason. And anyway . . . we both know better than anyone that this isn't the end. Not really."

He looked back to Death's baffled expression, realizing only now how incapable his old master was of change. He smiled at him with kindhearted pity, finding that his inability to look beyond the confines of his tedious daily routine made him seem much smaller suddenly, and far less threatening than he'd been before.

He's nothing but a slave, he realized, *chained to a great universal machine. He can't ever leave it, experience how rewarding a life of choice and free will can be. No matter how many souls he harvests, he'll never understand the essence of the lives he ends.*

"Death . . . ," he said, turning to the chamber. "I've forgotten. Show me, please, which light is mine?"

Death walked a few steps farther on, then pointed to the light beside him. It was a high one this time. One of the brightest in the chamber.

"This is your light, Nathaniel. It is a fine light, and always has been. I have grown used to its presence here over the last ten years." He paused, as if surprised himself by what he was thinking. "It will be . . . *strange* . . . to no longer have it here . . . To no longer have its . . . company . . ."

Nathaniel nodded, understanding what Death meant, even if his former master did not. He leaned forward to peer at his light. He could just barely see the reflection of his own face on the surface of the glass.

When he glanced up again, he saw a look of realization appear on Death's face.

"What?"

"I know now . . . ," said Death. "At last, I understand why I could never foresee your death. Because it happens here, in this chamber where no mortal was ever meant to be. This place is shielded from the rest of existence. So the details of your destiny could never escape it." He nodded. "Yes . . . That makes sense to me now. Even if the rest does not . . ."

With the final piece of the puzzle complete, Nathaniel reached out and shook Death's waxen hand to say good-bye.

"And you are sure . . . this is worth it?"

Nathaniel smiled at him again. But he saw no need to answer. Standing there, surrounded by the Lights of Life, of course it was worth it. *Just like every act of self-sacrifice is worth it,* he thought. *If it helps mankind move forward to a better place. And perhaps . . . Perhaps that's why all the Lights of Life are kept here so close together . . . So that each soul on earth has a chance to feel the others shining next to it, and realize that it is not alone. . . .*

Knowing that there was nothing else to say, Nathaniel turned away from Death and faced his own shining soul. With his one good hand, he carefully lifted the glass that covered it. He drew in one last sweet breath of air, then slowly leaned forward. And with a single puff . . . he blew out his light.

Death's Apprentice—A Grimm City Novel is inspired by the following tales and essays from Jacob and Wilhelm Grimm:

FROM THE COLLECTION *KINDER- UND HAUSMÄRCHEN:*
- ✳ *Der Gevatter Tod / Godfather Death.*
- ✳ *Der Bärenhäuter / The Man in the Bearskin.*
- ✳ *Märchen von einem, der auszog, das Fürchten zu lernen / The Tale of One Who Set Out to Learn Fear.*
- ✳ *Rumpelstilzchen / Rumpelstiltskin.*

FROM THE COLLECTION *DEUTSCHE SAGEN:*
- ✳ *Der Birnbaum auf dem Walserfeld / The Pear Tree on the Walser Field.*
- ✳ *Der Virdunger Bürger / The Citizen of Verdun.*
- ✳ *Tote aus den Gräbern wehren dem Feind / The Dead Rise from Their Graves to Ward Off the Enemy.*

FROM THE COLLECTION *DEUTSCHE MYTHOLOGIE:*
- ✳ *Tod / Death.*
- ✳ *Teufel / The Devil.*
- ✳ *Seelen / Souls.*
- ✳ *Zauber / Magic.*
- ✳ *Zeit und Welt / Time and the World.*
- ✳ *Schicksal und Heil / Destiny and Salvation.*